WITCH WOLF

by

Winter Pennington

2010

WITCH WOLF

ISBN 10: 1-60282-177-1
ISBN 13: 978-1-60282-177-4

This Trade Paperback Original Is Published By
Bold Strokes Books, Inc.
P.O. Box 249
Valley Falls, NY 12185

First Edition: June 2010

Credits
Editor: Victoria Oldham
Production Design: Stacia Seaman
Cover Design By Bold Strokes Books Graphics

Acknowledgments

This book would not have been possible were it not for the love and unwavering encouragement of my kith and kin. I feel that any words I summon will pale in comparison to the gratitude and love in my heart.

Thank you to my mother and father for your unfailing love, support, and generosity. I am truly blessed and proud to be your daughter. To Rebecca, my love, I am equally blessed to have you in my life and equally thankful for everything you've done. Without your love, my nights would be moonless ones. To Tony, my brother, for answering all of my weapon questions and for being the best big brother a little sister could ask for. To Desiree, for being the sister I never had and for being understanding when I've been kidnapped by the muse. To Dee, for the many conversations we shared over hot chocolate and for not being afraid of the dark. To Colette, for the words of wisdom and encouragement you offered when I needed to hear them the most. It is an honor to call each of you friend.

Last, but not least, my appreciation goes out to Radclyffe and Victoria (without whom this book would not have been possible). Rad, thank you for the belief you've shown in my work and for being a truly awesome publisher. Victoria, your input and guidance have been invaluable. I've enjoyed working with you and look forward to working with you on the books to come.

My sincerest thanks and appreciation go out to everyone at Bold Strokes Books.

Dedication

To Rebecca.
For the sacrifices you made in love's name,
I am deeply grateful.

Chapter One

"I need a gun that leaves a good-sized hole in a body." I emphasized the size of the hole I wanted by making a fist.

Rupert stared at me for several moments and then burst into laughter. "What in the world would you need a gun like that for?"

I tapped my foot impatiently against the tiled floor. "Is asking that sort of question part of your job description?"

"No, but it makes a man curious."

If ever there was a weapon—Rupert was your guy. We'd met when I was still on the force. He'd been working with us as a bounty hunter. It wasn't until I got to know him that I found out he used to be some type of professional assassin. Technically, even after the years that I'd known him his past was shady. So, to anyone else, he was a bounty hunter, a weapons genius, and the guy I got my guns from. I looked up at him and widened my green eyes pleadingly. Rupert wasn't built like a bounty hunter; in fact, he looked more like a computer geek with the dark-rimmed glasses. It amused me, because he didn't even need them. I'd know. He'd hunted with me enough times that I knew he could shoot yards away without them and still take his target down. It was just another part of his cover. He thought it made him seem more approachable. I thought it made him more like a target for bullying.

"Kass, don't bat your big green eyes at me," he said and crossed his arms over his chest. "I know how gay you are."

"Aww, shucks," I said. "Come on, Rupe, give me a good gun.

The firestorm isn't going to protect me from angry paranorms, and you know it."

"Being a werewolf doesn't automatically count as having an arsenal at your disposal?"

I frowned, but was glad he had kept his voice down. That was another thing my colleagues didn't know or need to know. After a bad accident three years ago I found out I was turning furry once a month. Oh, the joys of living.

A growl fell from my lips that sounded more animal than human. I narrowed my eyes at him. "Rupert, don't bait me."

The smirk he gave me was sarcastic. "Why not? It's so damn easy."

"Because I can still kick your ass from here to Nevada."

"That hasn't been proven."

I closed my eyes and took a deep breath of air. "Will you just find me a gun?"

"Fine, what kind are you thinking?"

"I already told you I need a larger caliber than the .380."

"Sawed-off shotgun?"

I stared at him in disbelief. "You've actually got one of those?"

"I've got a few of them. They're loud, obnoxious, and will definitely discourage any would be super-beastie."

"They're also highly illegal. Even with my concealed weapons license I couldn't pack that much firepower."

He shrugged. "You wanted something that would leave a fist-sized hole. The sawed-off shotgun would do the trick."

"It would also land my ass in jail," I retorted. "Let's think of something, um, well, legal for a start."

Rupert leaned over the glass counter looking thoughtful. I stared at the guns in the case below him.

"Think you've got enough Smith and Wesson guns?" I asked.

"They sell fast," he said. "There's a few guns in there that aren't Smith and Wesson. The Glock, for one."

"The Glock doesn't look bad, but I'm not fond of plastic and it's too big for my hands. It's also what every cop is carrying."

I heard more than saw the grin spread across his face. "Kass, you're not on the force anymore. I don't think you have to worry about that."

There wasn't any reason for him to remind me I was no longer a cop. It was his way of being a pain in the ass since I'd opened my own business and become a private investigator. I didn't have much of a choice. I couldn't work on the night of the full moon without my secret getting out. Oh, I'd tried to avoid quitting…I'd even entertained the thought of telling my boss I'd joined a coven and had a ritual every full moon.

In law enforcement that wouldn't slide, so I'd had to figure something out where I could create my own hours. In the long run everything had worked out for the best. My old boss still treated me like I was a member of the team.

I wasn't always open and honest about practicing witchcraft. Being a witch doesn't endow me with any magical powers. It's a spiritual belief, similar to Wicca, but not quite. It's still an earth-based spirituality, but I don't follow a specific tradition. A spell, to me, is like a prayer in action. Granted, I rarely cast spells, but I still keep up with my studies. I talk to my old mentor about once a year.

Once I finally came out of the broom closet, my boss realized he had one person on the team who knew something about the metaphysical and didn't believe it was evil and was willing to deal with cases that most of the other cops wanted absolutely nothing to do with.

"I still work with the force," I said, frowning at him.

"But you're your own boss now." The look he gave me was like that of a proud parent.

"That look." I shook my head.

"What look?"

"The look on your face…you look…proud or something."

"I am proud of you," he said. His tone was as serious as I'd ever heard it.

"Why? All I did was become a bitch in more ways than one."

"No, you became stronger, faster, and better."

I looked away from the intensity of his gaze. There wasn't a happy medium with Rupert. He was either lighthearted and funny, or deadly serious. He was rarely this serious.

"You need to stop being so hard on yourself," he said.

I looked at him then. "Rupert, if anyone knew, they would hunt me down and kill me."

"You don't know that, Kassandra."

"Yeah, I do. I've seen it."

He shook his head and dropped the subject. Rupert didn't work with the cops intimately enough to know what they do to animals. I did. I do.

The rule was that if it's more powerful than you are—you kill it. It helped that there weren't any laws protecting us, though there was a bill being tossed back and forth in the hands of congress. They just couldn't make up their minds yet. Did they really want animals to have legal rights? Would it make the world a better place if they couldn't kill us on sight? I didn't pay too much attention to it. I hate politics.

I heard him draw in a deep breath.

"I think I've got the gun for you."

Chapter Two

Black is a good color to wear when you don't want blood showing up on your clothes. I wear a lot of black for that reason. If you've ever tried removing a dried bloodstain, you know how difficult it can be, and some clothes are just not salvageable. On that day three years ago it had saved my life.

When the police showed up at the scene I had to hide my injuries. If there's a dead werewolf on the ground and a wounded officer—what does that tell you? It states exactly what it is—that the officer was attacked by the lycanthrope and is at a high risk of turning furry come the next full moon. Of course, that only happens if the person that was attacked survives the injuries.

It turned out to be a blessing that I'd left my jacket in the car that night. I'd carefully slid the jacket over my shoulders to hide the blood that was trickling down my back. With the leather jacket on, it wasn't noticeable that my T-shirt was torn and clinging to my skin like someone had poured a glass of water on it.

I lied to avoid further questioning, and the EMTs' attention. I told my fellow cops that the werewolf hadn't gotten anywhere near me. I caught her off guard when I shot her. Technically, when the silver bullet bit into her heart she *had* been caught off guard. She was too busy lapping at the bloody feast of a man below her to pay attention to me. The second bullet hit home and she collapsed to the ground. It didn't kill her, but I didn't know that until it was too late and I was too damn close. How did I explain the fact that her neck was broken? I told them it was a precautionary gesture to make sure she was well and truly dead.

It had hurt like a bitch when I slid behind the wheel. The world narrowed down to the pain in my back as the endorphins began to wear off. I clung to the steering wheel trying to keep the seat from hitting my back. When I pulled into the parking lot of Guns Unlimited it was still dark out. The streetlights were beginning to blur in my vision. I felt blood seeping onto the band of my jeans, soaking into the cloth and rubbing against my skin. If I didn't get help soon I would most likely die of blood loss. I forced myself out of the car. I stumbled to the door and inside Rupert's shop.

"We're closed," he said as the bell on the door jingled, announcing a customer.

I clung to the doorknob, struggling to get enough breath to speak. "Rupert," I said, but it fell from my lips, strangled. My back hit the door as my knees weakened and I bit my bottom lip to stifle a scream.

The sound made him look up. "I told you we're…" He leapt over the counter in a single bound and grabbed hold of my forearms.

"Kassandra," he said, "what the hell happened to you?"

"I need a doctor." I coughed. "Real fast, real private."

He pulled the cell phone out of his pocket and held it against his shoulder, keeping his arms free to help steady me. "Let's get you to the back," he said. I didn't ask any questions, because I knew he knew what I meant. When you're an ex-assassin you don't go to normal doctors. Which is why I'd come to him for help in the first place. Rupert could keep secrets. He had enough of his own.

The rest I remember in fragments like some shattered dream. Rupert hung up the phone. He helped me sit down in a chair. The pain shot across my ribs like a blow and I hissed. A fainter pain seared through my left leg.

"Where are you hurt?"

"Back, and leg, maybe," I said with what little strength I could muster.

He gently lifted the corner of my jacket to take a glimpse at my back. "Shit, Kass. You're bleeding everywhere. I'm going to go get some towels. The doctor will be here soon."

When Rupert returned there was a small dark-skinned man following him. I gave him a look.

"Fast," I said.

"I told you he'd be here soon."

"Where is she hurt?" the doctor asked. His voice held an accent I couldn't place.

"Her back is torn up and she said her leg might be hurt."

The doctor nodded and walked over to me. He dropped a first aid kit on the floor. "The jacket needs to come off," he said. "Put the towels you brought on the table."

The doctor shone a pen light in my eyes. "Do you feel faint?"

"I don't know," I said, gritting my teeth.

"We must do this quickly, or she's going to go into shock. I'm surprised she has not already."

I heard Rupert snort softly. "The only reason she hasn't is because she's too damn stubborn."

"Hand me a knife," the doctor said.

"What?" I asked.

"I must cut the jacket off. If you move more than is necessary you're going to lose more blood."

A moment later and my body jerked with the force of the fabric being cut. I refused to make another sound and dug my teeth into my bottom lip again. The doctor pushed the soaked material out of the way, exposing my back.

"I have to clean the wounds first. This is going to sting, but until I cleanse them, I cannot see what is going on."

I nodded.

The stuff he poured down my back stung and I couldn't stifle the small scream that followed. It burned like fire eating its way inside my skin.

The doctor made a sound. It wasn't a sound you wanted to hear from a doctor. There was fear in that sound, fear and shock. I looked at him. "What is it?"

"What did this to you?"

"Do you really want to know?" I asked.

Rupert stepped away from the table to look at my back. "I'd like to know," he said, "because if I'm seeing what the doctor is seeing, it looks like the wounds are trying to close up already."

"I have seen this only once before," the doctor said, and the look he gave me was full of a haunted knowledge. "What did this to you?" he asked again.

I looked at Rupert. He already knew, or had guessed. How could he not?

"It'll stay in this room, Kassandra. You said private."

"Lycanthrope," I said.

"That is what I thought," the doctor said. "Since the wounds are trying to close already you won't need stitches. I will clean them as best as I can, but the rest is up to your body."

My heart gave a panicked leap. "What do you mean up to my body?" I asked.

"You either live through the change or you die during it. However, since you are already beginning to heal—it looks like your body has decided the path it wishes to take."

"What the hell are you talking about?" My voice was soft and not quite real.

He ignored me and turned to Rupert. "It's only going to get worse from here."

Rupert nodded. "Tell me."

"She's already slipping into a fever." The doctor's voice grew distant as if I was hearing him from the other end of a tunnel. I felt my body relax and the chair slide out from under me. The dimness around my vision swallowed me whole and the last thing I remember was hitting the floor.

❖

I rolled over and opened my eyes. The room was dark. I sat up in the bed, pushing the hair out of my face. I froze when I heard a soft noise. Snoring? I looked to the corner of the room where the sound came from. There was a darkened silhouette of a person lying back in a chair. I tried to make out the rest of the shadows in the room. It looked like my bedroom. I leaned over and reached for the lamp beside the bed. Sure enough, it was there.

Light flooded the room and the man in the chair jumped up. He'd had a gun in his lap and was now holding it up. The man looked at me, a look of relief passing over his face.

"You're awake," he said.

"Who are you?" I let the demand slip into my tone. He was, after all, in my bedroom.

"A friend of Rupert's. He told me to keep an eye on you while he was away." He shoved the gun down the back of his pants and sat down in the armchair someone had pulled into the corner.

"Where is he?"

"He's at work right now. He should be back here in an hour or so." I watched as his eyes dropped below my chin. I looked down and realized I was only wearing a bra and panties. I grabbed the blanket and jerked it up over my chest.

"Get out so I can get dressed." I jerked my chin in the direction of the door.

The man stood and stretched with his arms above his shoulders. I arched a darkened brow. The dark blue tank top he wore left his arms bare. It was obvious he worked out by the bulk of muscles he flexed while stretching. The jeans he wore were faded and torn at the knees. I looked up at his face. It was more boyish than I thought it had been. The desperate need to shave had made him look older. His unruly blond hair fell in front of his eyes as he looked shyly at his own feet. I rolled my eyes.

"Can your shit and get out of my room," I said.

He looked up at me, either pretending to be shocked, or maybe really shocked, that I didn't buy into his little act. "What?"

"You heard me. I want to get dressed, and I don't want an audience." I gave him an expectant look.

"All right," he said, "I'll be in the living room."

He walked out of the room, shutting the bedroom door behind him. I rolled out of bed and walked over to my closet. I put on a pair of black lounge pants and dug a red tank top out of the top drawer of my dresser. I grabbed the gray flannel that hung on the closet door and put it on.

There were lights on in the house when I walked into the kitchen. I listened.

"Yeah, she's awake," the guy said.

"Good. Tell her I'll be there in a few minutes. I'm locking the shop up now."

"I'll tell her, but she's not very friendly," he said.

I heard Rupert's laugh. "She's always that way at first."

I quietly stepped into the living room when the boy hung up his cell phone.

"He's right, you know."

The kid jumped and turned. "Sweet Jesus. You scared the shit out of me."

I gave him an empty look. "You should pay more attention to your surroundings."

"I pay plenty attention to my surroundings."

"Which is why you were asleep when I woke up?" I asked, tilting my head to one side.

"I was bored and figured I'd get a little shut-eye." He plopped down on the black leather couch.

"I'm guessing Rupert hired you as a sort of bodyguard?"

"Yeah…"

"You need more practice," I said blandly. "Next time remember that you're supposed to be guarding someone's body, not ogling at it."

He looked up and I knew he'd been looking at me again. "Huh?"

"My point exactly."

When Rupert knocked on the door, I allowed the kid to get it. I sat at the kitchen table drinking a mug of coffee.

"You look like you're feeling better," he said.

"I am. Though I'm curious to know—how long I was out?"

"Three days," he said and sat down across the table from me.

"Shit. What about work?"

"They called when I was here. I told them you had the flu and were up all night vomiting. You should call them in the morning and let them know you're feeling better."

"Thank you."

"How's your back doing?" he asked.

"It feels better, but I haven't seen it yet."

"The wounds had already closed up by the time I got you here." He leaned back in his seat. "The wounds on your thigh were only scratches…nothing to worry about."

Nothing to worry about, I thought. *Yeah, right.*

Chapter Three

The phone rang, drawing me out of my memories. I put the mug of coffee down on my desk and leaned over to grab it.

"Lyall Preternatural Investigations," I said in the best courtesy voice I could muster.

"Heya, Kass. How's it going?" It was Arthur's cheerful voice leaking over the line.

I frowned. "It's going. What do you want?"

"Is that any way to talk to an ol' buddy ol' pal?" he asked and tsked softly. "Why do you always think I want something?"

"You never call me just to talk. There's always a string attached. So, go ahead and tell me what the catch is. What's going on?" I picked up a pencil and began tapping the eraser rhythmically on my mug.

"Harsh," he said, pretending I'd wounded his pride. "We need you to come out and take a look at something."

I took in a deep breath and let it out in a sigh. I looked at the large calendar on my desk.

"Shit," I said out loud.

"What?" he asked.

"You're in luck." My voice was flat. "There's nothing written on my calendar to help me get out of this. Tell me what happened, and why exactly I need to come out and take a look at it. You know, just because you guys treat me like I'm still a member of the team doesn't mean I am, Arthur. I've got my own business now," I reminded him.

He laughed. "You tell me that every time I call you."

"Then perhaps you should stop calling me?"

"You break my little heart," he said, and I rolled my eyes but didn't say anything. "Trust me, you'll want to take a look at this. They're keeping everything on the down low, but no one can decide what the hell murdered a man like this…" He sighed. "It's gruesome, Kass. I hope you haven't had lunch."

"Oh goody, a gruesome murder mystery." I mocked being thrilled. "You know I run strictly on coffee until around five or so."

Ignoring my sarcasm, he asked, "Will you come take a look?"

"Tell me where it is." I turned the pencil around and dug through my desk for a Post-it pad.

Arthur gave me the address. "Good Lady," I said, "the boonies? It'll take me forty minutes alone to get out there."

"I know, but we need you to take a look at this."

"Why, exactly?"

"I told you…No one has figured out what did this. We've got people running around talking about a bear. We need your preternatural expertise," he said making it sound oh so important by emphasizing the word "expertise."

I resisted the urge to roll my eyes again. "How does one get a bear killing and preternatural in the same sentence?" I asked. "Especially since bears are not native to Oklahoma."

"Exactly," he said. "So, yea or nay?"

"Yea," I said, "I'm leaving the office now."

I hung up without saying good-bye.

On my way out I stopped to do one of those little girly checks in front of the mirror that hung on the wall by my office door. I tucked the streak of white in my long black hair behind my right ear, tucking the long side-swept bangs with it. Unlike most side-swept bangs, mine were long enough that they swept across my face and past my chin. In my profession, it's a must that I can keep my hair out of my face. The white streak, on the other hand, wasn't bleached.

It had begun showing up gradually after every shift I'd made into wolf form. Ironically, it was the same color as my fur.

If someone asked me what the change was like, the melding of my human thoughts with those of the wolf and the sharing of my body with her, I would tell them it was beyond frightening. The first shift I ever experienced, I'd gone under alone, locking myself in the bathroom of my apartment on the night of the full moon. It was that night that I knew without a doubt that I was no longer human.

It was the first battle the wolf and I had. She ripped from my flesh as if she were tearing me apart. I'd passed out from the pain of it and when I came to on the bathroom floor it was morning. All I can remember are snatches, bits of memory, and my utter determination to stay on that bathroom floor.

I'd fought the wolf and won the first few times, but always at the price of my consciousness. I cannot remember if it was my third or fourth shift that I finally decided to try and work with the wolf. The cravings were too strong and lingering just a bit longer after each shift. So I drove out to the country hours before the full moon rose to hunt in a woodland area an hour away from my apartment.

And hunt we did. It was beautiful and tragic. The earth and moon and stars were my mother, were a part of me. I'd taken down a deer that night, running wildly, teeth gnashing.

If I think about it hard enough I can still feel the creature's pulse thumping slowly against my tongue as it died. I wasn't used to it and I didn't know if a part of me would ever get used to it, but I had to learn to live so that it didn't kill us both.

I stopped reflecting on my change and looked in the mirror. I had to admit—I looked pretty damn harmless. Of course, the shoulder holster and Mark III over my red blouse looked anything but harmless. I could see what most people saw: a petite woman with a heart-shaped face. The dark kohl looked good with my pale skin and green eyes. It helped to bring out the specks of gold around my pupils. I was the only person in my family who had black hair and green eyes. The rest of my family had brown hair and blue eyes. On my mother's side our ancestry went back to Ireland, and on my father's, England. I was the weird wolf in the family. My high school history teacher had used the term "Black Irish" to describe it, whatever that meant.

I grabbed the black pea coat from the back of my chair and shrugged into it. Once the jacket went on over the Mark III, no one would know I was carrying. I was going to see a crime scene. Yippee. I tossed the messenger bag over my shoulder and walked out of the office, silently cursing myself for wearing high heels. Three-inch heels and a crime scene are a disaster waiting to happen.

"June, I've got to go take a look at something for the cops. Can you manage locking the shop up by yourself if I'm not back by then?" I asked my secretary.

She pushed the gray tresses out of her eyes. "Will do," she said, "but I don't want this becoming a ritual." She looked down at the paperwork she was filing through.

I smirked even though she couldn't see it. June could be a little demanding at times, and an outsider might think she ran the place, by the way she talked to me. I'd come to realize she looked at me like one of her grandchildren. I liked having her in the office, because not only would she not take my shit—she wouldn't take anyone else's.

I walked across the street and spotted the solid black paint of my Tiburon. I slapped the sticky note with the directions on it on the dash and threw my bag on the floor in front of the other seat. When I turned the key in the ignition the gentle sounds of Within Temptation's "Mother Earth" drowned out the soft hum of the car.

❖

Everyone had been standing around twiddling his or her thumbs. It seemed they'd already looked at the body. *That figures.* I ducked under the tape as Arthur spotted me and approached. He led me through the mass of uniforms and to the body.

I knelt carefully, holding my hands out for the pair of latex gloves he offered. There wasn't much of a body left of this…thing. I had to call it a thing, or a body, because in my mind it wasn't a man anymore. It was a mutilated corpse.

The torso was barely connected to the rest of its body, hanging on by ribbons of flesh like the torn wrapping paper of a present that someone had opened a little too eagerly. White hipbones tipped with blood glinted in the afternoon sun. The ground was soaked with blood and other fluids. The stench caught in the back of my throat and I resisted the urge to cough.

"What body parts are missing?" I asked as Arthur knelt down beside me. I leaned over the torso and carefully examined the wounds there. The body's hips had claw marks engraved in them. I tried not to focus on the hollowed insides of the torso below me. The smell of blood and death made my stomach lurch.

"We found the arm over there." Arthur pointed farther into the woods that surrounded us. "And as you can see, there's nothing left of his intestines." He sounded like he was going to be sick. The human part of me agreed with him.

I took in a deep breath of air. It was a mistake this close to the body. I froze and tried to hold the pacing wolf inside me down. If I went apeshit at a crime scene I was not getting a Scooby Snack. The entire body was such a mess of red gore that all I could smell was blood. It flooded my senses and called to the beast inside me. I resisted the urge to roll around in it, to claim it as my territory, my blood, my kill. It wasn't my kill, and that just wouldn't look good, would it? I stifled a giggle at the ridiculousness of my thoughts.

Lesson number one: You don't giggle at a crime scene. It makes everyone else think you've lost your mind.

I closed my eyes as the scent of blood mingled with something else. Another smell hit my nostrils, something sour and acrid. "Werewolf," I said as I moved around the body, pretending to examine it as I sniffed out the area around it. It wasn't just the scattered pieces of human flesh strewn across the dying grass that made me say that. I stopped with the tree behind me. Turning, I pretended to cough. The movement put my face toward the tree, and I sniffed. There was a scent on the tree next to the body. The werewolf had marked the tree. Which meant that yes, he'd piddled all over the damn thing. How did I know it was male? Female urine does not smell that bad, and most females don't feel an urge to piss on everything.

I felt the beast pacing in her fleshy cage, nuzzling at the surface as the tide of anger rose within me. I stood too quickly and stumbled away from the body. It wouldn't be an unusual sight. A lot of people stumble away after seeing a dead body, and usually vomit. I had good control over the beast, but when she lurked this close to the surface—I knew better. She whispered not-so-nice things. Okay, not-so-human things. I wouldn't let myself touch the blood. That was too much temptation. In fact, I was getting away from the smell of sweet metal and raw meat. The thought alone made my mouth water and I swallowed a little too loudly. I was suddenly craving a bacon cheeseburger. Good Goddess. That sounded good.

At first, the cravings had freaked me out. It started with a desire for bloody food. I had learned, over time, that it wasn't always just the smell of blood that pulled the predatory instincts out of the wolf. The smell of fear could pull out the predator in me and I'd want nothing more than to taste that fear on my tongue. In fact, smell serves as a huge trigger. The smell of desire, the smell of fear, the smell of salt and sweat and human frailty, those things have a tendency to excite the wolf and make me feel terribly inhuman. For months, I was a stranger to myself, but with time, I began to learn the wolf and to understand her.

Well, in some areas. Getting hungry standing over a corpse still made me uneasy.

I headed back toward the group of uniforms and Arthur fell into step beside me. My stomach gave a fierce little rumble.

"Did your stomach just growl or are you about to upchuck?" he asked with a teasing twinkle in his eyes.

I looked at him with what I knew was a blank expression. "I'm hungry."

"Hungry?" The teasing fell from his face. "How can you be hungry after seeing that?"

I shrugged. "There's this place by my apartment that makes delicious bacon cheeseburgers. I haven't eaten all day."

"I cannot believe you could eat any kind of meat after seeing… that. You are definitely one of the weirdest gals I've met." The expression he wore was both shocked and curious.

"You have absolutely no idea."

"What?"

I smiled. "Nothing."

When we made it back to the uniforms they were standing as far away from the mess of man-meat as they could. Two of them were arguing back and forth about the bear theory. I felt the anger stir inside me. How could they try and slight this off as a bear attack? It didn't make any fucking sense. If they ever wanted to catch the real killer, they'd have to come to terms with the facts.

"That wasn't a bear," I raised my voice, interrupting.

"What?" one of the uniforms asked.

I looked to the man I knew was in charge of the investigation.

"Deputy Sheriff Witkins," I said, "it was a werewolf attack."

"How can you tell?" he asked, his voice deep and calm.

"The only wild animal that's native to these parts is livestock and deer, and unless mad cow disease just took a whole new turn, it was a werewolf attack. A deer won't snack on the insides of a man."

"What about coyotes, Miss Lyall?" he asked, and I ignored the "Miss" part.

"They're scavengers for the most part," I said, "but even then they're not going to do that much damage to a man. If you measure the claw marks around the hip, you'll see they don't match up with any animals in this area." I left off the part that they probably wouldn't match up with any animals at all.

"The couple that owns this ranch says they heard a wolf howl." He looked me up and down. "You may think it's a werewolf, Lyall, but I'm not putting my job at risk on your say-so. Not for a thing like that."

I looked at his pudgy face, staring into his beady brown eyes.

"That thing?" I crossed my arms over my chest. "That thing, Witkins, was a werewolf." I dramatically pointed in the direction of the body. "That was not the work of one Winnie the Pooh. It's seriously the Big Bad Wolf."

The deputy sheriff's dark brown eyes followed my pointing finger, and even with the tan his face paled.

"Miss Lyall," the deputy said, "if that's the case we have to figure something else out because the media can't have their hands on that version."

"That's Ms. Lyall," I snapped. So sue me, half the people I work with are idiots. I had a feeling I knew why the deputy sheriff didn't want the media getting wind of "that version." He didn't want the bad publicity if the shit hit the fan. I took a few steps closer to him, keeping my hand on the butt of my gun where it rested in its holster. As a deputy, Witkins got to handle the case out here in the boonies. It was his sandbox, but we'd been invited to play in it.

"Then I suggest you start finding out all that you can about your so-called Winnie the Pooh, because it's going to do this again, and within the next three weeks."

The other officer that had been talking earlier walked back to our group. He'd gone to throw up in the nearby bushes. He was so new I could tell this crime scene was going to haunt him for life. You never forget your first crime scene. He'd see pieces of that body floating around behind his eyes for days. Trust me, it'd happen. What really sucks is when you start dreaming about dismembered body parts chasing you and whimpering, "help me."

I turned my attention back to the guy in charge. Why some law enforcers asked for my expertise and then stood around arguing with me, I would never fully understand.

"Wait, why in three weeks?" Arthur asked.

I drew in a deep breath, counting slowly. I couldn't believe Captain Holbrook hadn't pushed for the Paranormal class to be mandatory for all officers on the force. I fucking would've.

"It's a werewolf, Arthur. Can you not remember any of the stories from your childhood?"

"I wasn't into that kind of thing when I was a kid," he said, grinning.

"The full moon. Aren't werewolves supposed to shift on the full moon?" the deputy asked, and I had to admit that at least one person in our corner of the world was beginning to go somewhere with the thought. Maybe he'd stop arguing with me.

"Bingo," I said, keeping it to myself that werewolves could shift even when it wasn't the full moon. "I really suggest you start studying all that you can."

"Lyall," he said gruffly, "I want your help on this case. I want you to get me all the information you can on werewolves."

"Deputy Sheriff Witkins, I'm a witch and private investigator. I'm not a werewolf hunter, unless I decide to be." I spoke the truth, but I sensed very strongly that the deputy was going to try and back me into a corner if I put up a struggle. Legally, he couldn't force me to take the case.

As a witch, I'm what most psychics would call a clairsentient. In French, "clairsentient" means *clear feeling*. I have moments when I sense things, without rational thought, and without a doubt. Most people have some type of psychic ability, whether they know it or not. Sometimes, people grow into adulthood and learn how to block out their own abilities, to the point where those senses become nearly nonexistent and undetectable. Instead of blocking mine, I developed them. It's part of what made me a damn good cop and a wickedly good investigator.

I gazed at the deputy and knew deep down in my gut that, intuitively, he knew I was right, but he was going to put me on the case because he just didn't want to spoil his pretty hands with it and didn't want his department taking the fall if there was one.

I realized at a very young age that I am much more sensitive than most people to subtle energy changes and spiritual energies within the environment. I cannot touch a person or an object and see visions of the past. I am not a clairvoyant, a psychic that relies on clear visions of things to come. I may not see images, but I have moments where I *feel* and *know*.

Looking into the deputy sheriff's dark eyes, I knew that he was sensitive, but I also knew that he ignored his intuition. In my opinion, it was a waste. If he'd harnessed the power that I felt coming off him in waves, like a warm breeze, he'd have been a better cop.

The deputy took a step back and I knew that he'd sensed me prodding around his shields. I gave a very slow blink. He had such raw ability, that if harnessed… I shuddered to think on it. I suddenly knew more than I wanted to know.

The trouble with abilities is similar to the trouble that comes with being a werewolf. If you cannot control the power, then the power will control you, and sometimes, when it comes to people that are as naturally psychic as the deputy sheriff standing in front of me, their own abilities could drive them to madness.

The cops couldn't force me to hunt and execute. That was a personal decision that came with being a licensed paranormal huntress. They could ask me to do it, but by law, I still had every right to tell them to go fuck themselves. I slammed my shields down tight, fearful of catching the attention of the beast within. I was still at a crime scene. The smell of blood hung heavy in the air and I wasn't going to risk unintentionally taunting her.

"I'm hiring you to investigate this crime. None of my men know how to deal with this. They don't have the training to deal with this. We've never had our noses shoved so deeply up paranormal ass. We need your help. Are you with us or not, Lyall?" The deputy's words were careful and slow.

Golly, put like that. "Fine. Where do you want me to start?"

"The Nelsons, who live on this farm, have already been questioned," he said, "but I want you to question them."

I narrowed my eyes at Arthur. "You so owe me for this."

He smiled a wide toothy smile. "You're just everyone's favorite witch, Kass."

"Oh, shove it where the sun doesn't shine, Kingfisher."

Chapter Four

It wasn't long before I was sitting in a brightly lit kitchen. Mrs. Nelson had offered coffee, and I'd graciously accepted a cup. I idly twirled my spoon before lifting the drink to take a sip. The Nelsons sat at the table staring at me like I'd sprouted a second head.

"You don't look like a cop," Timothy said. He was the Nelsons' youngest son. I knew that because they'd told me their oldest was out of state at the Texas University. I looked at the pink frilly drapes over the window. Mrs. Nelson's touch was undeniable. I turned my gaze back to the boy of sixteen. He looked a little bit older, one of those sixteen-year-olds who could pass for eighteen. His eyes were the deep dark brown of his father's, and they both sported the same light summer tans. Timothy's hair was a few shades lighter than Mr. Nelson's, but the height, the eyes, and facial structure were unmistakably his father's genetics.

Mrs. Nelson looked immaculately clean. Her blond hair was shoulder length and pulled out of her face to show startling blue eyes. The features of her face were soft and delicate. In size, she was tiny between her son and husband.

I took another sip. "That's because I'm not a cop."

"Then why are you here?" Mr. Nelson asked.

"I work with the cops and they want me to question you," I said flatly.

"But we've already been questioned," said Mrs. Nelson.

"You haven't been questioned by someone who knows about the preternatural."

"And you do?" Timothy snorted.

I stared into his rich brown eyes and he looked away first. "Yeah, I do."

Everyone fell silent. Mrs. Nelson leaned into her husband, narrowing her eyes at me. Her eyes kept flicking to the pewter necklace hanging over my shirt. I ignored it.

"What were you doing that all three of you noticed the werewolf?" I asked.

"Werewolf?" Mrs. Nelson laughed. "It was a wolf."

Great, she was going to deny what it was. I knew what it was based on the crime scene. I'd only seen one other werewolf killing, and that was a year ago on an out-of-state job. A single wolf wouldn't take down a man. They hunt in packs, and packs keep their distance from humans. Should I also mention that we don't have wolves in Oklahoma? Nah.

"Whatever you say," I said. "What were you doing?" I arched a brow this time.

"We were going to check on the herd," Timothy said. "I heard something howl and got my parents. We went out to make sure there weren't any wolves or coyotes trying to get past the fence."

Fuck it, I couldn't help it. "Just for your information, there aren't any wolves in Oklahoma. Wolves were hunted to near extinction so many years ago that they're only found in a few places in North America—Wyoming and other mountainous regions."

"It was a wolf." Mrs. Nelson's voice was harsh.

"Mrs. Nelson, I've seen a werewolf before. They're as real as you and me, but a hell of a lot furrier and scarier."

She just stared at me, mouth open. "When?" she asked boldly.

"I was on the job about three years ago. The werewolf's brother had reported her. Said that his sister was acting strange and he couldn't find her."

"What happened?" Timothy wiggled in his seat, eyes burning with a sudden interest in the story.

"The cops sent me out," I said, leaving out the part that no one had taken the call seriously enough to send me out with backup. "I found her in the woods near the house."

"And?" He pressed.

I shrugged. "And," I added, "that's all you need to know. The government knows about these things, but with the vampires taking over all of the media coverage, the people are kept in the dark. All we know is that not all of the wolves out there are hostile. If they were," I shrugged, "there'd be more bodies."

"Our government knows about this?" he asked, confused.

"Yep."

"Why don't they tell us? Warn us?"

"It's kind of 'don't ask, and they won't tell.' There are underground werewolf hunters out there, and most are unhappy that there's a new law going through that any werewolf in question has to go through a full trial before getting slammed with the death sentence. If it passes, it'll make them harder to kill. They'll be protected by our government."

"Cool." Timothy grinned. "That's so cool. I never knew they really existed. I mean, I thought when we saw the wolf out there, that it wasn't just a normal wolf, but I thought maybe I'd been watching too many horror movies."

"Timothy," his father said, and Tim closed his mouth.

"You're not a werewolf hunter," Mrs. Nelson said, and again her eyes dropped to the charm dangling off my necklace.

"No," I said, "I'm not. I'm a preternatural investigator."

She scoffed. "What is that?"

"I investigate crimes and cases having to deal with the preternatural."

Her eyes again lowered to my necklace.

"Is there a problem, Mrs. Nelson?" I said, and my voice didn't sound entirely friendly.

"Yes," she said, "I don't like having a devil worshipper in my house, lying to my son about werewolves. It's bad enough there are vampires!"

Fuck it. I took my cell phone out of my pocket and called Arthur's number. He answered on the first ring.

"Yeah, Kass? What is it?"

"I need backup before Mrs. Nelson gets out her Bible and tries to thump me out of her house."

"All right, we're coming."

"Thank you."

Arthur said, "No problem." I flipped the phone closed.

I smiled oh so sweetly while saying, "The cops are on their way so they can be witness to this investigation. How silly of me not to bring them in the first place. By the way, I don't worship a devil. You can't worship something you don't believe in."

Mrs. Nelson's face turned an angry shade of red. Her husband put a hand on her shoulder and said, "Honey…"

She jerked away from him. The expression on her face didn't look very sane as she spat, "I don't want this devil whore in our house!"

I took in a deep breath and leaned back in my seat. One…two… "I told you, I don't believe in a devil."

Arthur walked through the back door with two other officers. "Having trouble, Kass?"

"Yeah, apparently my new nickname is Devil-Whore."

Arthur looked at the obviously pissed-off Mrs. Nelson. She was leaning over the table glaring at me. She pointed at me dramatically. "I want this devil worshipper out of my house right now!"

Mr. Nelson and Timothy just sat there. Did I mention I don't like drama queens? I leaned back in my seat, taking another sip of coffee. I'd let Arthur and his backup deal with this.

"Mrs. Nelson, if you don't calm down and cooperate with us, we'll be forced to take you into custody."

"What for?" she practically screamed. "I haven't done anything!"

"For withholding information from the police and verbally harassing a law enforcing officer."

"She just said she's not a cop!"

"No, but when she's working with the force she's considered a cop. She's got a badge of her own and has every right to press charges."

Arthur looked at me and I shrugged. I wouldn't have pressed charges, but if Arthur's threat got her to sit back down, I'd go with it.

❖

I stood outside the Nelson's two-story ranch waiting for Arthur to wrap things up. A glance at my cell phone told me it was almost five in the afternoon. I really wanted to get home before rush hour traffic. Gods, I hate traffic. In order to keep myself from getting pissed at Mrs. Nelson, I had to remove myself from the kitchen. As much as I hated doing exactly what she'd wanted… She'd kept ranting and casting daggers with her eyes. It wasn't a good idea for me to let my temper out. Hell, even before I was infected with lycanthropy that was a bad idea.

The air around the house smelled like fresh grass and pine needles when I breathed. I heard footsteps falling somewhat hurriedly and turned around to find Timothy approaching. He smiled weakly, as if trying to be friendly but seeming more awkward in his youth.

"You're serious?" he asked.

"About what?" I leaned back against the car, crossing my arms over my chest.

"About the werewolves."

"Yes." I wondered where Arthur was and why it was taking him so damn long.

Timothy pushed the brown tresses of his hair back. "Sorry about my mom," he said. "She's pretty hardcore and anything she doesn't understand tends to freak her out."

I nodded slightly. "I'm used to it."

"I'm cool with it," he said. "I've got a friend in school and his mother practices witchcraft. She's really earthy, smart too."

"Nifty," I said, for lack of anything better.

"Look, I know I'm probably bothering you but I just thought we should talk. I'd like to know more about the werewolves."

"I didn't say I was an expert on the subject." In a sense it was true. I'm not an expert, just your average werewolf here, folks.

"You sounded like you knew about 'em in the house," he said, and I frowned at him.

I sighed. "Look, Tim, I only know what I've experienced, and trust me, you don't want to come face-to-face with a lycanthrope. They're not that fascinating. Scary, yes, but the whole fascination factor diminishes when they're trying to eat you."

He gave a slight nod. "I just wanted to hear more about what happened to you. Hey, you know what you said about the media and vampires? I saw on the news the other night that there was a vampire club that opened in the city a few weeks ago. Did you see that?"

He changed the subject so quickly it took my mind a moment to process what he was saying. I was obviously running low on caffeine.

"I don't watch the news," I said, "too much negativity."

In the United States, vampires had legal rights. It was the rest of us underground paranorms that were waiting for a law to pass that protected and treated all supernaturals as legal citizens. Of course, from an outsider's perspective, drinking blood might seem classier than using a human's arm as a chew toy.

In all reality, most werewolves keep to themselves or to a local pack. They don't usually brutally murder. Yet, with everything there are exceptions. The movies make it look like we lose all of our humanity when we shift. In actuality, we're not any different from humans. If a person of ill heart is turned into a werewolf, it's not being a lycan that makes them a bad person. It's being a bad person that makes them a bad person. It's like a gun. It's not the gun that hurts someone, it's the person holding the gun and pulling the trigger that does. I admit that the hungers and instincts arise and sometimes the animal sees through the eyes of the human instead of the other way around, but it is only the weak willed that fall victim to their inner wolf. Then again, maybe everyone's wolf is different. I wouldn't really know, because I never joined a pack. I know there's one in every city. At least, that's the case according to Jake, the Paranormal Hunter that helped me get my license, but I was too afraid joining a pack would risk exposure. Thus, I avoided the idea all together. Jake had told me that there are quite a few wolves that "lone" it. Well, I was one of them now.

I heard voices and turned to look toward the house. Arthur was shaking hands with Mr. Nelson. He turned, stepping off the porch. He was heading in my direction.

"Tim!" Mr. Nelson yelled from the porch.

Timothy smiled another awkward smile. "I guess I should go inside."

"Be safe, Tim," I said. "You should try and stay in the house until we find the lycanthrope that did this."

He began walking back toward the house. Unexpectedly, a little warning went off in my mind. This warning wasn't coming from outside danger, though. It came from deep inside and was loud enough that I called after him. "Timothy?"

"Yeah?"

"Do me a favor and don't try to go investigating on your own, okay?"

"Why would you think I'd do that?"

I couldn't tell if it was the emptiness in his voice, the way his shoulders tensed, or my intuition, but something in his dark brown eyes told me he'd thought about it. I only knew that there was an image in the back of my mind of a sixteen-year-old boy snooping where he shouldn't and getting himself hurt, or worse.

"I was sixteen once with an insatiable curiosity," I said, giving him a knowing look. I resisted the urge to say, "And look where it got me."

Tim nodded. "Yeah, okay."

Arthur watched me with a curious look in his eyes as he came around the car. "What was that all about?"

"He wanted me to tell him what I know about werewolves."

He nodded. "Well, truthfully, since you say that's what we're dealing with, enlighten me. You've faced one before."

I pulled the cell phone out of my pocket and looked at the time again. Damn it. "It's like I told the kid—I only know what I've experienced and what Jake taught me."

"How'd you kill that one several years ago?" he asked and leaned against my car.

"With a gun," I said. "And silver ammo. Kingfisher, get off my car."

"What? You were just leaning against it." His voice held an edge of shock.

"I've showered in the past month." I reached for the door handle.

He laughed. "I read that if I showered less, the pheromones to attract females would be stronger."

"That's a load of crap," I said, sliding into the seat. "The only thing stronger is your B.O."

He laughed again. "You're always good for a laugh, Kass." His hand rested on the butt of his gun. It was a habit most cops had. "So, what are you planning on doing next? We didn't get much out of the Nelsons."

"I know." I took in a deep breath. "I'll come back out here and do a little bit of trooping around within the next few days. The scene should be cleaned up by then and I'll be able to see if they missed anything."

"What are you going to do? Look for tracks?" he asked jokingly.

"That and a picnic basket," I scoffed. "I've got a friend that used to hunt all of the time. Ex–bounty hunter and licensed paranormal hunter," I said. I didn't know if Arthur would remember him. If he did, I didn't know it was a good idea to bring him up, so I stuck with being a little vague. "I'll probably call and see if he wants to tag along. He's a good tracker."

"I'll tell the deputy sheriff. I don't think he really gives a shit what you do as long as you're taking charge of the investigation and trying to solve it."

"That's my job, isn't it?" I asked. "I'll call you if I find anything. Tell Witkins the same."

I shut the car door before he could say anything else. It was a little after five. I cursed aloud. If I got stuck in traffic I was so chewing someone's head off. Figuratively speaking, of course.

I pressed the speed dial number and listened to the phone ring three times before Rupert answered.

"Guns Unlimited," he said, sounding tired.

"Hey, Rupe. Long day?" I asked.

"Hey, Kass. Yeah, it's been a hell of a day. What's up?"

"Not much. Are you busy tomorrow?"

There was long pause, as if he was afraid to answer. "I don't know," he replied carefully. "Why?"

"How's about you and I go do a little huntin'?" I said with a terrible accent.

Rupert laughed. "What kind of hunting are we talking about?"

"Why, the fun kind, of course. Camouflage, weapons, a nice stroll through the woods on the outskirts of town…"

"Who are we taking out?" He sounded calm and professional, as if he was already relaxing and polishing his gun. Wait, that was probably too close to the truth.

"The police assigned me to investigate a killing. The scene reeks of werewolf. I'm betting money his furry ass is still around here somewhere too."

"Sounds promising," he said. "What time?"

I made a left turn onto the access ramp to get on the highway. The Tiburon purred beneath me like a happy little kitten and I smiled. "I'll call you at nightfall."

"Talk to you then."

"'Til then," I responded and hung up.

The chances weren't that high that we'd find the werewolf, but it was best to be prepared. It wasn't being a preternatural investigator that gave me the right to execute a werewolf. Nor was it the fact that we didn't have the same rights as citizens. According to Oklahoma state law, a person found guilty for killing a werewolf had only one threat held over their head—if the family of said werewolf decided to press charges. That threat was animal cruelty. This meant that a murderer could walk away with either a fine, or imprisonment not exceeding five years in a state penitentiary. Now, here's the catch. If I were to kill the werewolf in human form, it's cold-blooded murder. That is until, I presume, scientists learn to recognize the lycanthropy virus. Unfortunately, they're working on it. Which would probably explain why one side is pushing to be recognized as human beings, and the other side is pushing adamantly against it.

No, what gave me the right to take this bastard down was the paranormal huntress badge in my wallet alongside the one that stated I was a preternatural investigator. My old boss tried to convince people to take the course and get the badge. Oddly enough, a good majority of them refused. There were maybe two officers in our department that had taken the course with me. The class was easy. In fact, it had been too easy. We listened to an already licensed Paranormal Hunter lecture us on the how-tos of "humanely" executing shape shifters and other super beasties.

My boss had wanted to cover his ass, but it was only another reason for me to cover mine after the incident.

The words on the actual license stated that I had the right to execute any paranormal that had committed a murderous crime when granted the authority or the proof. The downside was that it covered a broad spectrum of paranormals and unfortunately the class hadn't. You'd think that would make my life easier, but there are some things even I don't want to sniff out and hunt down.

Chapter Five

It wasn't until around six that I arrived back at the office. I wanted to get the Pro .40 out of my desk drawer tonight instead of tomorrow. If I did it tonight, my entire afternoon tomorrow would be free, since Rit was working. Her name is actually Avani Ritika. I fell into the habit of calling her Rit for short, and not long after that June started calling her by it as well. Oh, she was a bit irked with me for a few weeks, telling me that I made her sound like clothing dye or a lice-killing shampoo. I think it eventually grew on her, because she finally stopped complaining. Rit and I alternated days. She worked one day and I worked the next. It helped us both to keep a healthy balance between fieldwork and office work. Every P.I. works differently. It's what worked for us. There were days when I got called out of the office while the only person here was June. If that was the case, she told any potential clients to make an appointment. She tried not to schedule any appointments that would interfere with our days off, but as with any job, it happened.

I crossed the street and stepped onto the sidewalk, reaching for the door. My fingertips had just brushed the handle when the smell hit me. The breeze smelled of forest, of damp leaves and moist soil. It was an earthy scent, not the salty scent of a human. I let my hand fall away from the door. I didn't reach for my gun. My nostrils flared as I took that scent inside of me. It flooded my senses better than any alcoholic burst of air freshener. Being a werewolf, I'd recognize another werewolf from a mile away. This wolf was much closer than that. I turned my face toward the direction of the smell.

She stood about ten feet away wearing a yellow sweater and jeans. Her skin was lightly tanned, a healthy tan that only the sun could give. The breeze sent her shoulder-length auburn hair billowing, and she raised a small hand to tuck it behind her ear. Her rich amber eyes met mine and there was a moment of acknowledgment. Her chest rose and fell as she drew a long breath. I watched as her nostrils flared slightly, and her full lips parted. She tasted my scent on the air. Those lips curved into a seductive smile and she inclined her head, as if to say, "I know what you are," but neither of us needed words. I stood there for a moment and then slowly inclined my own.

The door opening startled me and I turned to find June about to run me over.

"Well, finally you return," she grumbled, "just as I was about to lock up."

"I need to grab something before you do," I said. I sprinted up the stairs and down the hallway to my office. I unlocked the door and went to my desk, opened the bottom drawer, and took out the Pro .40. I tucked it at the small of my back, pulling my blouse down over it. I made sure that the coat covered the bulk.

June was waiting at the door with an impatient look on her face. "Hurry up," she said. "I've got to get home and get dinner started."

I decided to be polite, instead of reminding her who signed her checks. "Sorry, June. I'll see you Wednesday."

She waved me off. "Yeah, yeah. I'll see you then."

I shook my head. People thought I was rude? Obviously, they hadn't met my secretary.

That trace of earth and pine still rode the wind, letting me know that the she wolf was still close by. I resisted the urge to draw my gun and focused on getting to the car.

I was almost to the car when a woman's voice stopped me in my tracks.

"Are you Kassandra Lyall?"

I spun on my heel to face her, drawing the Pro .40, clicking off the safety, and hoisting it in a two-handed grip. I looked down the sights, barrel aimed at her forehead. Her eyes widened.

"Why?" I asked as a strange sense of calm filled me.

"Because if you are," she took a brave step forward, "then I need to talk to you. Please," she said, eyes meeting mine over the gun, "I swear, I give you my most solemn oath that I mean you no harm."

I tried to sense a threat coming off her, and didn't. I had to admit that I was curious as to how she knew my name. There was no Kassandra in Lyall Preternatural Investigations. She had to have figured it out by other means. Call me foolish, but I wanted to know those means. Here's to hoping that phrase about curiosity only applied to cats, not werewolves.

I clicked on the safety and slid the gun into the back of my pants.

"What do you need to talk to me about?"

Her gaze darted around the empty parking lot. "I'd prefer somewhere more private."

❖

The Corner Café was a little coffeehouse and bakery a few blocks away from my office. The lighting was dim, as if the atmosphere was supposed to be romantic. It was clean and well kept, despite being the ideal place for high school kids to bring their dates. Then again, I wasn't feeling under the table for gum. The food was reasonably priced, too. There weren't very many customers. Even if there had been, the high backed booths gave the illusion of privacy, which was one of the reasons I liked it.

I found a seat in the far corner so I could watch the doors. It was quiet, with most of the noise coming from the employees doing their various tasks. Keeping my eyes on the front doors, I tore off a piece of croissant and popped it into my mouth.

She must've walked. If I had known her I might've offered her a ride. As it was, I didn't, and I'm not that generous toward strangers, especially when they could probably match me in supernatural strength.

I caught sight of a canary yellow sweater and leaned back, waiting. She slipped into the seat across from me.

"I apologize if I've made you go out of your way, but it was important that I speak to you where no one would see us."

I swallowed. "It's not that far out of the way." I motioned toward my plate. "I haven't eaten anyhow. What do you want?"

"Wow," she said softly. "You're forward, aren't you? Just cut right to the chase?"

I shrugged. "In my line of work, you lose patience with the cat and mouse."

"Well then, we should start off the right way. I'm Rosalin Walker."

I wiped my hands on the napkin in my lap, taking the hand she'd offered. "Kassandra," I said. "Kassandra Lyall." I smiled. "You already knew that. How?"

Rosalin Walker blinked a few times. "I'd heard you were to the point. I didn't think you'd be this to the point." She shook her head and then said, "I spoke with Avani Ritika the other day over the phone. I told her I'm looking for an investigator. She said she was booked solid." Rosalin folded her arms across the table. "I feel like I can trust you more, knowing what you are."

I gave a nod, urging her to go on as I finished the croissant.

"My brother is missing," she said matter-of-factly. "He's been missing for a few days now. I haven't heard anything from him, and his girlfriend hasn't seen him since last Sunday."

"When was the last time she heard from him?"

"Sunday evening, before he went to work. He works the night shift as a janitor at an elementary school."

"Which school?" I asked.

She smiled wide enough to show a row of perfect white teeth, "Jefferson," she said thoughtfully. "I'm pretty sure. I'll have to double check with Paula for one hundred percent certainty."

"Paula is his girlfriend?"

"Yes. He never made it back to the house that morning. Paula called me an hour or so after he was supposed to get home, before she went to bed. She asked me to try and get a hold of him because she couldn't reach him at his cell phone or work. I tried calling and kept getting voicemail. The last time I called was yesterday, and it was the same thing."

When she spoke her face showed worry, but not the concern of a woman who thought she'd never see her brother again.

"Before I agree to take this case…I need to know why you're being so secretive and having me meet you in private. Are you in trouble?" I asked.

The set of her shoulders stiffened and she leaned back. I thought for a moment that she wasn't going to tell me. "You know what I am," she said, "and I know what you are. You don't smell like pack. If you did, I wouldn't be talking to you about this."

"You belong to a pack?"

"Yes. I don't want the others in the pack to know I'm talking to a private investigator. It's too close to going outside of pack law." Her brown eyes hardened, carefully guarding whatever there was to see in them.

I understood that werewolf packs resembled traditional wolf packs. There was an alpha, a beta, and an omega. Due to lack of experience and the fact that most packs are very secretive, I didn't know a lot about them. And no, the secretive part didn't make me feel any safer about the idea of joining one. The whole idea of a pack seemed very power structured to me. I didn't want to have to answer to an alpha werewolf. It's one of the reasons I chose to go it alone.

"How does it go outside of pack law?" I asked.

"The alpha didn't approve it. She knows nothing about it. Can you keep it that way?" she asked.

I wondered for a few moments if it was a good idea. If the alpha found out, how much crap would I be in? I knew one thing without a doubt—the alpha's word was law, and Rosalin was breaking it. Either she believed in her capabilities as a werewolf enough that she could protect herself against the alpha, she had someone protecting her, or she was really putting her trust in me. Damn it. I had a feeling it was the latter.

I sighed. Without a contract, I was hesitant to take the case. The contract protects the client and the investigator. In the end, I wasn't the only one taking a huge risk.

"It's off the record," I said.

A look of relief flooded her features.

"Thank you. You have no idea how much I appreciate this."

"I don't do charity work," I said, "and just because it's off the record doesn't mean there isn't a fee."

She smiled, and it was a smile that probably got her anything she wanted. "Of course," she said. Her voice was a little too breathy. I frowned. I really hoped she understood we were talking about money.

Chapter Six

Rosalin had given me her cell phone number before she left so that I could contact her. She'd also given me the name of her brother and his girlfriend and their telephone numbers. Henry Walker and Paula Meeks. I assured her that I'd begin my investigation tomorrow. I no longer had the afternoon free. Damn it. At least I got a decent retainer out of her. Yeah, that made things a lot better.

There were two things I needed to do before I got home. The first thing was to call Rit and find out exactly what had happened. In my line of business you learn not to take anything at face value.

"Hello?" It sounded like I'd woken her.

"Hey, Rit."

"Oh, hello, Kassandra."

"Were you asleep?" I asked.

"Yes, but it's okay. What is it that you need?" She was soft spoken and polite, as always.

"Sorry for waking you up, Rit, but I need to ask you a few questions about a phone call you received the other day. Does the last name Walker sound familiar to you?" I wasn't going to give out Rosalin's first name. I'd agreed to keep the investigation on the down low.

"No, it doesn't," she said thoughtfully. "What is this about?"

"I can't give you all the details. A person that knows my first name has contacted me, and she said you gave it to her. Do you remember getting a phone call in the past three days that had to do with me?"

"On Friday June connected a call to my office. It did seem a bit strange, now that I think of it. She wouldn't give me her name, and she said that she specifically wanted to speak to you. I told her I was the only one available in the office, but that she could make an appointment with you. She declined and hung up."

Interesting.

"How would someone get my legal name?" I asked. The only thing publicly known was Lyall. Rit often gave her name out to potential clients to be friendly, but I liked mine remaining a mystery unless I was actively working a case. The only way a client would know my name was if we gave it to them. It meant a slighter risk of being harassed or attacked.

"Perhaps she was a former client?"

"No, it's not that. Well, thanks, Rit. I'll talk to you later."

"All right, Kass. If you need anything just let me know. Have a good night."

We hung up. Rosalin must've gotten my name from somewhere else. The police might've given it out, but I doubted that. They respected my privacy. I'd also managed to stay out of newspapers when I was working on the force. The only thing that ever showed up in print was my last name. Hell, my phone number wasn't even listed. So, that meant that Rosalin was either connected to someone that I'd worked for, or knew, or that she'd done her own snooping and figured it out. Either way, it made me wary. It made me cautious because she lied—and in my book, you absolutely cannot trust a liar.

CHAPTER SEVEN

It was midnight and I hadn't dug up any dirt on Rosalin Walker. She had a clean slate. At least, that's how it appeared. I'm just not one to be fooled by appearances. I'm suspicious by nature.

I closed the laptop and put the leftover pizza in the fridge. I walked into the bathroom, flicking the switch on the wall.

I washed off my makeup and started running a hot bath. My blouse fell to the floor as I looked in the mirror at the tattoo on my back.

"Should've gotten a wolf," I mumbled.

I got the tattoo about four years ago. It was before I'd been infected. The tattoo was of a raven with its wings spread wide. The feathers swooped out, tracing the line of my rib cage. The inside of its body and wings were woven with Celtic knot work. In the middle of the raven was a red Triskelion—the symbol of life, death, and rebirth. The raven's beak ended between my shoulder blades, and the tail feathers followed the lower line of my spine. Even if it wasn't a wolf, it was still something I was proud of and didn't regret. Becoming a werewolf hadn't changed the fact that the raven was my spirit animal. It was also the animal representation of the Goddess I dedicated myself to nine years ago. If anything, I was sure the raven understood the passage of transformation better than I did.

I stripped off the rest of my clothes and slid into the water, breathing a sigh of relief as the heat enveloped my body. I craved heat. It comforted me. It usually made me feel safe, but it suddenly felt like a false sense of security. I felt it in every fiber of my being as surely as I could feel the water holding me close. It was a growing sense of unease, a sense that something profound was about to happen. I sensed change before me and shuddered. I sank down deeper into the tub. I didn't want to face another trial, another opportunity for growth. Surely the Goddess understood that? Wasn't becoming a werewolf life altering enough?

"No," a small voice whispered inside my mind.

There wasn't any emotion to it. The voice was neither cold nor warm. It just was.

I shuddered, wondering what the Goddess had in store. The Morrigan is what a lot of witches would call my matron deity. A matron or patron deity is pretty much a feminine or masculine deity that a witch dedicates herself to. The spiritual connection is very personal. A lot of the time the witch is called to that deity through dreams or synchronicities. There are some witches who choose as their matron or patron the one they relate to most strongly. For example, a poet might be drawn to the Goddess Brighid due to her association with creativity and bards. The Morrigan is a triple Goddess of Battle who had called to me nine years ago.

I felt the breeze of beating wings against my face for an instant and quivered, as if the hand of her power caressed my aura. Weight like some great stone fell to the pit of my stomach.

Feeling deity in your personal space can be uncomfortable at best, and terrifying at worst.

I sank low into the water and closed my eyes, hoping that tomorrow would bring more clarity and less foreboding.

❖

My search for Henry Walker was proving to be as unsuccessful as my mission to find anything about Rosalin Walker. I'd called Paula Meeks earlier in the afternoon and spoken with her. I'd tried to schedule a meeting and failed. Why? Paula Meeks worked full-time as a telemarketer. She informed me that she was working overtime and was on call for the next couple of days. She gave me the name of her employer, a well-known telemarketer in the city.

I'd called to confirm her lack of availability, just to be on the safe side. There'd been worry in her tone and I could tell over the phone that she regretted not being able to drop everything. Which is how I knew she'd schedule something as soon as she was availabile. I didn't like it because it meant that I'd have to drop whatever I was doing to make it for an impromptu meeting, but I couldn't exactly throw a bitchfest over it, either.

Rosalin had told me before she left the café that both of their parents had passed away some years ago. I'd also checked into that, not wanting to take her word for it. Who knew if she was lying about that too? The birth and death records stated clearly that she hadn't lied.

I was meeting Rupert at Guns Unlimited in twenty minutes. I'd taken the time to shower and dabbed essential oil on my pulse points to cover my scent as best as I could. I was hoping that patchouli was woodsy and werewolf enough to go undetected in a forest. It wasn't guaranteed to work, but it was worth the try.

I'd chosen a pair of charcoal gray jeans. They were tight enough to fit into my knee-high combat boots. I slipped the black knife into the top of the boot, tying the lace and making sure the knife stayed in place. I strode across the bedroom, falling into a crouch and drawing the blade in a fluid motion. I flicked my wrist and the blade opened. It was only four inches long, but it'd do the trick as a last resort. It had been a present from Rupert. The blade had been coated in silver.

I closed the knife and slid it back into my boot. The black thermal was snug, but it was comfortable and easy to move in. I pulled the sleeves up and slid the other two knives into the wrist sheaths I wore. They were also high content silver, but fortunately none of the silver was touching my skin and each blade I had was made with a grip. I called it my safety grip. It wasn't losing the knives that I had to worry about it. I learned the hard way that silver and lycanthropy is a big no-no. I've got the pentacle-shaped scar on my sternum to prove it. Thank Gods, it hadn't burst into flames like the crucifixes in old vampire movies. After three days of itching and bitching, symptoms like an allergic reaction, I realized the pentacle was trying to melt into my flesh. Luckily enough, once removed it had only branded the skin. Well, guess I didn't need to wear the necklace anymore.

I don't think it would have killed me if I'd left it on. A wound inflicted with silver forces our bodies to heal nearly as slowly as a human's would. A mortal wound inflicted upon a human is a mortal wound inflicted upon a lycanthrope when it's done with silver. The scar was once red and angry, but now it was a white, faded memory. I'd proven the stories right that silver to a vital organ takes a lycanthrope down. I was pretty sure my healing abilities wouldn't cover my arse if that ever happened. It did make me wonder just how far those healing abilities went, but I'm not willing to test any theories. Maybe I could find a volunteer?

CHAPTER EIGHT

The September air was cool as the sun set on the western horizon. I'd put on a thigh-length leather jacket to cover the Mark III in its holster, the wrist sheaths under the sleeves of my thermal, and the Pro .40 tucked into the back of my pants. The day I bought my guns I'd remembered to get more silver-coated ammunition, but I'd totally forgotten about the fact that I needed a special holster for the Pro .40. I was surprised to find that the Mark III fit an old holster that had been stuffed in a box in the back of my closet. Hurray for pack rats. You never know when something might come in handy.

I stepped out of the car as Rupert was locking the shop door. He was wearing a black leather jacket as well, and I chuckled softly. His shoes were expensive motorcycle boots. A pair of dark jeans and dark blue turtleneck completed his outfit. He'd taken his glasses off and gone from geek to something deadly in a matter of minutes. He'd even put gel in his hair, making the dark brown tresses look more like stylish porcupine spikes. At first glance, it wasn't noticeable that Rupert worked out. When he was wearing plaid shirts or shirts with Hawaiian motifs on them, it was easy to overlook. When Rupert dressed to kill, it was clear he was a formidable opponent.

"Who's car are we taking?" I asked, noticing that the Hummer H2 was M.I.A. There was only one other vehicle beside mine. I'd ridden in the Hummer a few times. I'd even practically begged Rupert to let me drive. He wouldn't. It was his pride and joy. So, where the hell was it?

The minivan beeped and I realized it was Rupert's. I laughed. "Oh Gods, I need a picture of this." I went for my cell phone.

"Kass, get in the car."

"Oh come on, Rupe, you're dressed to kill and driving a Chrysler Town and Country. You're seriously not going to let me take a picture of this?" I grinned, putting my hands on my hips. I nodded toward the van and asked, "What happened to Phantom?" He'd named the Hummer "The Phantom" because it was swift, silent, and smoke colored.

"It's in the shop," he grumbled. "Get in."

"So, you got stuck with the soccer mom van."

"Kassandra," he said in his I'm-not-kidding tone.

I bit back another retort and climbed into the van.

"It's got more get up and go than you think," he said as he put the van in reverse, backing out of the parking lot slowly. He put the car in drive and then hit the gas. I hit the back of my seat with a loud thud and made a grab for the oh-shit handle.

Rupert laughed. "Now that was worth taking a picture of."

"You shithead," I said, but I couldn't help but laugh with him. "What is this thing for? Soccer moms with road rage?"

"Something like that." He leaned back in his seat. "I've got something for you." He grabbed a black duffel bag and threw it into my lap. I made a small *hmph* sound when it landed.

"It's in the bag," he said.

I opened the bag and widened my eyes. "Holy shit, since when do you need this many weapons?" There were two guns, a small collection of knives, and what looked like a large hunting knife. I pushed them aside to find a holster. I waited.

Rupert's blue eyes flicked to me and then back to the road. "It's for the Pro .40," he said.

"Oh!" I exclaimed. Gee, sometimes I'm slow. "How did you know I didn't have a holster for it?"

"Everything you've bought in the past few years has been from me, right?"

"Right."

He smiled flashing straight white teeth. "I remember what all of my customers buy, Kassandra. It's part of my job."

"Rupert, sometimes you're just plain creepy."

"You have no idea."

"That's my line," I said as I unfastened my seat belt. I unbuckled my black leather belt and slipped it through the holster. The Pro .40 fit perfectly. "Thanks, by the way."

"You're welcome."

There were a few moments of silence before he said, "Have you figured out where I live yet?"

"Crud, I totally forgot about the bet."

"How could you forget about the bet?" he asked with a look of disbelief.

"I've had a lot going on the past few days."

He nodded. "Start from the beginning," he said. "Tell me about the crime scene the police called you in on, and what we're going up against. Then get to the rest."

I told him what I'd seen at the crime scene and what I'd told the police. I explained what had happened with Rosalin Walker and the case she'd brought to me. Rupert kept his eyes intently on the road, but I knew he was listening to every single word I spoke.

❖

There was a small area at the edge of the woods where Rupert was able to safely navigate and park the van between two large trees. There were tire marks on the ground where cars before us had parked in the same spot. No doubt the tracks were left behind by people who had been doing something more nefarious than what we were about.

Rupert unbuckled his seat belt and began checking his weapons.

"I can never figure out how you manage to hide that much firepower," I said, watching him.

"Practice," he said, and then asked, "Do you have a map?"

"No, there wasn't a map available. It's the boonies," I said, adding, "literally."

"So what's the plan?" He pulled a gun out from under the seat. It had a scope on it. "Night vision," he said as if it explained everything.

"I don't need it," I said. "We need to stay close together. We need to mask our scents, in case the werewolf is still out here." I handed him the bottle of patchouli oil. I could tell he wasn't wearing cologne, as I had requested. Perfume and cologne will give your presence away really fast around a bunch of lycanthropes. When you're doing surveillance work, the obvious goal is to remain hidden while gathering information.

He dabbed the oil on lightly.

"I want to get a feel for the area, see if there are any other clues the cops missed." I stepped out of the car and shut the door quietly.

"Aren't you afraid of getting lost?" he asked.

I shook my head and ran my fingers through my hair before securing it in a long ponytail. "No. There's a horse farm a few miles away. In a place like this there are going to be trails. Are you ready?"

The look in his eyes was cold as he smiled darkly. "What do you think?"

"Great," I said, "try and keep up." I smiled wickedly before throwing myself into the woods. I had to force myself to keep to a pace that Rupert could keep up with. There was a certain temptation at the pit of my stomach, in the depths of my mind, to just let go and run like the wind couldn't touch me.

The smell of the wild called to me, called to the wolf within. The breeze whispered through high branches, louder in my ears than it should've been. Despite an inability to perceive color in the dark, my night vision is excellent. The woods stretched out before me like some beautiful black-and-white photograph.

I heard the soft *thud-thud-thud* of Rupert's footfalls. I could tell by the sounds of his breath that he was struggling to keep up, but because he was in shape and because I wasn't running as fast as I could, he managed.

I opened myself to the earth, and the scent of pine filled my nostrils. The woods have their own perfume. It was a scent so natural that it felt as if I could wrap myself in it. I could hear the soft hooting of a night bird. Crickets played their sweet music. I turned my head, hearing their song like a small orchestra. A brown rabbit bolted across the path in front of us. It stopped and sniffed the air. Beady eyes met mine and I could taste its heartbeat on my tongue. The rabbit darted into the thicket and I had to force myself not to chase after it. It wasn't that the wolf thought it would make a nice snack—it was more that the wolf thought it sounded like a jolly good time, chasing rabbits.

*That's not why we're her*e, I reminded myself, swerving around a tree and following a fainter path. It looked like it hadn't been traveled in years.

The murmuring of voices caught my attention and I stopped, listening.

I couldn't make out any words.

"Get down," I whispered, but the voice that came out of my mouth was deeper than usual. Rupert knelt beside me. About ten feet before us was a swell of bushes. I lowered myself to the ground and crawled to them, sniffing the air as I went. Rupert sat on his heels to my left.

"What is it?"

"Voices." I inhaled deeply. "Wolves." I placed my hand flat on the ground and felt the echoing of footsteps. It wasn't one, but many. I tried to find a hole in the bushes to see through, but ended up putting my hand into the bush to move a branch. I moved it slowly, then guided the branch back into place.

"It's a clearing."

I picked up a handful of dirt and decaying leaves and rubbed them all over my body.

Rupert followed, scooping up a handful of dirt and covering his clothes with it.

I whispered, "Stay here. I need to get where I can see. I don't think they'll smell us on the ground." I hoped he knew what I meant. We'd covered ourselves with the earth, but as we did we left our traces on it. If someone was trying to track us, they'd find our scents there. I crawled in a crouch away from the bush. There was another set of bushes off to Rupert's right. I sank lower to the ground and quietly made my way to them. I peered around the bushes.

Great, a werewolf fiesta. I frowned as I counted thirty-some weres in the clearing. Two were holding torches, standing beside what looked like heavy rocks piled up to make a basic throne. A woman with golden blond hair sat on that throne, decked in a white pantsuit with black pinstripes. Another woman knelt a few feet away.

What the hell was this? Werewolf mobsters are us? I frowned, thinking. Movement caught my attention, and a man with short-cropped brown hair strode up through the middle of the clearing. He wore a pair of baggy blue jeans and a faded black T-shirt. Judging by his attire, he wasn't mobster status. Yet, neither were the rest of the wolves, once I looked. In fact, it was the woman on the throne who stood out, drawing attention to herself like she was making some kind of statement with her bold attire. Then again, she was sitting on a throne. That in and of itself made a pretty loud statement.

As the male in blue jeans passed the kneeling woman, torchlight spilled across her features. Her dark hair came alive with bright red highlights.

Rosalin Walker. Shit. Shit. Shit.

I lowered myself and crawled to Rupert. "Van. Now," I said.

He had been peeking through the bushes, and slowly eased a branch back into place. I shook my head and offered a hand. "No time to crawl. Now."

He took my hand and this time I pulled him along for the ride. I opened myself again without holding back. I trusted that his feet would keep up with mine as long as I held on to him. The trees parted before me, easing me through, yielding to my presence. I darted between them like a shadow. I came to an abrupt halt as soon as I spotted the van.

Rupert's brakes didn't seem to be working. He skidded across the dirt and fell on his ass with a heavy thud. "I can't run like you do!" he hissed, getting to his feet. "You're going to throw me into a fucking coronary!"

"Rosalin Walker was one of the wolves in the clearing," I said.

His eyes went cold. "What does that mean?"

"I don't know," I said as he stood and brushed himself off. It was kind of useless considering we were covered in small twigs and bits of leaves. "Obviously it's her pack, but what else?" I shook my head. "I need to find out."

Was it suspicious that a strange wolf had sought my investigative services? It wasn't too suspicious for me. What was suspicious was the fact that the same wolf and her pack met in the woods near the crime scene the police had called me in on.

Rupert unlocked the car doors manually, and my respect for him grew just a little bit more at the small gesture. He was smart enough not to unlock them with the keypad, which would send nice bright headlights blinking through our corner of the woods. Then again, he'd started his career as something similar to a government assassin. He had to be smart.

Chapter Nine

It isn't unusual for Rupert and me to sit in silence. Our silence now, though, had more to do with us trying to work out different scenarios than not wanting to chitchat.

"What's the plan?" he asked finally. "This is your hunt."

"Well, we could follow her, but in order to do that we've got to figure out where she'll be. There's got to be someone driving a car."

"Do you think we should try and figure out where they parked?"

"That would be a start." I leaned back in my seat. "How are we going to do that without getting spotted ourselves?"

Rupert leaned over and reached toward me. I startled and backed up as much as the seat would allow. He laughed. "Chill out, I just need to get something out from under your seat. I'm not trying to grope at you or anything."

I nodded, still cautious and caught off guard. "Instincts," I explained. "You're reaching into my territory. Warn me next time, or you might get hit." I settled back down.

"Is it that bad with you guys?"

I moved out of the way so he could reach under the seat. "It can be. Usually, I can control it, but if you catch me off guard I can't guarantee which response you're going to get."

"Flight or fight?" he asked as half of his arm disappeared beneath the chair.

"Yes," I said, watching him curiously. "You better not tell me there's a bomb under there."

"Nope." He grunted and retrieved the item at last. "They're better than the scope," he said, handing me binoculars. They were heavy in my hands.

"I don't carry bombs around," he said. "There are grenades in a bag under one of the back seats, though."

"Why doesn't that surprise me?"

He looked out the window. "Do you think you could track them by yourself without being seen?"

I tapped the edge of the binoculars on my thigh. "Most likely. Why? What are you thinking?"

"I could drive down the road and find some cover to park under. You could go track them and find Rosalin's car. That way, you don't have to worry about me not being able to keep up."

It didn't sound like that bad a plan, but there was one problem. "What happens if I spot the car and it takes me twenty minutes to get back to you, let alone find you if shit hits the fan?"

If he hadn't been wearing the oil, I could have found him if something happened. Since he was, it would make it more difficult for me to track him.

"I could wedge the van deeper into the woods?"

I looked at the trees so closely knit together. "You'll scratch the van up and make too much noise."

He pointed at the corner of the windshield.

"I could park it between those trees right there."

There was a break in the trees that I hadn't noticed. It wasn't much of a break, but it would be enough to hide a small car. The problem was, we weren't in a small car, but if Rupert was confident that he could do it, I wouldn't doubt him. He'd taught me a lot in the past several years and I respected the fact that he had a lot more experience than I did. Granted, my trust in anyone's judgment only goes so far.

I grabbed the handle and pushed the door open. I turned to tell Rupert to wait in the car when I saw the headlights at the far end of the road. I ducked down in my seat. "Shit, duck!"

Rupert ducked. "What?"

"There," I said, lifting the binoculars to my eyes as soon as the light passed. I had good eyesight, but lycanthropy didn't grant me a bird's-eye view. The binoculars helped, even if they did cast a sick green glow. I instinctively aimed them at the driver's side mirror. If I was going to see who was driving, that was where I needed to look. Unless they didn't adjust their mirrors. If that was the case, I was screwed.

The face of the driver was familiar. It was the man that had been wearing the baggy jeans in the clearing.

I checked the passenger's side, and Rosalin's profile came into view.

I waited until I saw the car, a Cavalier, slow for the stop sign ahead. "Start the van, and follow them."

"And if we get spotted?" he asked but started the van and put it in reverse.

"Then we do what we do best."

"Which would be?"

"Confrontation."

Rupert's version of a mad scientist's laugh filled the van.

It was so horrible—I couldn't help it.

I laughed. It wasn't until my vision went blurry with tears that I wiped my eyes and shook my head.

Rupert followed about four car lengths behind the Cavalier. It wasn't until he'd sped up and navigated the van onto the highway that he flipped on the lights. We were three cars behind the one we were following. Rupert got into the far left lane. From there we were able to keep an eye on the car cruising down the middle lane. There wasn't too much traffic on a Tuesday night, but there was enough to provide cover.

I looked around the seat I was sitting in. "Surely," I said, breaking the long, tense silence,"you've got some CDs in here to listen to?"

Rupert spared a glance at me. "Check the glove compartment or on your side of the door."

I opened the glove compartment and my fingers curled around

something long and square shaped. Curious, I withdrew it from the glove box. There was a little button on it. I pressed the button and jumped as a spark of electricity zapped from the end closest to my body.

"Shit," I said.

"Leave it alone, Kass."

"Right." I put the thing back where it belonged. I don't like electricity—at least not on my body. Arthur had once given me a flashlight at a crime scene. The incident taught me not to take flashlights from him, or anything that could potentially backfire on me. When I'd turned the flashlight on, it'd shocked the hell out of me, leaving currents of electricity tingling up and down my arm for five minutes afterward. Sensational? Yes. Did it feel good? No.

I found a metallic CD case and unzipped it, flipping through pages of discs. It was a small case, and most of the music was either classical, heavy metal, or a combination of both. I plucked a Nightwish CD from the protective plastic and pushed it into the CD player. Rupert gave me a look before asking, "Nightwish?"

"I'm not really in the mood for Mozart," I said.

He nodded. I skipped through the first few songs on the album and stopped on track six. The song "The Siren" blared through the speakers as we steadily followed the car Rosalin was in. It began weaving in and out of traffic.

"It looks like they're in a hurry to get somewhere." I had to raise my voice over the music.

"I'm not going to play leap frog," Rupert said.

"Then don't." I watched as the Cavalier cut another car off, in a hurry to change lanes.

"I don't think they're on to us," I said lightly.

Rupert's gaze remained intently on the road ahead. "I don't either."

I leaned back in my seat, keeping my eyes on the car ahead and listening to the music to keep my mind from racing.

We followed the car downtown using other cars as cover. It didn't surprise me how busy it was. Downtown was Oklahoma City's pride and joy. It was party central. The food was hellaciously over priced, and the booze flowed steadily. By the end of the night, half of the population was wasted and broke. It was so not my forte. The car turned into a small parking lot next to an old building. It looked like it had once been a hotel, but it was obvious that wasn't what it was now. I blinked, gazing at the red and white sign that blazed brighter than the streetlights: THE TWO POINTS.

"That's cryptic," I said, grateful I'd turned the music off before reaching the city. I was no longer in the mood to raise my voice. "What is it?" I asked. "I get this feeling that The Two Points doesn't refer to natural land forms…"

Rupert found a parking spot and waited for an SUV to pull in next to us. I had to turn in my seat to see the entrance and the line of people gathering outside. A man stood just outside the doors. From this distance I wasn't able to see his face, but I could make out the swell of chest under his crossed arms. A woman walked up to him, dressed entirely in black and red Goth chic. The man next to her wore a black suit, complete with tails and a top hat. The bouncer nodded at the couple, pulling aside the rope and allowing them to go through. I looked at Rupert, still waiting for an answer. I was coming up with my own conclusion, and it wasn't a conclusion I liked.

"Don't tell me this is the Vamp Club." I made it a statement.

"Then I won't say anything." He unbuckled his seat belt.

"Morrigan's curse take it," I hissed. "If Rosalin is in league with the city's vampires, we are going to be sorely outnumbered."

"Only if we make a direct attack," Rupert said. "We'll go in and pretend we're having a merry time, but keep your eyes peeled."

There was a reason I liked hunting with Rupert. When I couldn't come up with a good idea, he always had one. It worked both ways, and we both found the faults and leaks in one another's plans. Neither of us took it personally; instead, we took it constructively. In fact, most of my training wasn't thanks to Jake, the paranormal hunter who'd helped me get my certification—it was thanks to Rupert.

Which is why I said, "We look like assassins, not Goths. I don't think that will work."

"Then do something to look more Goth." He drew a blade from his boot. "Hand the duffel bag to me." I reached behind my seat and tossed the bag to him. He opened a side compartment and pulled out a plain black T-shirt. He cut the sleeves off and drew the knife down the length of the neck to leave a long slit in it.

I looked at the line leading to the entrance of the club. It was slowly beginning to shorten, but there were still going to be about ten or so others in front of us. Something soft hit the side of my face and I looked down.

I held the material up. "You're kidding," I said and looked at Rupert. He was now wearing the torn shirt. It was skintight and torn in all the places that would catch a straight woman's eye, but more importantly, a vampire's. The cut-off sleeves showed the muscles in his arms, and there were three cuts running across his chest and stomach. I'd never again doubt that Rupert worked out. He'd cut the neck of the shirt to show the line of his collarbone, and the pulse beating steadily in his throat.

"Classy," I said. "You'll definitely distract someone tonight, but whether it's heterosexual Goth chicks, gay Goth boys, or vampires, I'm not so sure."

Rupert laughed. "Always be prepared. Put the shirt on, Kass." I looked down at the shirt. He turned away. The gesture was polite and respectful. The black fishnet shirt I held was not.

"How did you have a shirt that would fit me?" I asked.

He gave me one of his stubborn looks and said, "Let it go, Kassandra. It doesn't matter."

I left it alone. When Rupert did not give an outright answer, it meant you weren't going to get one. Of course, I wondered who the shirt had originally belonged to, but questioning Rupert about his personal life wouldn't get me anywhere. I could smell the laundry detergent on the shirt. It was clean, so who was I to bitch? I took in a deep breath and shrugged out of my jacket. It took a few minutes to remove the wrist sheaths, the shoulder holster, and the small-of-the-back holster, but I managed. Lifting the thermal over my head, I let it fall to the floorboard. The fishnet slid over my small curves like a second skin. I could feel it clinging to my most intimate places and thanked the Goddess I was wearing a black bra.

I left my jacket on the seat. The night air was cool, but not too cool. It would have been cold to me three years ago. I was always cold in what other people thought was comfortable weather. Now, the cold felt less harsh, as if my body had finally figured out that thing called body heat.

It irked me that I couldn't carry my guns or wrist sheaths. The only weapon I had was the boot knife. As if on cue, Rupert stepped out of the van at the same time I did. The van beeped as he locked the doors. I reached up to the high ponytail in my hair. I was about to take my hair down when I decided it was best to leave it up. We were going into a vampire club and leaving my neck exposed would probably help us blend in more. It was a dangerous game and we were left best undetected.

We stood in line for about twenty minutes. The security guard at the door was tall and well-built, wearing a black tee-shirt that had the word "Security" written in red bleeding letters. His brown hair was cut short. I met his hazel eyes, handing him my ID. He handed it back with a nod and repeated the gesture with Rupert's ID. He pulled back the rope and let us through.

Chapter Ten

I was right. The club had once been a hotel. We stood in the lobby, bathed in a warm glow of light. Beautifully carved black wooden lamps gave the room a cozy feeling. We passed a door with an Employees Only sign on it and continued until we stopped at a long counter that looked like black glass, sleek and reflective. A woman stood behind it. Her brown locks were pulled away from her face in a slick and professional style, pinned at the back of her head. Her face was thin and pale and she didn't wear any makeup. A crimson satin vest cinched over a black blouse with a high collar made her look far more proper than she probably was out of those clothes.

"How much?" Rupert asked.

She smiled, and it was one of those good but fake professional smiles. A smile that said, "I'm only being courteous because they're paying me to." She told Rupert the price and tilted her head. The tilt of her head drew the high collar away from her neck, exposing a white bandage over her carotid artery.

Rupert took the wallet out of his back pocket, counted a few bills, and handed them to her.

Unlike most clubs that seemed fond of stamps and plastic bracelets, the woman held up two adjustable woven cloth bracelets with "The Two Points" on them. One bracelet was black. One bracelet was red.

"Black or red?" she asked.

Rupert offered an unusually charming smile. "What's the difference?" he asked, curious.

I too, wondered.

"Red means you're a donor. Black means you're off-limits."

She held up her arm and pulled the sleeve down, revealing the red bracelet at her wrist.

"Black," I said. Rupert echoed me.

The woman behind the counter laughed and handed us our don't-you-try-to-fucking-bite-me bracelets.

He adjusted the bracelet to fit his wrist, slipping the end of it through the little plastic buckle. "How do you know I won't wear it again and try to sneak in?" The tone in his voice made me stop fiddling with my bracelet to look at him. He gave the woman a playful and almost flirtatious look.

I rolled my eyes and buckled the bracelet.

"Because you have to go through security first." She pointed out the obvious. If Security recognized a person and suspected they were trying to sneak in, chances were they'd either turn them away or ask to search. Rupert smiled again, but this time, it was a quick and embarrassed spread of lips. Kind of like, "Aw, shucks."

When he was done pretending to be just an idiot tourist, we headed in the direction of the large double doors at the far end of the lobby.

A wave of pounding industrial music battered my ears as we hit the ballroom beyond. Energy slammed into me and I stumbled, turning and catching myself against the inside wall.

Rupert reached out, as if he would try to help steady me. I shook my head.

"I'm fine."

"What is it?"

At the smell of sweat and arousal, the wolf stirred within me, pushing against the surface, stealing the breath from my lungs. I placed my hand flat against the concrete wall, trying to focus on my breathing. I drew in a slow breath. That was another mistake. There were so many smells—too many perfumes mingling with the salty scent of sweat and desire. I exhaled the breath through my mouth, eyelashes fluttering. I closed my eyes and saw the wolf inside my mind. She paced, back and forth, threatening to push against the surface. Her elongated ears swiveled and a growl trickled from her lips, from my human lips.

My eyes flew open as Rupert took a step back. "Kass?"

I had to shield. In order to shield, I had to get my breathing under control. I couldn't breathe through my nose, but I could steady my breathing through my mouth. I closed my eyes, breathing in through my mouth, out through my mouth, focusing on visualizing a tall tower that would metaphysically contain the wolf.

The wolf hit the wall of that tower and I clutched my side, sliding down the wall. I felt her eyes glaring at me. She thought one thing: *Food.* We were surrounded by so much food.

Then I felt something, a cooler energy that sent a shiver up and down my spine. Distantly, I heard Rupert talking, but for the life of me I couldn't make out what he was saying. The room reeled as the wolf took what felt like another frustrated yet invisible swipe against the insides of my body.

Cool fingers touched my cheek, spilling cold energy into my skin. The wolf went still, ears flattening against her skull. I could suddenly smell the scent of cool air, like a cold winter's night when the ground is covered with snow. Gently, the tips of those fingers lifted my face and her silvery eyes met mine.

She smiled down at me with lips the color of bloody pomegranates. My stomach sank. My heart skipped a beat.

I knew who she was. I didn't know her, know her, but I'd seen her on the covers of local newspapers.

Lenorre, one of the countess vampires of Oklahoma, stared down at me with the most glorious and surreal eyes I'd ever seen. Vampires, like werewolves, have their own hierarchy and social structure. As countess, Lenorre was their queen. She was the community's, or clan's, political link and leader. Fortunately, since ye olden times, vampire killings have diminished greatly. Murdering your dinner is generally viewed as déclassé, not to mention it's terribly bad for publicity, which most vampires care a lot about. That doesn't mean it doesn't happen. From what I know, the punishment system with vampires generally stays with the vampires, unless something has become such a problem that the government has to step in. In fact, there are even some vampires in our government. Thankfully, most of them aren't Republicans. Over the years, the vampires have managed to charm and seduce the media, granting their existence a moderate amount of political and social acceptance.

"Is that any better?" she asked in a purring voice that was only slightly accented.

I closed my eyes and finished visualizing the tower, leaving the wolf no bars or windows to peek through. I took a deep breath, and this time could breathe without the sensory overload. It seemed Lenorre was helping me to shield.

When I opened them she was still staring at me. I resisted the urge to push her away. She was nowhere near repulsive, but she was a stranger. Her long hair shone like polished onyx. When she turned her head, the clip that held the tresses in place winked in the flashing lights. The bands of the clip arched and entwined like Celtic knots, but the arches were too jagged, too harsh, and more tribal. Diamonds and amethysts absorbed the light, sparkling bright enough that I knew they were real.

"Kassandra Lyall," she said softly, and my heart gave another fierce beat. I was getting really sick of people knowing who I was.

"Lenorre," I said.

She leaned back on her heels and kept smiling. "What brings a preternatural investigator into my club?"

I didn't see a reason not to tell her the truth. So I said, "We're trailing someone."

"Oh?" she asked. "Whom?"

"Rosalin Walker," I whispered, feeling a wave of heat descend and the wolf look up. As if she could see it, Lenorre touched my arm, and her cool energy rolled through me like a caress to calm the wolf. The tips of her fingers trailed over the net material down my arm, brushing the black wristband.

"We should speak somewhere more private." Her silvery eyes met mine.

I didn't really like the idea, but anything was better than shape-shifting in public. My control of the beast was usually better than this. There were several things that I'd learned to recognize as triggers for the wolf, and there were certain things that helped me gain more control of it. One of the things that helped me gain control was constant practice; the second was consuming a lot of steak. It'd taken months, but I'd learned to partially shift as well. During a partial shift my nails were claws, my eyes turned gold, and my canines lengthened slightly. How did I know? That's what mirrors are for. It's quite disturbing to watch a partial shift. At least with a full shift the entire thing is fluid, the beast just rolls out of the body and voilà—it's a bipedal wolf. A partial shift is somewhere between human and animal. The partial shift takes stronger bars to stop her from spilling out completely, almost like holding a rabid pit bull at the end of a leash. You need a firm enough grip and enough discipline to keep her from breaking free and raising hell.

The thing was it didn't always work, especially not close to the full moon. The moon calls to the beast, and a werewolf has no choice but to shift. A werewolf can't stop it. Trust me, I spent months trying.

Lenorre stood and offered me a hand. I stood without taking it, pulling the fishnet T-shirt down over my hips. Her eyes flicked to the pentacle scar above my sternum, and then to my face. I stared at the hand she continued to offer.

The corner of her mouth twitched. "I promise you, little wolf, that I will not bite. I am only offering my aid."

"Oh, well," I said sarcastically, "since you promised."

She frowned. "You do not believe me?" Her shoulders rose in a slow shrug and suddenly my ears were ringing with the sound of the music blaring. My eyes widened in surprise as I felt the wolf's response, her furred body pushing against my shields.

I didn't take Lenorre's hand—I snatched it. I didn't care if it made me appear weak. The moment her cool skin touched mine, it was like she'd blocked out the entire world, so that we stood in a bubble of energy containing only the two of us.

"You may not be as prideful as I thought," she whispered and made to step closer to me.

I backed up a step, keeping her hand in mine, but putting some distance between us. "Don't test your luck," I said in a low voice.

The look in her eyes was one of amusement, not anger. "As you wish," she said. "Come, so we may talk."

She made to walk toward a large staircase along the southern wall of the club and I dug my heels in, unmoving.

Lenorre's head tilted curiously to the side and I watched as she thought about it, her grip tightening like hardened steel.

"I don't like commands," I said. "You may be a countess, but I'm not your bitch."

She went very, very still.

I felt her look go through me like a knife, and forced myself not to flinch. Why did I get the feeling that pissing her off shortened my life expectancy?

And then her look turned quizzical. She gave a slight nod, amethyst jewels glistening like purple tears in her raven hair. "Very well." She moved, bringing the train of her long dress to drape at the crook of her arm. "Would it help if I said please?"

"Yes."

Slowly, her grip loosened.

I was waiting for her to say please when Rupert coughed. We both looked at him.

"I am afraid," she said, "that this is a private conversation." She turned her surreal eyes to me. "You should have brought another wolf with you before coming into a club, Kassandra." She dropped her voice, and the music, in our little energy bubble, sounded like it was underwater. I could hear her words clearly, but I sensed that others could not. "Is it the first time you've tried your hand at shielding from this much?"

I thought about it and shook my head. "I don't know," I answered. "I've had to shield pretty strongly before."

"As strongly as this?" she asked. "You are surrounded by other preternatural beings and humans. You have dealt with both at the same time?" She didn't look like she believed me. Put that way, no, I hadn't. I'd never been around so many vampires, humans, and a few werewolves in one enclosed space like this.

"Now you know," she said. "Were you part of a pack, then the wolves would have come to your aid." She stepped into my personal space. "As you are not…" She laughed at the look on my face. "Oh, Kassandra, I have many spies in this city. I know you do not belong to a pack. Why do you think I am here, helping you?" She gave a coy smile. "I do not need the bad publicity."

"I'm glad to know you care."

She frowned. A second later she was against me. Her arm slipped around my waist as she pulled me to her. I put a hand on her shoulder, feeling the line of her like cool silk. I was suddenly very aware of the fact that only fishnet and bra were guarding my skin.

"You taste of power." She was tall enough, probably almost six feet, that she had to bend at the waist to whisper in my ear. Her breath tickled those tiny hairs, causing goose bumps to break out across my skin. "You have honed some of that power, Kassandra, but tonight, tonight you are drowning and your hold on the wolf within has slipped." She lifted our clasped hands between us, drawing back and gazing at me with intensity. "I care very much what would happen if your hold was to slip entirely."

I swallowed, breathing carefully to slow my erratic pulse. "Fair enough."

"So I thought," she said, and this time when she led the way, I went with her.

I spared a glance at Rupert and held up a hand.

I mouthed, "Wait."

He crossed his arms over his chest and shook his head like he couldn't believe I was actually asking him to wait while I went off with a vampire.

Lenorre led the way up a curling staircase, past rows of low tables and velvet couches, to a door in a darkened corner of the room. She held the door open and I went through.

I felt her withdraw her power as her fingers uncurled from my own. I took a deep steadying breath as she shut the door, drowning out the obnoxious music. The walls were soundproof, how nice. I took a deep breath and drew in her scent. Beyond that airy scent, she smelled of cinnamon and cloves. It made my head reel, but it didn't call to the beast.

The wolf didn't consider vampires to be a food source. Good to know.

I had a moment to give thanks to the lycanthropy that allowed me to see in the dark. The room was dark and empty. Everything looked like a black-and-white movie. Against the far wall was a long black couch facing a white leather love seat. The carpet was soft beneath my boots. I moved to watch as Lenorre plucked a box of matches from a table and began lighting the candles that lined the room's perimeter, bringing the color gradually back to my vision.

An opera cloak the color of dark plums graced her shoulders, falling down her back and bringing out the gray stitching in her corset. The corset was tight to her body and had enough lift to offer a demure amount of décolletage. She unbent her arm and let the train of her dress slither to the floor in a fall of silk.

Her eyes outlined in dark eyeliner were steel gray in the candlelight.

She sat on the couch, crossing her long shapely legs. A line of fishnet and pale skin peeked through the slit in her skirt. I was beginning to feel a little trendy. She placed her elbow on her thigh, resting her chin upon a slightly curled fist.

"You said you were trailing Rosalin Walker?"

I nodded, sitting opposite to her on the love seat. Against the blackness of the couch, her pale skin seemed even more unnaturally pale. She sat like some terrible beauty wrapped within the folds of a darkly delicious dream.

"Do you know her?" I asked.

Lenorre's red lips curved into a mysterious smile. "Yes," she said. "Though I've yet to figure out why you're trailing the woman who hired you," she added. "Surely she did not hire you to spy on her?"

This time, I was the one who went very, very still.

"How do you know that Rosalin Walker hired me?" I had not told her that.

"Who do you suppose told her about you?" She smiled deviously.

For a moment, I just stared at her.

"You know," I said, "I get that you have eyes and ears all over the city. I get that you may have heard of me. I don't get how, but I get that you might've. What I don't comprehend is why you would send Rosalin? What I don't fathom," I said, cocking my head, "is how you know Rosalin."

"How long have you been a werewolf?" she asked, and it seemed to me she was changing the subject.

"Why?"

"I suppose," she said, flicking her wrist negligently, "it is not that important. What is important is that I knew you were not intimately involved with the preternatural community." She leaned back, watching me. "Rosalin's brother went missing and neither I nor any of my vampires could find him. How I know of you is of little importance. What matters is that I advised her to approach someone outside of pack, where her alpha would not find out. You are outside of pack. You are not within the reach of the local alpha werewolf."

"What do the vampires have to do with the wolves?" I returned her unwavering stare. "What do you have to do with Rosalin Walker?"

She gave me an irritated look. "If you would listen, you would hear that I am getting to that."

"Fine, I'm all ears."

"Every city has a power structure," she said. "The more dominant community is the more powerful. The more powerful the leader, the more dominant the community. Most of the time," she said, "we, the vampires, are the ones that dominate the rest of the community. We keep the rest of the preternatural community," she hesitated for a moment before saying, "in check." The corner of her mouth curved. "If you hadn't noticed, we have quite the effect on lycanthropes."

I remembered the wash of cool energy, calming and soothing the beast.

"Oh, no." I smiled despite myself. "I hadn't noticed."

Lenorre laughed and my stomach did a little flip.

"So," I said, "the vampires pretty much govern the rest of the preternatural community? That's your connection to the wolves?"

She dipped her head. "Precisely."

"How do you know Rosalin?"

"She works for me."

"Here?" I asked.

Lenorre gave me a look. "Where else?"

The door opened and I had one of those speak-of-the-devil moments as a woman came in, talking in a familiar voice.

"I did what you suggested," she said. "I…"

I met Rosalin's honey brown eyes.

"Kassandra," she said.

"Rosalin."

"What are you doing here?"

I crossed my legs, turning to look at her. "What were you doing earlier tonight?" I asked.

"Stuff," she said.

"What kind of stuff?"

"You're not a member of the pack," she said, smiling.

"I know where you were," I said.

Rosalin swallowed loud enough that I could hear it.

I patted the couch. "Sit down," I said, "I think we need to have a little chat."

Chapter Eleven

Rosalin sat at the far end of the couch, away from Lenorre, away from me.

"What do you want to know?" she asked. "You know there's stuff I can't tell you."

"I know," I said. "Lenorre told me that she suggested you hire me." I rubbed my temples. Rosalin hadn't committed the murder, but someone in her pack could have. There was a chance, a slight chance, that it was a wolf outside of the pack. Yet Rosalin and her little werewolf buddies had been in the woods near the scene of the crime.

"How close are you to your pack?"

"We're close," she said. "Why do you seem so worried?" She leaned forward and reached out toward me. I looked at her hand and she stopped. "This isn't just about my missing brother, is it?"

"No," I said, "not entirely. Does your pack hunt in those woods?"

"Yes," she admitted freely. "Why?"

"How many of them like to munch on humans?" I gave her a hard look.

Her eyes widened in disbelief. "None," she said defensively. "My pack mates didn't eat my brother, if that's what you're implying." The edge of a growl rolled out of her mouth.

That growl did it.

I felt the wolf pushing against the wall of my shields. My lips parted and a trickling growl fell from them, echoing Rosalin's. It was a call, a challenge from one wolf to another. Rosalin's growl deepened. Mine held the edge of a warning.

"I'm second in command to the Blackthorne Pack," she said confidently. I felt the energy of her beast rise, as if I could reach out and touch it. Her energy called to my beast and it rose to the challenge in a rush of energy.

Rosalin moved forward, and that was all it took. I'm not a bully, but in that moment I understood what the wolf understood, what I'd carefully avoided for the past three years. One wolf is always more dominant than the other.

I was not about to let myself get dominated.

I looked the second in command in the eyes and felt my hair stirring in its ponytail, in the heat of energy that emitted from my body. Rosalin stood from the couch with a growl. The beast rose, standing at the surface, at the brink, ready to push forth. I closed my eyes and took a deep breath, counting to ten. I was not going to allow myself to shift just because I couldn't control my temper. I felt my nails lengthen, felt my canines sharpen against my lips. I curled my lips back and growled.

For a second, I felt her wolf hesitate and then she didn't. Her shoulder connected to my stomach, knocking the air from my lungs. My back hit the wall, knocking another lungful of air out of me. I had a heartbeat to take the upper hand. I put my foot behind her heel, grabbed her by the shoulders, and pushed. It would've worked, but Rosalin grabbed a handful of my ponytail and pulled me down with her.

She snapped at my neck in a half sitting position and I thrust my elbow out, hitting her in the eye with its point. Her human nails clawed at my chest. I pushed out with my arms, trying to keep her away from my midsection. She grabbed my shoulders and pushed and I knew she wasn't using all of her strength. She could've knocked me across the room, but what she did was shoved me on my back. I brought my left knee up until it met her stomach. I'd succeeded in returning the favor of knocking the air out of her. She gasped and I thrust her off me, rolling on top of her. We were close in size, she and I. Rosalin was only a few inches taller.

I dug my claws into the back of her wrists and pinned them to the floor, giving one last warning growl to the wolf below.

Finally, Rosalin whimpered her submission. When she didn't move, I stood.

"Do that again," I said carefully, so that my words were clear, "and I can't promise you I won't rip your throat out, Rosalin."

She gave me a considering look. "You know I didn't mean it like that."

"Yeah, well," I said, closing my eyes and focusing on my breathing, replacing the bars with bricks, "I don't like being provoked, let alone fucking attacked."

"We had to establish where we stand with one another at some point," she said.

Lenorre spoke, and her voice crept like a chill throughout the room. "Rosalin, Kassandra can partially shift and you cannot. That should have told you where you stand with her." She stood from the couch, tossing the train of her dress over one arm and looking down at the other woman. "As should the fact that Kassandra bears the mark of an alpha, which you do not."

"Sheila doesn't either," Rosalin spat.

"No," Lenorre said and looked at me. "She does not."

"She's our leader," Rosalin whispered.

"And a weak one at that," Lenorre said.

"She's led the pack for eight years. How could she lead the pack for eight years and be weak?" Rosalin's eyes widened with the question. She still lay on the floor.

Lenorre looked at me when she said, "Sheila finds others to do her dirty work, and given her history for sadism, very few of the wolves wish to challenge her, for fear of losing and falling victim to her," she gave a dramatic pause and said, "skills."

There was a deep and thoughtful look in her silvery eyes. She was telling me something. What she had just told me was something very important.

"Sheila?" I asked.

"Rosalin," Lenorre said, "it is time for you to leave."

Rosalin didn't challenge Lenorre, she simply got to her feet.

She stopped near the door and looked at me. "I'm sorry," she said. "Please, try to find my brother."

"I will," I said.

"Kassandra?"

I turned my attention to Lenorre, but said, "What?"

"If you need anything, another wolf to talk to…I'm here."

I heard the door close behind her, not bothering to watch her go.

"Sheila Morris," Lenorre said, "is the alpha female." She sat back down on the couch. I leaned against the love seat, resting my butt on the arm. Lenorre's eyes dropped for a second and then met my gaze again. "I fear that whoever has committed your murders may be the same person that has taken Rosalin's brother."

"The thought crossed my mind," I admitted. "There's a chance it's a lone wolf."

Lenorre stood in a fluid movement and came closer.

"A chance," she whispered, looking down at me.

I looked up into her beautifully surreal gaze. I wondered how much I should tell her. If I didn't tell her that I knew for a fact that the urine near the crime scene had been left behind by a male werewolf, was I leaving too much out? If I did tell her, would she help me? What it ultimately came down to was how much I had to gain versus how much I risked.

She smiled. "Kassandra?"

"Hmm?"

"What are you thinking?" The words themselves were innocent, but the tone in her voice seemed darkly intimate. It made me shudder to hear it.

"If I tell you something," I said, holding her gaze, "will you give me your aid?"

"My aid?" she asked, and then smiled. "I've already given it once tonight, have I not?"

I nodded. "You have, but…"

She touched my jaw with the tips of her fingers and I resisted the urge to look away from the intensity in her gaze.

"You have my aid."

"The werewolf that committed the murder claimed the kill," I said. "It was distinctively male."

Lenorre looked thoughtful for several moments before she spoke. "There are several male lycanthropes within the pack."

"Oh goody," I murmured sarcastically. "That narrows it down."

Lenorre lifted her pale shoulders in a shrug. "I know Sheila has introduced one new male member to the pack within the past month," she said.

I stared at her, suddenly wondering why she was helping me. Why would a countess vampire give her aid so easily to someone she didn't know?

"You wonder why I so freely offer my aid to you?"

"Yes." I gave her a look. "You didn't read my mind, did you?"

"Oh, no." She laughed, moving closer. When I didn't back up, she trailed her nails lightly down the side of my neck.

My pulse sped in response.

"Body language," she murmured. "The rhythm of one's heart. These things offer clues and answers to what one is thinking or feeling." Her last words ended with a purr.

I jerked to my feet and side-stepped, putting the arm of the couch between us. If I didn't, I was going to end up leaning into her touch. I hadn't been affected by another woman in a long time. In fact, I steered clear of relationships and sex altogether, ever since I'd been infected. It just wasn't safe. One thing I was sure about was that Lenorre affected me. She called to something inside me that'd been long sleeping.

I narrowed my eyes. "Why are you toying with me, Lenorre? Why are you helping me?"

Lenorre moved with lethal grace, following me as I backed away from the couch. "Toying?" The question sounded innocent. The devious look in her very gray eyes was anything but that. She kept moving toward me.

I changed the subject. "You know I work with the police?"

She grinned. "Is that some kind of veiled threat?"

"No," I lied, "but you do know I work for them?"

"Yes. You were a police officer, once. You quit when you were infected, did you not?"

I stopped. "Has anyone ever told you that you're a little creepy?"

Her eyes shone with amusement. "No." She lifted the corner of her mouth in a half smile. "Why would they?"

"You're telling me that you're completely oblivious to the fact that normal people don't find out someone's entire life story?"

"I do not know your entire life story, Kassandra," she said, giving me a look. "I am also not people." She smiled a quick smile, giving me the briefest glimpse of her dainty fangs. "How long amongst your humans have you spent in hiding?"

I didn't answer that.

Lenorre filled the silence that followed. "When I take an interest in a thing, I like to learn what I can about it. As an investigator, I am sure you can relate."

I understood—what I didn't understand was why she'd taken such an interest in me.

"You are frowning," Lenorre said, searching my face. "Why?"

"I'm not sure whether to feel insulted that you just referred to me as a thing or to feel positively confused at the fact that you took such an interest in me to begin with."

One minute Lenorre was standing there—the next, she was gone. I took a step back. Arms slipped around my waist from behind.

I jumped.

Her breath was warm against my neck. Some part of my mind screamed, *Run, run!* But I didn't.

"Suffice it to say," she whispered against my hair, "I have my reasons." Her mouth moved behind my ear, lips touching my skin.

I forced myself to focus on my breathing. In through my nose and out through my mouth. I could taste her smell of cinnamon and cloves like a piece of candy on my tongue.

"I will send Rosalin home with you," she whispered. "There are things that you may learn from her, things that are pertinent for you to know."

A second later her arms slipped away from me. It was strange, the profound sense of loss I felt at their removal.

I looked at her. "Are you doing something?"

"Doing what?" she asked, offering a slow blink that showed off the glorious length of her eyelashes like onyx butterfly wings.

I closed my eyes, taking another deep breath and taking stock of the energies in and around me.

"Nothing," I said. "Thank you, for your aid."

Great, if she wasn't using vampires' wiles on me it meant the shit was real. Not good.

Lenorre looked amused. "It is my pleasure," she said.

My stomach did another little flip. It was time to get the fuck out. I was getting way too comfortable. Or uncomfortable. Whatever.

I stopped at the door, turning to look at her. "Why, again, are you sending Rosalin home with me?"

Lenorre gave me a look, as if to say, "isn't it obvious?" but what she said was, "Rosalin knows the details of pack structure and can inform you about everything that you have so willingly chosen not to be a part of since you were infected. It is easier. She is trustworthy," she said as if to reassure me. "If we are to work together, if I am to give you my aid, then you must trust me, as I must trust you, Kassandra."

At first, it made sense. It was logical. Then it didn't make any sense at all. My mind went over it, and then it made absolute perfect sense to me.

"You're using her to spy on me," I said.

"If I am?" she asked, raising her chin. "Tell, what would you do about it?"

"I could simply refuse to take her home with me."

"I could simply refuse to offer my aid," she stated plainly.

"How manipulative of you," I said.

Lenorre smiled, and since I had no idea what the smile meant, I opened the door and stepped out into the boisterous energy of the club. I closed my eyes, visualizing a dark cloak surrounding my aura, a cloak that would keep the energy out. I didn't know how long it would last. I wasn't sure if the wolf would try to rise again or not, but thought it best to hurry. I made my way down the steps, scanning the pulsing crowd of people, looking for Rupert. I spotted him against the far wall and waited at the end of the stairs as he pushed through the dancing crowd.

As he made his way toward me, I noticed the bruise blossoming under his left eye.

"What happened?" he bent toward me to shout over the music.

"What happened?" I shouted back. "What the hell happened to your face?"

"I tried to follow you. One of her vampires got physical trying to stop me."

"Is the vampire still alive?"

"Yes," he grumbled, very unhappily. "I know when it's my own damn fault."

"Thanks for trying to make sure I was safe."

"No problem." He touched his cheek, wincing. "I didn't expect her to take a swing when she told me no. What happened? What did she want?"

I held up a hand, keeping the image of the impenetrable cloak in my mind. "Later," I said, "I'll tell you later."

He put a heavy hand on my shoulder. At the waft of oil and sweat that hit my nostrils, I focused on drawing my shields down tighter. "Are you okay?" he asked.

I shrugged his hand off my shoulder. "Not a good idea to touch me," I said. "Not here. Let's go."

"All right," he said. "You better tell me what happened. I just freely admitted that some tiny chick with fangs clobbered my face with her itsy-bitsy fist."

Under any other circumstances I probably would've started poking fun at him, but now wasn't the time. I started working my way around the crowd. I was almost to the doors when a tall man with chin-length black hair blocked my way.

His eyes were a light blue, like the eyes of a Siamese cat. He smiled and his labret piercing caught the light, winking, but that wasn't what caught my attention. It was the pair of fangs he was showing off. His hand went to the door, as if he would open it.

"Sure you don't want to stay for a bite?" he asked in a drawling tone. His smile broadened to a grin.

The cool airy scent of vampire caressed my face.

I held up my wrist with the black band. "Not unless you're offering," I said.

I watched as the knowledge of what I was slid through his eyes. He threw his head back and laughed.

Rosalin's voice rang clear above the thrumming music. "Stanley," she said, "leave them alone."

I didn't take my eyes off the vampire in front of me. I sensed Rupert standing by like a quiet and deadly shadow.

Stanley flung the door open and stepped out of the way. He bowed and swept his arm back in a dramatic gesture.

"I'll not cross fangs with you, daughter of the moon."

I shook my head and walked past him with Rupert and Rosalin not far behind.

CHAPTER TWELVE

Rupert drove back to Guns Unlimited so that I could get my car. Rosalin buckled her seat belt, sitting behind him.

I leaned back between the seats and fished out the black duffel bag I'd stuffed my knives and guns in, putting the wrist sheaths back on, sliding into the shoulder holster, looping the small of the back holster through my jeans, and plucking the jacket from the floorboard. I buttoned the jacket up over the weapons and put on my seat belt.

Rupert turned the key in the ignition.

"So," he said, flicking his gaze to the rearview mirror. "why is she in my backseat?"

I shot him a blank look. "She's helping me."

"She's not connected to the murder?"

I looked at her then. She didn't say anything.

I sighed. "No," I said, "but someone in her pack might be."

Rosalin spoke up from the backseat. "Sheila didn't do it."

"I know that," I said.

"How?" Rosalin and Rupert asked in unison.

I smiled darkly. "'Cause I do." I wasn't going to tell Rosalin. I might have told Lenorre, but I didn't trust Rosalin, not just yet.

"Well, I guess that's good," she mumbled. "Sheila doesn't kill her victims."

"Who's Sheila?" Rupert asked, taking his eyes off the road for a second.

"The alpha female of the local werewolf pack," I answered.

Rosalin said rather cryptically, "You're lucky we didn't know you were there, Kassandra."

"Rosalin," I said, "part of my job description is not getting caught." I turned back to Rupert. "Here's the breakdown," I said. "The countess vampire, Lenorre, has agreed to help me with this case. Rosalin is also helping me."

"You think your case coincides with her missing brother?"

I shrugged. "I don't know. I can't be sure." I turned to Rosalin. "You agree to talk to me, correct? You do realize that in order for me to find your brother I have to know more about your pack?"

Rosalin muttered under her breath. "If one of the pack members touched him, they're dead." Her voice shook with anger. "Yes. I'll talk, if it's the only way to help you solve your case and for you to find my brother."

"Do you think it's safe taking her home with you?" Rupert asked as if Rosalin wasn't in the seat behind him.

"Rosalin?" I asked.

"If you think I'm going to tell someone where you live, I won't. Lenorre has made it perfectly clear that you are under her protection—even the pack wouldn't risk challenging her. I certainly wouldn't risk it alone," she said. "Besides, to break the trust of another Lykos goes against pack law, whether you're a member or not."

"Lykos?" Rupert asked.

"It's Greek for 'wolf,'" I said.

Rosalin nodded.

"You're not involved with them," Rupert said. "How do you know?"

"I took mythology in college, remember? A lot of the studies we did covered a very broad spectrum of mythos."

"I know the pack structure of a wolf pack is similar to the wolf packs in the wild," Rupert said, "but just how structured are they?"

Rosalin met his gaze in the rearview mirror. "I can't share that information with you."

Rupert smiled. "That answers my question."

Rosalin frowned at him.

"What does the Countess of Oklahoma want with you, Kassandra?"

"I'm not exactly sure, but I'm guessing she's trying to stay on the good side of publicity and in everyone's good graces."

Rosalin laughed from the backseat. "Lenorre," she said, "trying to stay in everyone's good graces." She laughed. "That you think so shows you don't know her very well."

I frowned. "I don't know her." I turned as much as the seat belt would allow. "Which brings to mind," I said, "how do you know her and how well do you know her?"

"I work for her," she said. "I wait tables at the club." She grinned. "I make good tips. I also happen to live with her, so yeah…I know her fairly well."

"You live with her?" Rupert gave her a disbelieving look in the mirror.

For some reason, the idea of Rosalin living with Lenorre really didn't sit well with me. Were they lovers? Was that why she lived with her? I frowned.

"Yes," she said, "I live with her. I take care of her house. She offers me a place to stay."

"Why aren't you living with the pack?" I asked. "Are you lovers?"

Rosalin's honey brown eyes sparkled, even in the dark. "I'm happy where I'm at," she said. "It works for me. No, we're not lovers. Lenorre doesn't take lovers."

It was my turn to give her a disbelieving look. Lenorre, the countess who had oozed her sex appeal all over me, didn't take lovers. Right. I don't turn furry once a month, either.

If you asked me, that seemed a little absurd.

When we arrived at Guns Unlimited I wondered: If she wasn't looking for good publicity, what in the world did Lenorre want with me?

❖

Rosalin was silent on the drive back to my apartment. I'd spent five minutes reassuring Rupert that I would be fine with her. He didn't seem to think so. I disagreed with him, because even though Rosalin's wolf had challenged mine, I'd understood it. It pissed me off, still, but I couldn't say I didn't understand. Rosalin and I knew where we stood with one another now, and on the human level she'd been nothing but polite and friendly. Hell, she was worried about her brother. That she couldn't fake.

I trusted my gut and my abilities. Whether it's foolish or not, they haven't failed me yet.

I parked the car and got out, carrying my thermal draped over one arm. Rosalin followed, and when I heard her door close I hit the lock on the keypad, climbing the stairs to my apartment.

I hit the switch on the wall and the light flooded the room. I shut the door, locking it behind her.

"Shit," she said.

"What is it?" I asked watching her take a cell phone out of her pocket.

"I was in such a hurry I forgot to bring stuff."

"That's fine," I said tiredly. "We're about the same size. I'm sure I can find clothes and a spare toothbrush."

"You don't mind?" she asked, uncertainly.

"Right now, I'm too tired to mind."

She went to the couch and sat down. "It seems strange, doesn't it? How all of this has happened? You're not used to it."

"I'm not used to what?"

"Putting your trust in someone else," she said.

"No."

"I meant what I said." She held my gaze. "I won't betray your trust, Kassandra."

"Good," I said, "I'm a bitch when crossed."

She smiled. "I find that hard to believe."

I ignored the sarcasm in her tone and went back to my bedroom. I found a pair of shorts and a gray shirt with a white dragon on it. I handed the clothes to Rosalin and went to the closet at the end of the hallway to procure a black comforter. There were pillows already on the couch that she could use. I dropped the comforter on the arm and set about starting a fresh pot of coffee.

If I was going to question her, I really needed some freaking caffeine.

"Do you want some?" I asked, turning just in time to see her shirt fall to the floor.

"Sure," she said and my gaze dropped to a line of white scar tissue that decorated her back.

She pulled the shirt down and turned to look at me.

I got two mugs out of the pantry and carefully poured the coffee in, adding milk and sugar to mine.

"Milk or sugar?" I asked.

"Milk," she said.

I handed the white coffee mug to her. "What happened to your back?"

Her eyes met mine. "Silver," she said and dropped her eyes to the pentacle scar at the top of my sternum.

She smiled. "I'm guessing that was silver, too?"

"Yeah." I sat down, nursing my coffee. I grinned over the brim of my mug. "Fortunately, though, the chain wasn't."

She laughed and it seemed to lessen the tension between us.

"You don't want to tell me more about your back, do you?" Leave it to me to bring the tension back.

"No."

I nodded, dropping it. I curled my legs under my body, resting back in the chair.

"How did Sheila become your alpha?" I asked.

"She's stronger than the rest of us."

"I'm taking it that's your way of telling me she wasn't elected by democratic vote?"

Rosalin laughed. "Elected? Lykos don't elect their leaders," she said. "That's a pretty idea, but it doesn't work that way."

"Why not?" I asked.

"In order to be an alpha," she said, "you have to be able to prove to the rest of the pack that you're more dominant than the rest of us.

Most of the time, it's about power and bluffing. Personality plays into it as well. There are wolves in the pack that are submissive to the core. They'll never aspire to climb the pack ladder because they enjoy the safety of being under the rest of the pack's protection."

"Like an omega wolf?" I asked. In the wild, the omega wolf was the lowest-ranking wolf in a pack. It was the wolf that got picked on the most. The wolf that didn't get to eat until the rest of the wolves were done eating. Yet, as badly treated as it appears the omega wolf is, he or she is still under the protection of the rest of the pack. Which is why I asked, "It just looks like they're treated poorly? The wolves in the wild usually don't actually cause any physical harm to the omega, they just snarl and humiliate him or her."

"That is how it is supposed to be, yes." Something in her voice made me meet her gaze. "With werewolves, it doesn't always happen that way."

"What are you thinking that you're not telling me?" I leaned forward.

Her eyelids fluttered closed and she whispered, "Sheila has led the pack for eight years, and throughout the years she's held the pack together and followed the rules in every way. Lately, her hold is slipping."

"What does that mean?"

"She's let her darker desires cloud her judgment," Rosalin said. "She's a sadist, Kassandra. She has issues."

"You're not talking a little slap and a bit of hair pulling, are you?"

"No," she said. "She's abused those who are meant to be under her protection. It's gotten worse since her brother arrived." A growl trickled from between her lips.

"I take it you don't like him?"

"No one does," she said. "The only reason the pack has accepted him is because we have no other choice. It's not unusual for a new wolf to come in flaunting the Rite of Challenge. He hasn't done that…yet."

"The Rite of Challenge?" I asked.

"One werewolf challenges the other to a duel," she explained.

"If the wolf challenging a higher-ranking wolf defeats them, then they get the higher-ranking wolf's position. It's a way to move up in the pack hierarchy."

"So, if someone challenges you, they get to be beta wolf?"

"Yes," she growled, but her eyelids flickered nervously.

"Don't worry," I said, "I'm not going to challenge you. How is the duel fought?" I asked.

"By shifting," she said and her gaze lowered.

I sat my mug on the table and slid to the floor, looking up at her. "It's to the death, isn't it?" I spoke what I sensed.

"Not always," she whispered.

"But most of the time?" I whispered. "Is that how it is?"

She put her face in her hands, auburn tresses hiding whatever expression she wore. "I don't know," she whispered. "Usually, it's to third blood. There are some that hold to the older customs, which yes, is to the death."

A single tear dripped from her chin. I moved to her without thinking.

I pressed my lips against her damp cheek, catching that tear on the tip of my tongue. I closed my eyes, savoring its salty sweetness, breathing my breath against her skin. Her scent came on my exhaled breath, the smell of moist soil and earth, the smell of wolf. Somewhere inside me I felt the wolf stir. *Pack*, she thought, and a fierce yearning gripped my heart.

Rosalin's fingers stroked my hair, lifting the white streak.

"Doesn't it get lonely?" she asked, smiling with soft sorrow.

"What do you mean?" I whispered, leaning into her touch.

"Being without a pack. Especially with the mark of the alpha on you." She tugged at the white streak.

"I haven't been around any other wolves to know," I said, suddenly understanding why most other wolves didn't have a punk-rock hairdo like mine.

She murmured, "But, you feel it, don't you?"

I turned, rubbing my cheek against her fingertips. "Feel what?" I asked, dipping my head and sliding my cheek across her jeaned thigh.

"Kassandra," she said with a hint of laughter in her tone that the wolf and I were happy to hear.

She smelled good. I wanted to carry that smell with me. I wanted to make her smell like me. I opened my mouth and sank teeth playfully into her thigh. She gasped above me.

I could smell the subtle and clean smell of detergent on her clothes, could taste it, but the scent I focused on drawing into my lungs smelled of that damp soil, of pine trees, of rich earth and patchouli. I dug my teeth in a little rougher, growling my frustration around a mouthful of jeans.

"Kassandra," she said and I rolled my eyes up to her. She touched my face and the scent grew stronger, less tainted. I turned my face toward her wrist. Yes, that's the smell we wanted.

I froze feeling my heartbeat pounding against the side of my neck.

"What's going on?" I asked.

"Nothing," she said. "It's your wolf, Kassandra, just go with it. What does it feel like she wants?"

My eyelashes fluttered closed. Her scent spiraled in the air around me. What did I want? What did she want?

"Smell," I said and Rosalin began taking off her shirt.

I wrapped my hands around her shins, digging my nails into her calf muscles. "No."

With a nod, she did what I asked. She left the shirt on. I climbed up onto the couch. Rosalin lay back and I gave her a distrusting look. It seemed so natural just to lie down with her, to lie next to her and smell her. I tried to argue with the wolf, but Rosalin moved her wrist to my face again and the wolf followed that smell. Where the wolf went, my body followed.

I pushed myself up off the couch in one fluid motion, breathing heavily, scrambling to my feet and nearly tripping over the coffee table.

She watched me with those compassionate honey eyes.

"Why are you scared?" she asked. "It's only natural."

"No." I hugged myself. "Rosalin, no, I'm not ready."

"Your wolf seems more than ready."

I felt her as she paced inside my mind. The wolf didn't try to slam into any metaphysical bars. She didn't want out. She just wanted the comfort of another wolf. She didn't understand why I didn't agree with her. It confused her. It didn't confuse me. Rosalin might have been another wolf, but as a human, she was still a stranger to me.

I asked, "What if I wanted to join the pack?"

"Is that what you want?" She gave me a disbelieving look.

I opened my eyes. "No," I said, "but it'll probably be necessary."

"Oh," Rosalin said, "because you suspect…"

I nodded. "Yes."

"Sheila would be going against pack law if she didn't at least meet with you," she said. "I can take you in and introduce you, if she gives me permission, but you're going to have to play it like you're seriously considering joining."

"I know. If that's what it takes, Rosalin, I'll do it."

CHAPTER THIRTEEN

My cell phone rang from its place on the nightstand. I rolled over, blinking at the bright little window on the phone's face. I flipped it open.

"Arthur," I grumbled sleepily, and rolled my eyes toward the clock. "It's almost four o'clock in the morning. What the fuck?"

"Guess again, Lyall." Instead of Arthur's voice, someone else's gruff voice grumbled in my ear.

I sat up in bed. "Deputy Sheriff Witkins," I said, wondering why the hell he was calling me from Arthur's phone. The only explanation I could think of was not a good one. "What happened?"

"There's been another murder," he said, then asked me if I remembered how to get to the Nelsons'.

"For the most part," I said, leaning over and finding a pen and legal pad in the top drawer of the nightstand. I put the pen in my mouth, taking the cap off, speaking around it. "Give me the address."

"Go about two and a half miles past the Nelsons'," he said, "When you pass Cole Road, you're going to make a left onto Southeast Twenty-sixth Street. My men have got their lights on."

I kicked back the covers, tearing off the sheet of paper with the directions on it. "Deputy," I asked, "may I speak with Arthur?"

"Yeah, but make it fast," he said. "The scene is getting cold."

I bit back the retort that the scene was always cold by the time they called me in.

"Hey, Kass," Arthur said.

"If there's not a steaming cup of coffee in your hands by the time I get there, Kingfisher, I'm going to kick you in the balls."

I closed the phone, hanging up before Arthur could reply. My feet hit the floor as I stumbled around the room grabbing what I needed: shirt, jeans, bra, socks, shoes, and my shoulder holster. I went into the bathroom, relying on my night vision as I slipped the nightgown off, allowing it to fall to the floor. I shimmied into the jeans, pulled the bra straps up on my shoulders, and slid the shirt on over my head.

A crime scene at four o'clock in the morning—there's more than one reason cops despise bad guys. I plucked the directions off the bathroom cabinet, shoving them deep into the pocket of my jeans. I grabbed the shoulder holster, shrugging into it on my way out.

I stopped in the living room, eyes flicking to the sleeping werewolf on my couch. Sighing, I went into the kitchen and tore a piece of paper off the magnetic notepad on the fridge.

I hastily scribbled:

Rosalin,
Had to go out. Be back soon...
Don't touch anything.

There, that worked. I carefully slid the piece of paper onto the coffee table, listening to the languid sound of her breath. I grabbed my jacket off the chair. My keys jingled and I quickly muffled them with my palm, slipping out of the apartment as quietly as I could.

I knew my apartment like the back of my hand. If Rosalin touched anything, I'd know. The fact that I'm a werewolf and could trace her scent if I tried hard enough also came in handy.

❖

I took I-40 to I-44 like I was going out to the Nelsons' home. The drive turned out to take a little over forty minutes. I followed the directions Witkins had given me. The paved road turned into gravel that made an obnoxious grinding noise beneath the Tiburon's tires. Over the crest of the hill, nestled behind an old wooden fence surrounding a trailer home, the lights from two police interceptors cast a blurry blue and red haze out over the land. I guided the car through the open gate, parking next to one of the squad cars. The cops had left their headlights on and I watched as they helped one another string the black and yellow tape from the right side of a double-wide trailer to the wooded area on the southeastern part of the land.

I spotted Arthur and Deputy Sheriff Witkins standing in front of the trailer. Arthur saw me approaching and started heading toward me. Goddess bless his little heart, he was holding a cup of coffee.

"Here," he said, eyes sparkling. "I'd like to have kids someday, you know."

I took the cup of coffee, taking a sip. I nudged my head in the direction of the trailer. "Who lives here?"

He pulled a little notebook out of his pocket. "The trailer belongs to a man named Carver White. Twenty-five years old. Works in a clothing store. Single. He lives alone and has lived here for five years. He heard someone scream around three o'clock. Ran out and found the body. Said he ran back in and called us. No sign of the murderer," he said, closing the notebook and stuffing it back in his shirt pocket.

"Wonderful," I grumbled, taking another sip and making my way toward the guys with the crime scene tape. Arthur followed as I lifted the tape and ducked.

Beyond the tape the land sloped down toward a small creek. There were trees lining the area, and enough cops standing around that all I had to do was play connect the cops to find the body. Arthur pointed to a large cypress as we approached.

"There," he said.

The body was propped up against the base of the tree. A breeze stirred and the smell of blood and feces hit my nostrils. I coughed, lifting my shirt and covering my nose with it, not that the material would help much.

I breathed in and out of my mouth, holding my coffee close.

"I need gloves," I said, stopping in front of the body and looking down. Her hair was long and brown, falling down over her breasts and matted with blood. Her lavender-colored blouse was so thick with blood that it had turned the color of dark plum. The woman was posed against the tree, like a trophy. I knelt, turning my head enough to see the blood that originated at her throat, spilling out over the front of her body.

"Here," Arthur said, kneeling with me.

I handed him my coffee and put the gloves on. I reached out, touching the woman's jaw. Her face was pale and wide-eyed with death. I used two fingers under her chin to guide her head upward. It moved easily, which meant that rigor mortis hadn't begun to set in.

"Oh God," I whispered, looking at what had once been the woman's throat.

It was an empty cavity that still seeped blood at the edges. Ivory bone glistened sickly at the back.

I let her head fall back down, taking another deep breath through my mouth. The wolf didn't rise. I felt in her a certain amount of disinterest, cold neutrality. I traced the edges of the wound with two fingers. The edges were jagged and I stifled a shudder as a wave of nausea hit me. The beast's ears perked inside me, like she was curious. I slammed my shields in her face, not willing to risk tempting her. She could remain neutral or she could get hungry. Only one of those could be an option right now.

Not tonight, I thought.

I scuttled around the body: brown boots, bloody jeans, charm bracelet on her right wrist, empty hazel eyes.

"Any ID?" I asked.

I heard Arthur take out his notes. "Veronica Monroe," he said.

"Late twenties?" I asked.

"Twenty-eight," he said.

"Have you contacted the family?"

"Yes."

"Good."

"Kass, is it another werewolf attack?"

I gestured for him to come closer and brought her jaw slowly up to show him the victim's throat.

Arthur paled, but forced himself to look. "Here," I said, the tip of my finger tracing the jagged wound. "You see these? At the edges of the wound?"

"All I see is blood," Arthur said, sounding disgusted.

"Look closer," I said, and touched the tip of my gloved finger to one curving piece of torn flesh and then another. "Here and here," I said, "these are where the upper incisors clamped down."

The medical examiner could precisely calculate how many teeth marks there were. Obviously, I couldn't. Werewolves have more teeth than humans. Humans generally have thirty-two teeth, while wolves and werewolves have forty-two. Definitely one aspect of shifting that hurts like a bitch. Figuratively speaking, of course.

Arthur swallowed, loudly. "You're saying this is another werewolf?"

"'Fraid so," I said and then motioned for him to follow me as I moved farther to the right, pointing toward the base of the tree. There were five very deep, very distinct claw marks etched into the bark.

"Shit," he said loudly, getting to his feet. I watched as a bit of my coffee sloshed out of the cup.

"Arthur, you're wasting my coffee." *Not to mention contaminating the scene*, I thought.

"You want to hold it?" he asked.

I held up my bloody fingers and wiggled them. "Can't."

He paled again.

I sighed, casting my gaze toward the creek. I took an unthinking breath through my nose and coughed as that horrible smell hit me again. Anyone that has smelled death will tell you, you never forget it. It clings to your hair, your skin, your clothing. The blood itself didn't smell all that bad, but the feces, that made my stomach turn. I got to my feet, carefully stripping the gloves off, avoiding smearing the blood with years of practice.

"Where's the trash?"

"It's up on the porch."

I walked past Witkins and climbed the wooden steps to throw my gloves away. They were using a brown paper sack as a trash bag.

"Well?" Witkins grumbled. "What does your little witch think, Kingfisher?"

Arthur stood at my side and handed my cup of coffee back to me. I took a sip, grateful that the smell helped mask all of the other smells in the air.

"Ask her," he said.

"You still think it's a werewolf?" the deputy asked.

"I don't think it is, Witkins. I know it is." I intentionally left off his title.

"Hmph," he grunted and walked away.

I gave Arthur one of those what-the-fuck looks.

He shrugged. "It's your job to hold our hands and walk us through the preternatural stuff."

I stared at the deputy's back and said, "It doesn't really look like he wants to go for a walk, not through this. What the hell is his problem?"

Arthur's eyes sparkled. "He thinks you're evil."

"You're joking?" I asked.

"Maybe. If he does, he might be right about y—"

He oofed as I drove my elbow into his rib cage. I did it lightly, just enough to make him shut up.

"What was that for?"

"You don't want to call me evil, Kingfisher."

His mouth split into a wide grin.

"Why not?" he asked.

I narrowed my eyes and glared at him. The glare elicited a rumble of masculine laughter.

"You know," he said, "I'm glad you're short. If you were taller that look might actually work on me."

I rolled my eyes and took another drink of coffee. "I need to question Mr. White," I said, ignoring his amusement.

He gestured toward the door. "He's in there with two of our men."

"Your men," I corrected him as I opened the screen door and stepped inside.

Chapter Fourteen

Two men in dark blue uniforms stood in the middle of the living room. A young man with white-blond hair was seated on the couch. He lifted his head when he heard the door open. When his eyes met mine, I saw that they were blue with striking gold around his pupils. His expression was unflinching as he watched me.

"Carver White," Arthur said, "this is Preternatural Private Investigator Lyall."

"I told you what I know," Carver said in a deep voice. It was a voice that didn't match the youthfulness of his appearance. Then again, neither did mine.

"Mr. White," I said, smiling as professionally as I could. Given the fact that they'd woken me at four in the morning, it probably wasn't as professional as I hoped. "I have a few questions to ask you."

Carver stood from the couch, moving until there were only a few feet between us. He looked down at me. "I told you," he said, voice deepening, "I've already told the cops everything I know."

The smell of pine and moist earth hit me like a brick to the face. I stepped back, but it was too late.

Carver's blue eyes widened as an unseen breeze of energy tickled the hairs on my arms.

My heart gave a fierce thump that echoed through every pulse point in my body.

Arthur moved forward and his hand hovered above the gun at his hip. "Stay on the couch, Mr. White," he warned.

Carver sat back down, but his gaze hadn't left my face. "Fine," he said, eyes flicking to Arthur. "If I have to talk again…I talk to her."

"Duh, boy," one of the cops, an older man with white hair circling a shiny bald spot on his scalp said. "That's kind of what the nice detective here is trying to get you to do."

Carver leaned back and smiled. "Alone," he said.

I let out the breath I'd been holding. Arthur asked the question with his eyes and I nodded.

He and his men went to wait on the porch. They didn't look happy about having to stand out in the cold.

I placed one of the chairs from the kitchen opposite to Carver, and sat down.

"So," I tilted my head to the side, "out for a midnight snack?"

His eyes narrowed. "I didn't kill that woman."

"Under the circumstances, I find that terribly difficult to believe."

"I didn't do it!" his voice took on the edge of a growl. "I don't even know her!"

I met his blue gaze. The sunny gold around his pupils expanded, fluctuating. He dug his hand into the arm of the couch hard enough that the wood creaked.

I leaned forward and hissed, "I don't believe you."

A deep bass growl trickled from between his lips. "I…did… not…kill…her."

His chest was rising and falling too fast. He was angry, and that's not a good thing when you're a lycanthrope trying to stay in control. I wondered how bad Carver's temper was. Should I push him? Should I wait for him to lose control and shift all over the place? Then let the cops cuff him and stuff him? The problem was, if I did that, I knew without a doubt he'd out me.

He had to be the killer. It was his land. He was a werewolf. Gods, he was sloppy, but it made perfect fucking sense. He'd lost control.

I stood from my chair, pacing. "What happened, Carver?" My gaze flicked to him. I heard the wood pop again. "What did you do? Did you invite her back to your place? Bring her home for a nightcap and decide to munch on her?" My eyebrows went up.

Carver growled and said, "No."

I went to stand over him, leaning my face close. "What was it, Carver? The smell of her sweat?" I whispered. "Or the knowledge of hot blood pumping through her veins like sticky syrup? What made you lose control?"

Carver screamed. His hands hit my shoulders as he rushed me, shoving me across the room. My back hit the wall and the trailer shook with the impact.

"I didn't fucking kill her," he growled in my face.

"Liar," I hissed, waiting for him to hit me, waiting for his temper to finally erupt.

Carver backed up, curling his hands into fists. His entire body shook. The energy of his beast made the air seem thicker.

I felt the wolf stir in answer to that power and a warning growl started low in my throat.

The front door clattered open, cutting off my growl.

Arthur yelled, "Hands on your fucking head, now!"

Carver glared at him, and then slowly, ever so slowly, put his hands on his head.

He turned that light blue and gold gaze to me and I watched as his breathing steadied.

"What happened, Kass?"

"I pissed Mr. White off," I said, getting up from the floor. Carver hadn't put all of his strength into rushing me. If he had, I knew for a fact I'd be sitting ass first in the grass outside of the trailer, with a little hole left behind in the wall, like in one of those children's cartoons.

Carver stared at me as if he thought he could burn a hole through me.

"Go back out, Arthur," I said. "I think Mr. White will keep his temper under control now, won't you?"

Carver said one word. "Yes."

"Are you sure, Kass?"

"I'm sure. If I need your help, trust me, Arthur, I'll scream."

"Don't scream," Arthur said, "just shoot the bastard."

I smiled darkly and turned that smile to Carver. "There is that," I said.

The trouble was, Carver had already caught me off guard once. He'd been so fast I hadn't had time to go for my gun. There was no way I going to match him in strength around the cops. I wouldn't risk exposure.

Arthur holstered his gun. A moment later, I heard the door click shut behind him.

"They don't know you're one of us, do they?" This time, it was Carver who smiled darkly.

"That's none of your business," I said. "Sit down."

Carver sat and smiled at me like a happy four-year-old who'd finally managed to find the stash of hidden lollipops.

"I'll tell them," he growled. "If you arrest me, I'll take you down."

I let the coldness I felt seep into my eyes and said, "I know."

Carver frowned.

I went to the kitchen, retrieving my neglected coffee. "Which is why I am going to tell you something that I rarely tell people, Carver."

"What's that?" he asked.

"Go to hell."

I went to the door. I couldn't arrest him. If I arrested him now, in front of the cops, he was going to spill my beans. Damn it. Damn it. Damn it.

Then again, I'm a licensed paranormal huntress and a preternatural investigator. Arresting isn't what we do.

We dig for facts. We hunt and execute.

Carver White had just made it to the top of my shit list.

Chapter Fifteen

I woke out of a dreamless sleep wondering why. Someone was touching my hair. The realization hit me with a rush of fear, and I rolled out of the bed in a fluid motion that had nothing to do with human grace. The pads of my feet landed on the floor with a soft thud and I looked up into Rosalin's honey-colored eyes.

Her hand stopped in mid-motion and she let it fall into her lap. "You're cute when you're asleep," she said and curled her legs up under her body. She leaned back against my pillows.

"Why did you wake me up?" I asked, sounding grumpy.

"Lenorre called. She wants you to meet with her tonight. She has a reservation at Francesca's."

I just looked at her. Francesca's was an Italian restaurant in the city. It was by reservation only, and they usually put a person on a weeklong waiting list. I'd been there only once and that was for a friend's birthday party. I never knew food could be so expensive. It was classy as all get-out…fine dining for the best dressed and the richest. I couldn't believe what Rosalin was telling me.

"You look shocked," she said. "You don't believe me, do you?"

"I would say no, that I think you're joking, but I'm afraid you're not."

"Lykos's honor." She grinned. "She wants you to meet her there at seven." Rosalin crawled out of bed and headed for the door. She stopped in the doorway, turning to look at me. "You'll want to wear something nice."

“What if I don’t go?” I asked.

“Trust me, Kassandra. You don’t want to test her kindness.” The look in her eyes was very serious. I nodded. Surely, I could find something nice?

I looked at the clock. I’d slept through the entire day. The red numbers glowed brightly in the dim lighting. It was six o’clock.

“You’re fucking kidding me!” I hissed at it. I had less than an hour to get ready. I still had to take a shower, find something to wear, and get there. I took the dress that I’d worn once to a witch’s ball off a hanger. It was one of the few expensive outfits I own.

I grabbed everything I needed, trying to hurry.

Rosalin peeked around the corner of the door. “By the way,” she said, “where’d you go last night?”

I’d gotten home just as the sun was rising. The note had still been on the coffee table. I’d thrown it away, thinking that she’d slept through the whole thing.

“Police business.”

She nodded, turning to go.

“Rosalin,” I said, catching her attention. She paused.

“Hmm?”

“Do you happen to know a wolf named Carver White?”

Her eyes widened. “Why? Was there another murder? Do you suspect him?”

“Answer my question first,” I said, “and then I’ll answer yours.”

“Yes,” she said, leaning against the door frame. “I know him.”

“How?” I asked.

“He’s the pack’s gamma.”

“Gamma?”

“Alpha, beta, gamma, delta, epsilon…”

“Ah,” I said, “the whole pack is based on the Greek alphabetic numerals?”

“Yes.”

“So, he’s third?” I asked. “Just below you?”

She gave me a look. “I keep telling you more than I should,” she said. “I can’t tell you any more than that, Kassandra. Besides, you never answered my questions.”

“Yes,” I said, “there’s been another murder.”

“Do you suspect him?”

I wanted to tell her, yes, I did, but I didn’t know how much to tell her, so I decided not to give her a yes or no answer.

“I don’t know. What do you know about him?”

She looked thoughtful. “He’s a nice guy,” she said, “but he’s got a horrible temper.”

I hadn’t noticed. “How horrible? Horrible enough that he’d kill someone?”

Rosalin shook her head. “Honestly,” she said, “I don’t know.”

“Rosalin, you can’t tell anyone in your pack about this conversation.” I walked toward her, giving her a hard look. “Give me your oath that you won’t.”

She laughed. “God, first Lenorre makes me give her my oath, now you. I’m beginning to feel like no one trusts me,” she said.

Strangely, I did trust Rosalin, but for the life of me I couldn’t tell you why. There were some people in my life that I’d met and trusted on an instinctual level. It happened very rarely, but Rosalin was one of those people. Being a witch could come in handy when trying to figure out if someone was likely to try and kill you. Lenorre I wasn’t so sure about. Oh, I trusted that she would help me. I just didn’t trust her motives for helping me.

“Rosalin,” I said.

“You have my oath, Kassandra. You have the oath of the beta of the Blackthorne Pack. I will not tell anyone in the pack what you have told me here.”

“Give me your oath that you won’t tell anyone,” I said, “period.”

She shook her head. “I can’t.”

“Why?”

She gave me a look. “If Lenorre asks me then I am bound by my previous oath to her. I am not an oath breaker, Kassandra.”

“Fine,” I said, “but no one else. Promise?”

"I do so swear."

"Good," I said. "If you do, Rosalin, there will be hell to pay. I promise you that."

"Are you threatening me?" she asked, blinking.

"No," I said, "I'm simply stating fact."

❖

The dress was a nice combination of medieval gothic and modern Goth fashion. The corseted bodice was lined with red trim. The same bright red material peeked through the lace that crisscrossed up the front of my torso. Two thin black straps were more for style, as the dress was tight enough it would've clung to my body without them. The off-shoulder sleeves looked like a splash of blood against my very pale skin. The rest of the dress flowed gracefully to my feet.

I knew it was inevitable that I was going to be late. If Lenorre hadn't made the reservations at Francesca's it probably would've been a different story. She had, and that meant that unless I wanted to stick out like a sore thumb, I had to look my best. It took two hours minimum to look my best.

I leaned over the counter by the sink and applied the kohl to my eyes. A light coating of black shadow added dramatic effect. The gray eye shadow in the crease made them smoky, and white beneath my brows made them stand out. I'm not one of those women who wear makeup like icing on a cake. Makeup is supposed to enhance, not cover. I put on mascara and brushed the ivory powder across my face, smoothing it out with the palms of my hands. A little bit of sparkling clear lip gloss and I was done.

I went to the closet door at the end of the hallway, pulling out a trench coat that matched the outfit. The trench was unmistakably feminine. The back of the coat cinched at the waist. The hood of the coat was lined in faux fur, as were the sleeves. I put it on and buckled the front straps.

"Meow." It was Rosalin's voice.

I spared a glance at her, tucking my hair behind my ear. "Aren't you portraying the wrong animal?" I asked with a hint of sarcasm to my tone.

"Would you prefer I bark? I'll bark if that's what you want."

She was still wearing the shirt I'd loaned her. I watched as her hips swayed. The muscles worked beneath her skin as she came to me. I froze with my hands hovering over the last buckle and closed my eyes, listening as she stopped in front of me. With a gentle touch she lifted the white streak of my hair. It slid through her fingers before falling back into place.

Her breath was warm against my lips. "You look beautiful."

I opened my eyes to argue with her when she leaned in. My entire body went rigid a second before her lips brushed my cheek.

"Have a wonderful evening," she said with a light in her eyes. She'd meant for me to think she was going to kiss me.

I grabbed the keys and put my cell phone in the pocket of my coat. There's one problem with wearing a dress, and that is there's usually no room for concealed weapons. I left my guns and knives at home and prayed to the Morrigan I wouldn't regret it. I stopped with my fingers hovering above the doorknob.

"There's a spare key in the cabinet above the sink," I said looking over my shoulder, "use it if you leave."

Rosalin sat down on the couch. "I will."

CHAPTER SIXTEEN

The clock in the car read 7:38 when I arrived at Francesca's. It was a large restaurant nestled in the heart of Oklahoma City. Stone steps led up to the entrance. The walls of the building had dim lights shining on it, just enough light to show it was a pretty cream color. A large patio was located several feet from the steps. The fence around the patio was made of curling wrought iron. Too many places around the building were hidden in shadow. It made me uneasy. Probably not something most patrons were concerned about when they came for dinner here. But I wasn't like most patrons.

I was glad that the four-inch heels were the tallest ones I owned, since I likely would have broken my neck in anything higher trying to navigate the damn stairs.

"Kassandra." Her voice purred my name, sending a shiver of chills up my spine. I turned to find Lenorre bathed in the dim glow of an old-fashioned street lamp. She'd left her hair down so that it fell to her waist like a cloak of black silk. The wind stirred a few curls, causing them to dance. We were both wearing trench coats, except hers was velvet and midnight blue. The pants she wore were tight and formfitting, highlighting every curve of her body to perfection. A line of lace strings crisscrossed down the length of her legs, disappearing into slender knee-high boots. I couldn't tell, but the boots looked like they were black suede. The shirt she wore was the same velvety material as her coat. The collar of the shirt was high, hiding her neck behind black velvet and white lace. My eyes followed the line of white lace to her cleavage.

A smile spread across her garnet lips. I looked down at the steps, hoping the appreciation hadn't shown in my eyes.

She was suddenly in front of me, offering her arm. "Shall we?"

I looked at her gloved palm. The silk gloves disappeared into the sleeve of her coat so that I could not tell just how high they went.

I walked past her and the arm she offered.

Her smile hardened slightly, but kept an edge of humor. As we walked through the door, she watched me intently. It took more effort than I'd like to admit to keep my knees from buckling. Was it just Lenorre, or did all vampires have the ability to caress with a look? I really, really fucking hoped not. If so, I was going to stock up on vampire repellent. A lot of it. That is, once I figured out what would repel them, not kill them. Unfortunately, the whole garlic thing is a load of crap.

We made our way through the dimly lit interior to a table in an intimate alcove. Lenorre sat across the table. I fought against the urge to fidget under the weight of her gaze. Our coats had been taken at the door. The restaurant was filled with the soft murmuring voices of couples enjoying a romantic night out. I cradled my hand delicately around the stem of my wineglass. When we ordered, Lenorre had told the waiter to bring her the usual. The usual had turned out to be a dark liquid in a long-stemmed glass. I didn't have to smell it to guess what it was. Blood in a champagne flute—who would have thought? I wondered if it was some type of vampire etiquette.

So far, dinner was turning out to be a highly uncomfortable experience. At least, it was for me. Lenorre seemed quite content to just sit there and watch me. I'd never in my life been so aware of every move I made, every bite I took. It was unnerving. If I had hoped she'd reduce the tension with polite small talk, I had hoped in vain.

I tried to return her unwavering stare and failed, eyes flicking to the glass in her hand.

"Does every restaurant have that on their menu?" I asked, interrupting our silence.

I could see her smirk out of the corner of my eyes as I took another sip of my own wine.

"No," she said, "I've known the owner for some years. It's an acquired taste."

"I just bet it is," I mumbled. I was full after eating the manicotti, but Lenorre had insisted that I order dessert. I'd gone with the tiramisu. Tiramisu and Lambrusco were on the top of my "orgasmic foods" list. Every woman I've ever met has had a sexy food that tastes so good they equate it with either foreplay or an orgasm.

The waiter returned bearing the gift of tiramisu and put it down in front of me. He looked like he was in his early twenties and I guessed he was working his way through college.

"Anything else?" he asked. The look in his eyes when he looked at Lenorre showed a certain curiosity.

"No, thank you." Her tone was reserved but polite.

He glanced at me and I shook my head. I picked up the fork and focused on my dessert.

The tiramisu melted on my tongue, coating my mouth in the taste of cream and coffee liqueur. I took a sip of wine to enhance its flavor. The wine was sweeter than before, mingling with the richness of the dessert. I licked my lips, savoring the sweetness it left behind.

When I opened my eyes Lenorre was watching me. Her stormy eyes seemed to glow with an otherworldly silver light.

"Would you stop staring at me? You've been watching me like a hawk all night," I said between bites.

"If you were not so fascinating, I wouldn't feel the need to watch you." Her voice was low as she took a drink. There was an edge to her words that made my heart skip.

"You have an accent," I said, changing the subject.

"Barely. I have been in this country long enough that it is not as noticeable as it once was." She gently swirled the ruby liquid in her glass, staring into it as though she could see some aspect of her past.

"England?" I asked, taking another bite. It sounded almost British, but softer, smoother…more like tiramisu.

She nodded and then asked, “What are you thinking?”

“What?”

“A look just crossed your face. What were you thinking a moment ago?”

I was in trouble. I’d just compared the vampire’s voice to tiramisu. I put my fork down. I was suddenly no longer hungry. It was nearly gone anyhow. The comparison was a bad sign. The only person you should compare to a decadent food is your lover.

“I’m not sure,” I said, but it came out too quick.

“There was fear in your eyes.” She put down her glass. “The only look you’ve had in your eyes since the first sip of wine was sensuality, not fear.” She gave me a questioning look.

I shook my head. “It’s nothing.”

She let it drop and pushed her chair back, signaling that our dinner was done. Lenorre paid for the meal and retrieved our coats. She held mine open for me to step into, and I didn’t bitch when she helped me to put it on. The least I could do was allow her to be courteous without bitching. At least, that’s what I told myself as we left the restaurant.

I unlocked the car door and finished buckling my coat. The nights were beginning to get cooler as the autumn equinox approached. Lenorre looked out into the darkness with watchful eyes.

I didn’t know what to say to her so I opened the door and slid behind the wheel.

“Are we going to your apartment?”

I nearly jumped out of my skin. “Sweet mother!” I exclaimed and looked at her. She was sitting in the passenger seat sideways, watching me with those cloudy eyes.

“Do you have to do that?” I asked.

“Do what?”

“Poof,” I said. “Poof, you’re there. Poof, you’re not.” I demonstrated with my hands.

She gave me an amused look.

“It’s not amusing,” I said. “It’s downright creepy.”

Her laugh slid down my spine like heat. My hands clenched and the steering wheel dug into my palms. I tightened my jaw.

"Let's go for a walk," she said.

"Are you telling me, or asking me?" My voice was angry.

She smiled. "Both."

"How can you be doing both at the same time?"

"I'm asking you to go for a walk with me. I'm telling you not to make me ask twice." She leaned back in her seat, crossing her long legs.

"Are all vampires as bossy as you are?"

"Kassandra, is it truly that much trouble just to go for a walk with me?" The gentleness in her tone made me turn to look at her. "I would like very much to go for a walk beneath the light of the crescent moon, and I would greatly enjoy having your company while I do."

Damn, she was good. It was my turn to laugh.

Her facial expression hardened. "I ask you nicely to go for a walk with me. I do exactly what you want me to do, and yet you laugh?" There was anger in her tone, and her accent was more noticeable as it grew.

I shut my door and put my seat belt on.

"Put your seat belt on," I told her.

She just looked at me.

"I'm not starting this car until you put that damn seat belt on." I crossed my arms over my chest.

"You seem to forget something," she said.

"What?"

"I am a vampire."

"We could still get into a wreck. You could get thrown out the windshield and get decapitated by the hubcap." Hey, it could happen.

She didn't even blink.

I kept my arms crossed. "It's still the law, vampire or no."

She opened her mouth to argue and then shut it, putting on her seat belt. Smart vampire. I started the car.

"Where are we going?" I asked.

"There is a park a few blocks from here. The one with the gardens?" I knew which park she was referring to. I held the turn signal down with my fingers and made a left onto the main street, heading in the direction of Heartland Park.

The sounds of the car filled the silence that stretched between us. I spared a glance at Lenorre. A flood of light from a street lamp spilled across her features, illuminating one side of her face. Braking for a red light, I stared out the windshield, waiting for it to turn green.

"You're doing it again," I said.

"What?" she asked.

"Staring," I said.

"It truly bothers you?" She sounded curious and perplexed, as if she couldn't understand how being stared at would ever make a woman so uncomfortable.

"It feels like you're dissecting me with your eyes."

"And that is such a bad thing?" she asked.

"I don't know," I said. "It depends on what kind of mental notes you're making."

"Do you wish to know?"

I eased my foot back on the brake, slowing down enough to allow a couple to cross the street. The man had a little blonde in jeans and heels tucked into the crook of his arm. He raised his hand in my direction, a gesture of thanks. I offered a nod in acknowledgment, whether he could see it or not.

"Sure," I answered.

"I am thinking that you find it so uncomfortable being stared at because it makes it nearly impossible for you to ignore the person that is staring."

At that, I couldn't help it. I grinned. "You're not charging by the hour, are you?"

She raised both of her brows, giving me a look. "That was cleverly evasive."

I smiled softly. "I have my moments."

"The light is green."

I turned my attention back to the road. "So it is," I said, and started scanning the street for a place to park.

Chapter Seventeen

Heartland Park is a swell of hills nestled just below the heart of the city. The buildings and skyscrapers towered above us like metal giants. Legally, the park would be closed to visitors at eleven in the evening. It was about twenty minutes until nine, so we had plenty of time. Lenorre was silent as we walked down the three flights of stairs that led to the pond. The path wove intricately around the large body of water. Old-fashioned lamp posts arched above the winding path, and what the lamps didn't illuminate, the lights of the city brought into view.

I walked across the wooden bridge and stopped for a moment to enjoy the view. The lights and foliage reflected off the water like a surrealist's painting, bent and distorted, but no less beautiful for it.

The path led us on an incline up the side of the hill and around the pond. The smell of juniper was strong on the breeze. I ducked away from a spider's web as we walked under an old wooden archway. Lights that were set into small stone pillars replaced the lamplights. Lenorre stopped and turned to look at me. I almost bumped into her.

She'd taken her gloves off and left them in the car. Her fingers brushed my neck as she tenderly guided the tresses of hair behind my shoulder. I could feel the effects of the wine flooding warmth throughout my body, calming my mind like a comfortable blanket. Her eyes were dark as she looked at me. She reached up, hesitantly at first, and when I didn't step back, she touched my face. I had a moment to wonder if she was going to kiss me before her eyes cast downward. It didn't take a genius to figure it out. She stared at the pulse in my throat like it was something she wanted to unwrap.

I stepped back then. "Oh no," I said, "just because you bought dinner does not mean I have to open a vein and provide you with yours."

Before she could open her mouth to speak, a scream ripped through the night air like the wild and terrible cry of a banshee.

Lenorre snapped out of her trance as she turned and looked into the night. I watched as her nostrils flared slightly. I felt the hair at the back of my neck rise. Goose bumps marched down the length of my arms. Another cry pierced the silence, and the fear in that one cry rode so thickly in the air that I thought I was going to choke on it. I felt my senses sharpen. The wolf stirred in her den, peeking out into the world with eyes that were my own. I couldn't think as a sense of helplessness and fear slammed into me. I couldn't shield against it. I flung off my heels and I began running toward the garden, leaping over a flight of steps and landing on my feet. I didn't stop running. The trees stretched toward the sky. I slipped silently between their trunks. I could hear small helpless sounds from within the dense gardens, but those weren't the only sounds I heard. A low guttural growl vibrated through the night.

Hands caught me and shoved me against one of the trees. Lenorre was suddenly there, pinning my shoulders.

I whispered, "What are you doing?"

"You are not the only wolf in this park," she said.

I placed my heel against the trunk and pushed off. "I know."

She saw the movement and moved away so quickly that I stumbled. I looked between the trees. The light in the area beyond was scarcer, but by the light of the crescent moon and the wolf's keen night vision, I could make out two shapes.

Lenorre kept her voice at a whisper. "What are you going to do?" she asked. "Swoop in and save her? Risk exposing yourself?"

"No," I said as I began taking off my coat. "I'm not going to expose myself." I started unlacing the bodice of my corset. "But I am going to save her." Carver? I wondered. Could it be? I shrugged out of the dress. It fell in a heap of cloth at my feet.

If it was, I would find him. I would stop him.

I knelt on the ground wearing only my undergarments. I didn't care if Lenorre was staring at me. I let go of all of my cares. I drew the smell of the night into my lungs. The smell of juniper clung to me. I opened myself, like I'd open a door, a window, or the lid on a box. I had to open something in my psyche to let her out. As soon as I opened that part of myself that kept her inside, she came running down the line of my soul and out of my physical body. Once it had been painful. It had been so painful I'd passed out. Now I gave myself to the shift like a woman giving herself to orgasm. Every muscle in my body clenched like a fist a second before the change took me under. There was a second of agonizing pain as every muscle went rigid, and then the wolf pushed out against the surface of my skin, breaking free of her fleshy prison.

Distantly, I heard the sounds of my bones grinding and popping. I felt my nails lengthening, pads forming where palms once were, felt things moving like a wave gathering in the ocean, and spilling, spilling out of my skin, spilling out of my mouth in a howl and a tidal wave of white fur.

I collapsed on my side, snout in the dirt, maw agape, panting, trying to catch my breath, to remember how my lungs worked.

I stood on my rear paws and turned to look at Lenorre. I couldn't hear her breathing. My ears swiveled in her direction, listening for a heartbeat and not finding one. Her stormy eyes met mine, and there was something in them that I couldn't read. I lowered myself to the ground, and flung myself through the trees. I had forgotten how good it felt to feel the earth colliding under my paws, to feel the world as it melted into so many scents and sounds.

The wolf's growl grew louder and my hackles rose to attention. My paws hit the ground like war drums. The gray wolf grew in my vision. I lowered myself and pushed off the earth with all of my might. I flung my furred body into the air and hit the other wolf like a bullet nailing its target. The impact sent us both scattering to the ground.

Another scream pierced the air. I scrambled to my paws as the gray wolf did the same. A deep bass growl sent a shudder of power down my spine like a line of hot flame.

I drew my lips back, snarling, but I did not spare a glance at the screaming woman.

Slowly, the gray wolf in front of me stood on its hind legs and erased any doubts from my mind that it might not have been a he. By rising, bipedal before me, his maleness dangled in plain view. I made a disgusted noise low in my throat.

"Small," I said very carefully with the wolf's tongue. It is possible to speak in animal form, but the words always sound distorted. A wolf's mouth is not made for human words. It is our human selves that give us the capability, our knowledge of words and shaping vowels.

He took a step toward me. "Bitch."

I gave a bark of laughter, drawing my ears back in challenge. "Obviously."

He leapt. I flung my body to the left, rolling across the grass and springing to my feet, trying to dodge the blow. He was there, suddenly, clawed hands seeking my face. I growled, snapping, just barely managing to evade his attack.

My heart sped. I'd never fought another wolf in wolf form. I knew how to fight hand-to-hand combat. I knew how to fight with knives and how to use a gun. I'd hunted in wolf form. I'd dominated Rosalin, but at this I was untried. The gray wolf saw it and took advantage, putting me on the defensive. His massive furred body sank low to the ground and his gold eyes watched me as he circled, predatory and deadly, more like some great cat waiting for the right moment to leap in on its unsuspecting prey.

The wolf and I saw that look, and her power sailed through me like a physical blow, forcing me to dig my clawed hands into the earth. I had pushed her down in human form, but this form was hers and she would not be distracted or banished, not now.

I closed my eyes for the briefest moment. She did not doubt. She was not afraid. She was not uncertain. She was the power of the full moon and no eclipse could stop her.

I opened my eyes and rushed the gray wolf, slamming into him again in what I knew was a blur of motion. My claws found him first, cutting skin like incredibly sharp blades. He reared back and howled in pain, exposing his neck in a long line. I dove and sank my teeth in. The blood burst in my mouth like warm syrup. Claws raked down my arms, causing my jaw to slacken as I stifled a howl of pain. His claws sank into my skin and I bit harder, jerking my head back and tearing his throat out in a shower of hot blood. I felt the piece of his skin dangling from my lips. I tried to look at him. A moment of panic washed over me. There was blood in my eyes, obscuring my vision. I heard him coming.

Kicking out with my legs, I caught his body. Claws the size of small knives raked across my hip. In the heat of battle, the pain was dull. I swiped at him again, catching the side of his face.

I tried opening my eyes again but all I could see was red. I shook my head, reached up to wipe my eyes with clawed hands. He caught me off guard and my breath went out in a whoosh as I hit the ground. I felt the tension string his body like a bow on top of mine, like a snake just about to strike. My own body tensed, but this time, in fear.

The air above me was suddenly empty. A heartbeat later and the sound of something heavy and solid sent a shudder through the ground beneath me.

"Get up." It was Lenorre's voice. I sat up, wiping blood out of my eyes and blinking. A pile of werewolf huddled at the base of a large oak tree some ten or fifteen feet away.

I managed to lift myself to all fours.

"Where's the woman?" I asked.

"She ran when you interfered."

I began slinking toward the wolf man's body.

I heard Lenorre say, "I won't save you again."

But the wolf and I weren't looking at Lenorre. No, we were looking at the gray wolf at the base of that wide tree. The wolf thought *Kill*, and I didn't disagree with her.

Lenorre was suddenly blocking my path. I looked up into her misty eyes. A growl of warning trickled from my lips.

"Kassandra," she said very slowly, very carefully. "Kassandra, control your beast. You cannot allow her to make this kill, not if you wish to live in accordance to your human laws."

I growled at her.

Lenorre was quick. She was faster than my eyes could follow. So much faster that I had a flicker of a thought—were all vampires faster than werewolves? Her hand sank into the fur at the back of my neck.

She grabbed a handful of my scruff and jerked me roughly to her. Her other hand caught my jaw in a near-bruising grip.

"No," she said, and there was command and power in her tone. A weight of cool power pressed heavy against my mind. I flinched as she shook me. "No."

I closed my eyes and focused on my breathing, focused on drowning out the wolf's cries for vengeance, for justice paid in blood and death. When I opened my eyes, Lenorre asked, "Do you have control?"

I did, but somewhere inside me, in this wolfish body, the wolf paced unhappily.

"Yes." The word was only slightly tinted with that edge of growl.

She was right. I couldn't kill him, even if it was Carver. If I'd been in human form, and had a gun, then I was Kassandra Lyall, P.P.I. and Paranormal Huntress, but right now I was the wolf.

I heard the sound of sirens far off in the distance. Lenorre turned her face toward the direction from which they sounded.

"We need to go," she said.

"Who?" I asked, but she was pulling me to my feet.

I looked at the wolf huddled beneath the base of the oak. The sides of his furred body rose and fell with each inhale and exhale of his shallow breath.

I stood, torn. Did I run or did I stay and make sure the cops found him? Lenorre went and picked up a bundle of something from the ground. It took a moment for me to realize that the bundle she carried was my clothes.

"Kassandra, you cannot stay," she said, as if reading my thoughts. "We must go, now."

I made my decision and turned away from the pile of unconscious werewolf. If I stayed, I knew what would happen. I was wounded, but I was still a shape shifter, and more than likely, shape shifter was all the cops would see.

The sounds of sirens drew nearer, several blocks away, but quickly approaching.

Lenorre fished the keys out of my coat pocket. My nails clicked softly against the pavement. I stayed close to her. It wouldn't exactly hide me, but in the dark, someone might mistake me for a Great Dane.

She turned and walked to the driver's side door. I tilted my head, looking beyond the reflection of snowy fur and through the tinted glass. I sat back, waiting for her to realize that she was going to have to open the door for me. I watched as she slid behind the wheel. She looked at me and seemed to understand. The door opened and I hopped into the seat. I tried to get comfortable, and finally settled for sitting like I normally would, with my butt in the seat and feet on the floor. My clothes and shoes were a small heap in the backseat of the car.

She started the car and I made a noise low in my throat, almost a growl, but not quite.

"Happy?" she asked after putting her seat belt on.

"Yes," I said and put mine on, though it was awkward and uncomfortable brushing up against my fur.

She put the car in drive and hit the gas. Before I could say anything she was turning out of the parking lot. I leaned my weight against the turn to avoid hitting the door.

"Watch it!" I growled. Just because she was a vampire didn't mean she had to drive my car like a bat out of hell. I grunted as the Tiburon lurched over a bump in the road, wondering which was worse: near-death experience by policemen with silver bullets, or possible near-death experience with Lenorre driving.

❖

Lenorre's driving improved. I wasn't sure if it was because I'd told her to drive more carefully, or because we were trying to look like good citizens, and not a vampire driving with a werewolf passenger. She made a left onto a street I didn't recognize.

"You're going in the opposite direction of my apartment," I said.

"We are not going back to your apartment."

I tilted my head to look at her. "Where?"

I knew she wasn't going to the Two Points. In order to get to the Two Points we had to hit the service road and go farther north into the city. We would've taken the service road and gone south to get to my apartment.

"Where I live." She stopped as the light turned red and looked at me.

"Why?"

"Do you really want your neighbors seeing you thus?"

She had a point. I settled back in my seat.

"Rosalin will meet us there. She will bring some of your clothes."

I stared at her in disbelief. "I'm staying the night?"

She looked genuinely perplexed. "Why not? How long will it be until you are able to shift back?"

Instead of focusing on the "why not," I answered the other question. "I could shift now."

She gave a reserved smile. "Are you bragging at long last?"

"No. The only reason I'm not is because of the side effects." I didn't always experience side effects, but I kept that part to myself. It was usually only when I forced myself to shift back after a full moon shift that the side effects kicked in. The body aches and tiredness were similar to having the flu, and so not my idea of fun.

"Most lycanthropes cannot shift so soon." She glanced at me. "I have known only a few that were capable of such a feat."

"Are you saying I'm abnormal?" I growled.

"I never said such a thing." Her voice was more than calm. It was damn near soothing. "I am only stating that you have an ability few possess."

I grumbled unhappily, "I can go home later."

"You are covered in blood and need a bath. By the time you shift back, you will be too tired to go home, correct?" The dark curve of her brows raised dramatically against paleness of her skin.

I'd forgotten about the blood. I lifted my hand. The blood had dried around my face and neck, leaving my fur stiff and clumped with it. I tried to see the wound at my hip beyond the matted fur. It was already healed. I turned in my seat as much as the seat belt would allow, trying to examine the wounds high up on my arms. One was long and jagged, with blood still seeping out of the opening. The other arm wasn't that bad, but this one looked angry. It was deep enough that it would take longer to heal. I ran my tongue across the wound, slipping it gently along the edge of the jagged cut. It stung, and I did my best to ignore the pain. The sweet metallic taste of blood helped me to slip into that quiet place within. It was a place inside my mind where I was able to turn small pains into pleasurable sensations. I rolled my eyes upward and met Lenorre's wide-eyed gaze. I saw the hunger in her eyes a moment before she turned to look back at the road. It made me uncomfortable. I stopped trying to clean my wounds.

"Are you healed?" she asked.

"For the most part."

Lenorre offered a slight nod. I turned to gaze out the window. The lights of the city fell behind us as we drove out of its reach. I should've guessed she lived away from the hustle and bustle of everyday life.

"Do you think the police will find him?" I asked.

A long pause followed my question.

"I do not know," she said at last.

I suddenly wished I hadn't shifted. I wished that I'd thought to carry a gun with me, but I never imagined that what had happened would happen. If I'd had a gun with me and pumped a few rounds of silver bullets into his chest and called it self-defense, would that have solved the murders? Of course, there was the possibility that there was more than one killer. I tried to remember what Carver had smelled like and failed. If I'd had a piece of clothing I might've been able to trace the smell back to him, but that didn't help me any. In the heat of battle, the wolf had overshadowed my abilities to think like an investigator. Why hadn't I just shifted back into my human form, donned my clothes, and waited for the police? After my fight with the bitch that infected me those three years ago, I'd practically had to beat the EMTs away from me with a stick. I'd narrowly averted the suspicion of my colleagues. I had hidden the pain and the blood and gone to Rupert. If I'd stayed and the EMTs had looked at me… they'd have suspected that I'd been infected.

Even if I shifted back and waited, the cops would know that I'd been attacked. Also, there'd been a witness that had seen me in wolf form. The wounds might heal during the transition, but there's still the issue of being covered in blood. Sure, I could've jumped in the pond after the shift and washed the blood off, but personally, that would look suspicious to me. Cops are a suspicious lot. I don't blame them, but I don't want their suspicions directed at me either.

If I showed up on a scene and found an unarmed woman still standing after a fight with a werewolf I'd be looking for one damn good explanation. Lenorre being a vampire wouldn't work as that damn good explanation, especially if my wounds weren't healed. The whole thing pissed me off and made me bitchy. It was such a no-win situation. The only "win" we had was the woman's safety.

Lenorre drove in silence as I gazed out the window watching the white painted lines in the road streak by. I gave myself to my mood and dark thoughts.

"We could have put him in the trunk," I said, giving voice to one of my thoughts.

Lenorre's eyes strayed from the road as she gave me a look. "And if he woke?"

I thought about that. If we'd stuffed him into the trunk and he'd woken I'd probably be missing half of my car. I frowned. He'd still been breathing when we'd left, which meant his body was already beginning to heal. If he was awake when the cops found him, they were in a bunch of shit. I said a small prayer that the cops arriving on the scene would be safe. I had no doubts that the sirens we had heard were on their way to Heartland Park.

"Someone must've called the cops," I spoke carefully. I'd started to ask her if she knew who had done it earlier, hadn't I?

"My guess," Lenorre said, "is the woman, as there was no one else there."

"You're sure of that?" I asked.

Lenorre guided the car onto the highway.

"Very sure."

I closed my eyes and whispered, "Thank Gods."

I was glad that we had saved the woman. Yet the fact that the killer was still out there left a bitter taste in my mouth. It was the bitter taste of defeat, and I hated it.

Chapter Eighteen

There was a high black fence circling the property. Lenorre had to enter the security code on a keypad so that the gate would draw back and let us through. The house was gigantic. Lenorre pulled into the circle driveway and parked the car. I stepped out and stared at the giant house.

It was a building of dark gray stone. The stone put me in mind of a castle, but it was just a small mansion with a very gothic feel.

The only lights were two sensory lamps that blinked on when we approached a large wooden door. A gargoyle hung above the stone archway, arms spread out like it was crawling out of the building. Its wings swooped upward, large and impressive. The lips of the gargoyle were drawn back to reveal elongated canines.

We walked through the wooden door and I looked up. The ceiling was a good fifty-some feet above our heads. I spotted a casual lounge room to my left. It was covered in soft cream colors and white furniture. The carpet leading up a wide staircase was a dark burgundy. There were silver vines painted on the white wooden rail.

Lenorre walked past the flight of stairs. We rounded a corner down a large hallway. The carpet matched the carpet on the stairs. Hugging the wall were Greek statues that were tall enough I had to look up at them. I knew enough mythology to know who the statues were. As we passed the Virgin Huntress I lightly trailed the tips of my claws across her arched bow. A deer slept at her feet, sheltered and protected.

I lingered at the statue of Venus. A fall of hair tumbled down one side of her body like a veil. The only cloth covering her was the material draped around her womanly hips, trailing across a slightly bent leg. There were seashells scattered at her feet.

It wasn't until I stopped to gaze at the bust of Medusa that Lenorre spoke. "Do you like them?" she asked.

"How could I not?" I'd stopped in front of a mirror. My ears swiveled and flattened against the back of my skull.

Fingertips brushed the fur on my cheek and I resisted the urge to lean into their gentle touch. "You are as beautiful as a painting."

The fur on my ears was more lynx than wolf. Eyes the color of burning gold stared back at me. I ran a clawed hand down the length of my body, turning slightly to look at the bend in my knees. On all fours the hip shifted into place and locked higher up on the body than any other dog. The femur tilted inward more at the knees, creating that graceful arch that allowed us to transition from all fours to bipedal. It was indeed strange, but I had gotten used to looking at myself this way. If the wolf was not trapped somewhere within me, then I was trapped somewhere within her.

Lenorre stepped behind me, meeting my reflected gaze in the mirror. "You disagree?" she asked, bowing at the waist to place the side of her face against my furred shoulder. Her black curls cascaded down the front of my body, standing out starkly against the white of my fur. Her eyes like storm clouds remained steadily on my features. I tilted my head to the side, thoughtfully. I gazed at her reflection in the mirror for a long time. On some level, I did disagree with her. There was a tragic beauty to the wolf. A wild beauty, but when I thought of the wolf as myself, my ears swiveled back, flattening against my skull.

I opened my maw, speaking very carefully. "Somewhat."

She offered a gentle smile, burying her fingers in my fur, sliding her hands up my arms, seeming to ignore the drying blood. "Somewhat?" She chuckled softly, breath tickling my fur. "You disagree because it seems so strange?"

I closed my eyes, nodding.

"Ah well," she mused. "'Tis not so strange to me. Rosalin is waiting." She spared a glance down the hall. "You may use my personal bath. Come."

I wasn't in the mood to argue so I followed her down the hallway, trying to keep my distraction to a minimum, but with so many nifty things to look at, it was difficult. Lenorre turned down another hallway and I trailed quietly behind her, watching as she unlocked a door at the end of the hallway.

"A closet?" I asked.

The vampire looked at me and then opened the door. She stayed in front of me as we walked down a wide staircase. The lighting dimmed in comparison with the brightly lit hallway. I stopped, allowing my eyes to adjust.

"Basement?" I whispered into the darkness, waiting for my night vision to take over.

"You shall see, my questioning wolf." The sound of metal sliding made me jump. The concrete walls were white in my vision, and behind the stairs was a large door. The doorway was the size of a small garage door. Lenorre walked through it and I followed.

"Stay close behind me, along this side of the wall," she said. I nodded even though she couldn't see it, because she was in front of me. The hallway was the same gray concrete floor and white concrete walls. After rounding another corner Lenorre knocked softly on the door. A wash of blinding white light spilled over my face and I shielded my eyes with a blood-covered hand.

"It took you guys long enough," Rosalin said. "Kassandra, I've put your stuff in the guest room."

The room was a drastic change from the basement and entry hall. The walls were a light gray. The carpet was the color of dark ash. A large couch sat against the far wall. A glass coffee table was placed in the center of the room. There were two bright red armchairs on each side of the table. I looked at the back of the love seat. Both couches were a darker gray than the carpet, but not quite black. A huge crystalline chandelier hung above the circular coffee table, and rainbows of light bent through each crystal. It was fancy.

A man and a woman sat on the couch that was against the wall. They sat close enough to be lovers. It wasn't until the male looked at me that I recognized him from the forest. He stood up, smiling brightly and wiping his hands on his jeans. "I'm Trevor, Rosalin's friend."

He pushed the light brown tresses of surfer hair out of his face. "I've heard you're interested in joining the pack." He held his hand out to me.

"I'm thinking about it," I said, doing my best to ignore the hand he offered.

Rosalin leaned over and whispered. "You're going to have to learn how to greet other pack members if you decide to join."

Trevor looked at her. "She's not very friendly, is she?"

"She's just standoffish." They both laughed and I frowned.

"The proper way to greet another member is like this," Trevor said. He reached for me, and before he could touch me I grabbed his wrist, sweeping it up behind his back. I shoved my left knee into the back of his leg, catching my heel on his right ankle. I pushed my body into his like a punch and the momentum took him down. It wasn't exactly graceful, but I rode the back of his body until I felt him hit the floor. A rumbling growl filled the sudden silence, and I realized it was coming from me. My lips pulled back from my teeth and I kept them close to his neck, the wolf still irritated with having to give up her earlier fight.

"Rosalin!" Trevor yelped.

Rosalin put her hands up in the air. "Hey, I told you not to test her strength."

The female had suddenly moved from the couch and stood beside me. Her voice whispered hauntingly. "Get off him." I loosened my grip and Trevor instantly tried to throw me off. It made me come back to myself, and I slammed his wrists roughly into the carpeted floor.

"Try to manipulate me again," I growled, tail lashing angrily, "and I'll dye the carpet a new color."

The woman's eyes widened a touch and she backed away,

hands fiddling with the edge of the blue miniskirt she wore as if she had nothing better to do.

"Kassandra." It was Lenorre's voice that made my body shudder like a chord being struck. Her fingertips brushed across my cheek as much as they had earlier. "You need a bath. If you come with me I will show you to it."

She was trying to calm me down, to offer a distraction before somebody got hurt. My eyes went to the man I was sitting on. His eyes were closed and he whimpered helplessly. A wave of satisfaction went through me. The small helpless noises he was making were like sweet music to my ears. The thought scared me enough that I slowly climbed off him. I took the hand Lenorre offered and allowed her to help me stand. Her eyes caught mine for a moment, but I quickly looked away. I didn't want her to see what was in them.

I sank down low in the tub. It was deep enough that bubbles tickled the edge of my jaw. Once I was alone I had forced the beast into her cage and shifted back. It was best to shift before taking a bath. When I shift it leaves a film on my skin a lot like sweat resin. I found a bottle of soap that smelled a little too soft and feminine for my tastes. The blood had dried in clumps at the ends of my hair, so that I had to scrub the strands between both hands to get it out. The sweat from shifting back had washed some of the blood off, but not all of it.

Lenorre's bathroom was as generous and classy as the rest of the house. The tub sat in the corner. The marble steps surrounding the porcelain tub were tricolor. Silver, black, and white stood out starkly against one another. The countertops matched the marble around the bathtub, offset by the white marble tile on the floor and light gray paint on the walls.

The door opened and I jumped, sloshing water and bubbles over the side of the tub.

Rosalin smiled. “I thought you might want this.” She put a black fluffy towel on the cabinet by the sink.

“Would you learn to knock?” I asked. “How did you get in? I thought I locked the door.”

She held up a small silver key. “Why knock when I have the key?”

I laid back against the edge of the tub. “Because it’s rude just barging in.”

“Lenorre told me to bring you a towel.” She lifted her shoulders in a shrug. “I’m just doing as I’m told.”

She crossed her arms over the tight white T-shirt she was wearing. A pair of snug-fitting jeans hung low on her hips, showing the slight arch where they began.

“Aren’t you old enough to do what you want?” I asked.

She smiled, and it made her honey brown eyes twinkle in the light. “Who said I’m not doing what I want to do?” She leaned back against the cabinet and stared at me brazenly.

“Very nice.” Her voice was breathy as the grin split into a wide smile. My eyes followed her gaze and I realized Rosalin was getting a show. The bubbles had decided to congregate at the foot of the tub.

“Shit.” I sat up, trying to pull the bubbles over my body like a sheet.

Rosalin pouted once I had arranged the bubbles back into place.

“Why’d you have to go and do that? I had a good view.”

“I wasn’t offering you the view,” I said.

“Would you offer it to Lenorre?” she asked. It sounded too forced, too steady, and too much like she was trying to be calm. I turned to look at her, and even though her expression was blank it was obvious how much effort it took her to keep it that way. It was the set of her shoulders, the look hidden within the depths of her eyes that told me she wanted to know not for curiosity’s sake, but for other reasons.

“Rosalin, is it any of your business?” I asked. “You’re not my lover or my girlfriend.” It sounded harsh, but I wanted her to know where we stood. I didn't want to hurt anyone's feelings. I found her attractive, but that didn't mean I knew her. Nor did it mean I was ready to have another relationship. It wasn't just that I didn't want to hurt anyone's feelings. The truth was that I didn't want to get hurt either.

Rosalin pulled herself up so that she was sitting on the marble countertop. "What if I wanted to be your lover or your girlfriend?" she asked, tucking a tendril of auburn hair behind her ear.

I shook my head. "I'm not interested."

"Why?" She looked genuinely curious.

"I have my reasons," I said and then asked, "Will you hand me the towel?"

She picked the towel up and slid off the counter. She stopped in front of the bath, holding the towel in the air. The only way for me to get it was to stand up out of the water. I frowned at her.

"Fine." She sighed, lowering the towel where I could take it from her hands and then moving back to her seat on the counter. Opening the towel, I stood when I knew I could wrap it around my body without flashing her again. The towel was large enough that it hit my knees, and just by the feel of it I could tell it was one hundred percent cotton. I walked carefully down the marble steps, and was surprised to find that they weren't as slippery as I thought. I stopped once I felt the cushioning of the rug beneath my feet. It matched the walls, as if that was a surprise.

"How long has it been since you've made love to a woman?" Rosalin asked.

I looked at her, tilting my head to the side. "What's with the twenty questions?"

"Why won't you answer me?"

"Because I don't think my personal life is really any of your business."

"It's been a while, hasn't it?"

I drew a deep breath, telling myself that I wouldn't get angry. If she kept persisting…then I might.

"Will you just get off it?" I asked in the nicest tone I could muster.

I watched as she slid from her perch and approached me. She was only a few inches taller, and I realized I didn't have to crane my neck to look up at her.

"I think that's your problem," she stated in a low voice."You need to get laid." Before I could respond she leaned in, closing the distance between us. Where her lips met mine they were smooth and gentle. She smelled of some clean perfume, but beneath that was the smell of musk and fur, earth and forest. A flicker of acknowledgment shuddered through me as Rosalin opened her mouth, pressing the entire length of her body against mine. Her hands went to my shoulders as her tongue parted my lips.

I hesitated. Rosalin pressed into the kiss, forcing her tongue deep within the cavern of my mouth. Power like divine honey slid down my throat. I suddenly found myself returning the kiss, tasting it, rolling that power like candy on my tongue. Her energy pulsated against mine, calling to the shadowy creature that dwelled within my flesh.

Any thoughts I had before, any reservations that I held, turned to ash in the fire of her touch. The palms of her hands swept across my ass, causing a moan to build in my throat. Our tongues danced against one another like two velvet serpents twining.

I felt her beast rise ghostly and unseen, felt its energy pouring over me like warm water. A growl vibrated against my lips, and I drank it.

Rosalin broke the kiss, lifting me and carrying me with supernatural ease. She placed me down on the countertop. Beast ridden, I craved. I desired. I cupped her face in my hands and an echo of longing howled through me—a wolf's mournful song. I felt her furred body beneath the bones in her face. Though she did not shift, I felt her beast. I felt her wolf. I felt her.

I tried to wrap my legs around her and growled my frustration when the towel got in my way. Her hands found the edge of the towel, pushing it up over my knees. She pushed it higher until my thighs were free. The tip of her tongue teased mine, until I leaned over to catch her mouth in another deep kiss.

Her skin was warm where her hands lingered on my shoulders.

She lowered her hands, trailing the tips of her nails across my skin. I closed my eyes, chest rising and falling with each breath. The scent of her desire rolled over me, took me under.

"Fuck," I whispered as she leaned over and caught the skin of my neck in her mouth. Her tongue was hot and moist as she licked a wet line across my collarbone. The force of the towel being ripped open made my body jerk. I moaned as she kissed the dip in my shoulder with lips as light as a feather.

Yes. It was the wolf's thought, not mine. I froze.

"Rosalin," I whispered, but it was breathy, a vain plea whispered in the heat of passion. If she didn't stop, I wouldn't be able to stop. The heat between my legs grew as she nibbled and sucked on the skin around my breasts.

"You don't want to stop." Her breath was hot against my breast, and my nipples grew taut. "Your beast doesn't want you to stop." I felt her shudder against me. "Oh God, Kassandra, don't you feel it?"

As I pushed myself off the counter, I seized the towel in my hands. I stumbled and realized she was holding the other end of it. Her eyes were like amber gems, and my body tightened. I felt it.

"Rosalin." I shook my head, trying to think, but she kept moving toward me with that unnatural grace, and I couldn't think. My back hit the wall and she leaned forward, putting a hand to either side of my face. Then she lowered one hand and placed it between my legs. A startled cry escaped my lips and then I moaned for her.

The tip of her finger slid into the wetness between my legs. She circled my clit lightly at first, teasingly, and then her rhythm changed until my back arched against the wall.

One arm snaked around my back, and she lifted me, holding me against the wall. I dug my nails into her shoulders, growling my pleasure into her mouth. Heat rose from the center of my body, spilling out of my mouth in a muffled cry as I came against her hand.

My knees buckled. Rosalin helped lower me to the ground. I leaned back against the wall, eyes narrowing.

"Why?" I asked, trying to get my lungs to work properly. Her power left the sweet taste of cool ginger in my mouth. Her scent lingered in my senses like patchouli.

She knelt in front of me, gazing at me with eyes that were sincere and warm. “You needed it,” she said softly.

I stared at her for several moments, eyes narrowed, unsure of how I felt. I was angry with her, angry that she had pursued, but more pissed off with myself. I’d given in. I’d allowed the beast to override my sensibilities. I closed my eyes. I knew if I gave in to that anger, there wouldn’t be any stopping it. It would rear its ugly head, and there would be hell to pay, because once my anger found a target, it wasn’t easily satiated.

Her touch was light as she took my hands in hers. “Kassandra?” She made it a question. “What’s the big deal? It was just sex. You enjoyed it…”

I threw her hands away, snatching the towel as I stood. She watched as I wrapped the towel around my body. My hands and words shook with anger. “It’s never just about sex, Rosalin.” I opened the bathroom door and walked out. Once the door slammed shut I stopped in my tracks. I had a moment to wonder which was more frightening—facing Rosalin, or the scene on Lenorre’s bed.

CHAPTER NINETEEN

Lenorre was like some dark mysterious dream caught between the folds of erotic and horrifying. Her eyes rolled upward, reflecting the candlelight as I walked into the room. Why did I suddenly feel the urge to turn tail and go back the other way? Her eyes were like silver mist, deep, intense, and untouchable. The power I felt in the room was thick, making it hard to breathe, like an overpowering smell in a small area. There was a woman in her lap. The woman's neck bent back at an awkward angle. I expected to see pain written across her features, but what I saw was the look that really good sex will give a person.

Lenorre watched me while she fed. Her onyx lashes fluttered, as if she found it pleasurable. The blood pounded in my ears. I tried to reason with my body. One foot in front of the other, that's the way to go, but my legs didn't seem to be working.

Lenorre stroked a hand down the woman's back, cradling her, comforting her. It was too gentle a gesture for what was happening. I tried to move, but my body felt too heavy, too solid. The hairs on my arms stood on end. I felt the magic riding in the air, coming for me a second before it hit. The pain that shot through the side of my neck was sharp and cramping.

The magic spilled across my skin like something liquid, filling my blood like sweet poison. A hand stroked down up and down my back. Every muscle in my body relaxed while her mouth worked at the wound. Each flick of her tongue against the wound was long and sensuous. I felt weightless struggling against a pleasure my body wanted to accept. My mind did not want to accept it. I felt the metaphysical bars of her power and screamed.

Someone was drawing deep ragged breaths. I knelt on the floor as my vision blurred around the edges. The candlelit room slowly came into view as the spinning in my head seemed to slow down.

I was the one who had sounded like she was about to hyperventilate. Closing my eyes I took meditative breaths, counting each. It helped to push some of the panic away. I opened my eyes to find Lenorre kneeling in front of me. Blood painted her lips and the sight made my heart bang against my ribs. I tried to move out of reach, but she was too fast. Her lips caught mine. With her tongue she pushed the taste of blood into my mouth. The beast stirred at that promise.

I touched her hair, twining a handful around my fingers. I ate at her mouth as the hunger rode me, ate at her mouth like I was dying for it. The edge of her fangs brushed across my tongue and I hesitated, about to pull away when the beast howled through me. How could we refuse such a prize? How could we not honor such a gift? I pressed into the kiss, no longer worried that she might bleed me. I cleaned the blood from her mouth, licked it from her lips.

The metaphysical bonds that held the beast in place relaxed. We were one.

"You smell of sex." Lenorre breathed against my mouth.

"You smell like blood," I said. If we were going to point out the obvious, might as well start there.

"So do you," she said and I looked at her. Her eyes were their usual cloudy gray, no longer misty with vampiric powers. The robe she wore was silk, sleeves ending at the elbows in a spill of black lace. It draped open down the middle, revealing the low neckline of the nightgown underneath. The beginning of her sternum peeked through all of that black, making her skin look inhumanly white. A jolt of longing cut through me. I clutched the towel tightly to my chest.

"Was it worth it?" she asked, freeing the white streak in my hair. She twirled the wet strand around her finger, tugging lightly.

"It wasn't my idea," I said.

Lenorre stood in a swish of black silk. "You say that it was not your idea?" She looked at me. I nodded.

"But did you enjoy it?" she asked, eyes intent.

"Yes," I said, then thought about it. "No."

"Kassandra, choose one. I want the truth from you, not a mixed message."

I glared at her. When did it become her business? Better yet, why was everyone suddenly up in my business? First Rosalin, now Lenorre.

"Yes," I said and watched as her face hardened in disgust. I wasn't going to lie to her. Whether it was the wolf, or me, some part of me had enjoyed sex with Rosalin. I hadn't enjoyed the fact that my longing, the beast, and my groin had gotten the best of me.

I heard the bathroom door open. Lenorre's gaze went to it, eyes full of an anger I couldn't understand. I seriously doubted the vampire harbored any jealousy toward me. More than likely, I suspected her ego was bruised that she hadn't gotten to me first.

I moved so that I could keep both the werewolf and the vampire in view. Rosalin's hair was wet like she too had taken a bath. A matching black towel was tucked around her body, and I knew she made the situation look twenty times worse.

Rosalin looked at me, and then the vampire. The expression on her face told me she was completely lost, but she had to have heard some of the conversation. Our kind have excellent hearing.

"I did not say that you could use my bath." Lenorre gave the other werewolf a look the put a chill of coldness in my heart.

"I didn't think you would mind."

Lenorre closed her eyes and responded with two words, but the command in her tone was hot enough to make me flinch.

"Get out."

Rosalin looked at me as if asking for sympathy. I was too upset to feel particularly sympathetic. I felt like an idiot who'd allowed myself to get caught up in a moment of careless passion.

A look of pain crossed her face and she hesitated at the door. She looked back at me.

I shook my head. "No," I said when she opened her mouth to speak, "not now."

She left.

My hands trembled where they held the towel in place. Lenorre turned away, looking up at a painting on the wall. In the glow of candlelight it was beautiful. The painting was many shades of deep swirling blues and black. There were tiny pinpricks of light trapped in the sky, small silver stars. A horned crescent moon hung low on the horizon, stark white against the darkness. The edge of a gray cliff jutted out, welcoming the moon. The lighter shade of the sea below reflected the moon's luminosity, tides curling in welcome to her light.

The woman Lenorre had fed upon lay back against the thick dark pillows. As if she felt my gaze, she looked at me. Her skin was as pale as mine, but not quite the unnatural paleness of Lenorre's. I couldn't tell if it was some trick of light or contacts that made her eyes look like amethysts. She turned her head and I noticed there was a purple tint to the fall of her straight black hair.

"Zaphara," Lenorre said.

"Yes, m'lady?" The voice didn't quite purr like Lenorre's, but there was breathiness to it that hinted at more nefarious things.

"Show Kassandra to her room."

The woman nodded to the vampire's back, climbing out of the pile of massive covers. She buttoned the top two buttons of her blouse, smoothing out the material with the palms of her hands. The dress slacks she wore were wide enough and had enough give that they made her legs look long and slinky. Her heels were muffled against the thick-carpeted floor. I looked up at Lenorre, and then followed the woman out into the brightly lit hallway. I squinted until my eyes adjusted.

Zaphara walked ahead, putting a sway in her walk that would turn every head in a bar. I frowned and forced myself to stare at the fall of her black hair, deciding it was a bad idea since her hair ended right above her ass. I'd had enough preternatural drama for one night. It wouldn't do to stir the cauldron even more.

We passed several doors before she turned a corner.

"This is your room," she said.

I walked into the room and nearly dropped my towel. It wasn't as large as Lenorre's room, but the space was generous. The room smelled of rosewood, sweet and spicy at the same time. Thick green material was pulled back and tied to each post on the canopy bed. The pillows were a combination of greens and cream colors. A rosewood armoire was placed in the corner of the room, matching the wooden posts of the canopy and the mirror diagonal from the bed. There was a Victorian vibe to the room, but beneath style was the energy one only finds in natural elements like wood and stone.

Dark gray yoga pants and a white tank top were spread out on the bed. I guessed that Rosalin had taken them out and left them for me.

"Rosalin put the rest of your clothes in the dresser," Zaphara said from the doorway and I nodded.

"If you need anything I'm down the hall and to the right." She left, shutting the door without waiting for my response.

I went to the dresser and opened a drawer. Rosalin had brought more than one outfit for me, all of which were neatly folded. I dug through them, finding a pair of black underwear. I opened the doors on the side to find that the dress and coat I had worn to dinner were hanging on wooden hangers. They smelled like they'd been cleaned.

I tossed the towel over the large mirror and changed. I was glad the tank top had sort of a built-in sports bra so that the shirt wasn't see-through. After I dressed I went back to the armoire, remembering my cell phone. It wasn't in the pockets of my coat, where it should've been. I frowned and headed for the door, nearly jumping out of my skin when my mind registered the vampire leaning her tall frame against the door. I wondered how long she'd been standing there.

"I told you to stop doing that." I narrowed my eyes at her.

"Doing what?" She looked genuinely perplexed.

"Poofing. You did the poof thing again."

"I apologize for…poofing." She gave a slow blink. "I wanted to give this to you. You had a phone call." Extending her arm, she offered my cell phone.

"Why do you have my cell?" I asked, and the suspicion in my voice was obvious.

"I used it to contact Rosalin." She shrugged, as if that explained everything. I took the phone and stood there, staring at her.

She motioned at it with a graceful flick of her wrist. "You might want to get that."

I looked at it and realized it was on. "Shit, now you tell me."

"I told you a moment ago that you had a phone call."

I shook my head and took the call. "Yeah?"

"Who was that?" Arthur asked. "Did I interrupt some bow-chicka-bow-wow?"

"A friend, and no you didn't interrupt anything." That was, like, thirty minutes ago, right? "What do you want, Arthur?"

"To hear your sexy angry voice," he said, laughing loudly over the line. I had to move the phone away from my ear for a second or risk injury to my eardrum.

"Arthur, cut the crap. Why are you calling me at two in the morning?"

Did he catch Carver? I wondered. I hoped.

"I'm not telling you until you tell me who answered *your* phone."

"I told you, a friend."

"She sounded hot."

I looked at Lenorre, who sat on the bed smiling. No doubt she was hearing the entire conversation.

"Maybe," I said and her smile faltered a little around the edges. I smirked. "Your turn. What's going on?"

"We've got our first official werewolf complaint," he said in a singsong tone.

"Really?" I asked in my best you-are-boring-the-shit-out-of-me tone. A complaint? Not the actual werewolf? Damn it.

"Holbrook wants you to come in and help question her," he said, serious.

"Her?" I asked.

"Yep," he said. "Can you be here in twenty minutes?"

"Yeah, if you want me to get pulled over for speeding."

"What? Your apartment isn't that far away…Ooh." There was a pause as it dawned on him. "You're not at home, are you?" He laughed.

"That's none of your business," I said.

"Aww," he said, "spoil the fun. How far away are you?"

"From the station?" I asked. "If I take the highway, only half an hour or so." I was guessing. I hadn't kept track of time when Lenorre drove us out here. Who would with a vampire driving?

"I'll let Holbrook know, but you should hurry. You know how impatient he is."

"Yeah, okay," I said, remembering. Captain Holbrook was bossy, loud, obnoxious, and had zero patience. If he said to get something done, he meant get it done in 2.5 seconds. His wife was the complete opposite, polite, soft spoken, and with what seemed like an unending amount of patience. Usually, people that project a sweet image to the world have a horrible temper lurking somewhere in the depths, but not Lillian. She was the epitome of kindness and ladylike grace.

"Hurry up, all right?" he said.

"Give me time to change and then I'll leave," I said.

"Can I—"

I hung up the phone before he could finish.

Lenorre stood from the bed. "As well," she said, "I need to change my clothes."

I frowned as she began walking toward the door. "Why would you need to change?" I opened the top drawer in the dresser, taking out a pair of stylishly destroyed jeans and red hooded henley. Rosalin had been thoughtful enough to put a pair of solid black skate shoes in the armoire. I silently thanked her. I was so not in the mood to wear heels.

"Your undergarments are not there because they were not retrievable," Lenorre said matter-of-factly.

An image flashed through my mind of the entire squad finding the remains and sending them in to forensics. So not cool. I was ninety percent certain the woman was reporting the werewolf in Heartland Park. It wasn't a comforting thought that I might end up on that complaint. I certainly hoped not, since I had saved her butt. If that was a possibility, why was I going in to interrogate her? I was also ninety percent sure the wolf in Heartland Park had been Carver, and judging by Arthur's call, they hadn't caught him. Any information I could get would be valuable to the case and taking him down.

"You didn't leave them, did you?"

She gave me a look. "Of course not."

I nodded, but said, "I don't think it's a good idea if you go with me."

"Ah," she said, "but I am going to go with you."

"Why?" I asked.

"You asked for my aid, did you not?"

I tried to see if there was a trap in her words and failed to see one. "You're right," I said carefully, "I asked."

"So," she said, lifting her shoulders in an elegant shrug, "I am giving it." She gave a victorious smile. "I'll leave you to change. It will not take me too long."

She left, kindly shutting the door behind her. I changed into the clothes I'd set out on the bed. Digging through the drawer and ruining Rosalin's fold job, I managed to find that she had packed an extra bra for me. It wasn't the same as the bras I usually wore, which molded to my body. This bra was a push-up with two tiny shoulder straps. It was the only bra that made it look like I actually had cleavage.

I hoped the henley would be warm enough. The material was thick, but it had been chilly earlier tonight. I slipped my feet into the shoes, pulling the white socks up so they didn't bunch at my toes. If there was one thing that would drive me neurotic, it was bunched-up socks. I laced the shoes and put my cell phone in my right pocket.

There was a light knock.

I called out, "Come in."

Lenorre walked in. "Better?" She asked.

"Yeah, much better." My gaze traveled over the length of her body. The denim pants she wore were tight and neatly tucked into a pair of strut-your-stuff boots. The word *delicious* came to mind.

The shirt she wore was modest and faded, but the design that peeked through the opening of her dark jacket made me laugh.

"The Grateful Dead?" I asked.

She grinned wide enough to flash the tips of her fangs. "I am glad you notice the humor in it."

"Shit, I couldn't miss that a mile away," I said. "At least you look somewhat human. Let's go."

As we stepped into the hallway she walked past me and looked over her shoulder. "So do you."

"So do I what?" I asked, lost.

"You look somewhat human."

"A wolf in sheep's clothing," I jested.

"That is more true than even you know, Kassandra."

I gave her a look at that cryptic comment, but decided it was best if I left it alone, for once. There was a nearly unnerving silence to the house as we left. It felt as if the walls were holding their breath. I couldn't quite put my finger on it, but something about the house felt strange.

CHAPTER TWENTY

As Lenorre sat in the passenger seat guiding me toward our destination, I tried to memorize the area. This, at two-something in the morning, wasn't easy to do. Everything always looks so different at night. I knew that if I tried to drive back to the house in the morning I'd have to try and remember street names. The problem with that was there were none. They had all been painted over in various shades of spray paint.

"Why aren't there any street signs out here?" I asked.

"There was a house down the road where teenagers used to party. They replaced the signs once, but the kids vandalized them again."

"That explains why the past two stop signs we've passed have 'Go' written on them," I said.

"Indeed," she said. "It does."

"They should really replace the signs. Fine the kids or throw them in juvey."

She lounged in her seat. "They would most likely give them community service."

I nodded in agreement. "True."

"The kids would do it again."

"Oh, look." I leaned over the steering wheel while easing my foot down on the brake for a stop. "Elderberry," I said, reading the first sign that was graffiti free.

"If you keep going straight it leads to the highway," Lenorre said.

I spared a glance at her. "Forward," I corrected. "When you're in a car with someone that's gay, it's the polite term to use. If you say 'straight' we just come up with smart-assed remarks."

The corner of her mouth trembled for a second in what I thought was an effort not to smile. "Forward, then."

I wondered if Lenorre was a lesbian. I mean, come on, she'd taken me out to dinner. Wasn't that a date? Well, that and the scene in her bedroom. I tried to think back to my first impression of her at the club. It's easy to visually spot the obviously gay—the stereotypical butch and gay male. The women that go into clubs scoping out other chicks, shoulders held tight, as if they're ready for a fight at any moment. In all reality, stereotypes do not trigger what is commonly known amongst homosexuals as "gaydar." I've met butch and tomboy women who were married and men who were extremely feminine but loved women. There's a lot more to homosexuality than a trend or appearance. Appearances, as they say, are deceiving. Very deceiving. Like knows like, and a lot of us can sniff one another out almost on a psychic level. Kind of like the way I could scent another wolf nearby, I realized.

I glanced again at Lenorre, trying to figure her out. I was betting she was a lesbian, even though it wasn't physically noticeable.

"Kassandra." Lenorre's voice called me out of my thoughts.

"Hmm?"

"You failed to stop at the sign we just passed."

"There's a stop sign behind us?"

She nodded and then looked curiously at me. "What were you thinking about?"

Should I tell her, or do I just ask her, "Are you a lesbian vampire or a bisexual vampire?"

I drummed my fingers against the steering wheel…Hmm.

I decided to tell her. "I'm trying to figure out if you're a lesbian or not."

Her lips curved into a soft smile. "Why would you try to figure that out?"

"I'm curious," I said.

"Mmm." She tilted her head to the side."What do you think?"

"I think yes," I said, this time remembering to stop. I followed the street under the overpass and made a left onto the service road that would eventually spit the car onto the highway.

Lenorre was silent.

I looked at her. "You're not going to enlighten me, are you?" I asked.

"Why should I when you already know?"

"So, are you admitting to it?"

"That I am a lesbian?" she asked.

"Yeah."

"Yes. Though I prefer the title 'Lover of Women.' It has a more sensual ring to it."

"It sounds a little polyamorous to me." I gave the car a little more gas when taking the onramp.

"I can see where one might get that impression," she said. "I am, however, a highly monogamous creature when I am in a relationship."

"When you're in a relationship?" I laughed.

I heard more than saw her shoulders lift in a shrug. "I have been alive long enough that I have tasted a casual encounter at least once, Kassandra."

I ignored the fact that, technically, she wasn't alive. She was undead.

"Once?" I asked.

She smiled, reservedly. "Or twice."

"I'm not a casual person," I said, placing my cards on the table.

"Are you saying that what happened with Rosalin was not a casual encounter?"

I stared at the stretch of highway before us and tried to figure out how to respond. In a sense, it had been casual. Rosalin had been the pursuer, but I had ultimately given in to my wolf, to the energy between us. Could I have stopped it? If I could have, would I? I didn't know. There wasn't any sense in blaming anyone or trying to push it off as an accident. Those were both lies. I wasn't angry with Rosalin, I was angry about the fact that we'd had casual metaphysical sex and I didn't feel as terrible as I thought I should. In fact, I felt okay. Did I see myself having a relationship with Rosalin? No. The energy was amazing, but something was missing, some deeper craving wasn't there with Rosalin. In that moment, I'd felt plain and simple erotic hunger brought on by the wolf. It was nice, but fleeting. It was, in fact, purely animalistic.

I looked at Lenorre.

"I don't take it seriously, if that's what you're asking."

"Good."

"Good?" I asked.

"If she had won your heart…it would have diverted all of my plans." Her voice was low and purring.

I shuddered. "And what plans are those?"

"You are a smart woman, Kassandra. I am sure you can figure it out."

❖

The police station was a large red brick building located on the opposite side of the highway. It was hard to miss, and was the only two-story police station I'd ever seen. I parked the car and got out. Lenorre followed my lead. Arthur stood outside by the double glass doors that read *City of Oklahoma Police Department*. He threw his cigarette down in an old coffee can as we approached.

"Took you long enough," he said.

"My broom doesn't work like it used to," I said sarcastically.

He laughed. "Tell that to the boss man."

I stopped and stared at Arthur as he opened the door for Lenorre and me. He was wearing a pair of dark brown wrinkled slacks and a white dress shirt. The collar of the shirt was unbuttoned, as well as the cuffs.

"Why aren't you wearing a uniform?" I asked.

He saluted me. "You're looking at Detective Kingfisher," he said in a singsong voice. I laughed and shook my head.

"They were safer keeping you in the blue suit.".

I looked back at him when he didn't respond. He pushed the sandy brown hair out of his face and stared at Lenorre. His hair was the longest I'd seen it, just beginning to brush the edges of his ears. I watched as recognition dawned across his features.

He held out his hand. "Detective Kingfisher. I don't believe we've had the pleasure of meeting." His tone was suddenly serious. I realized that even with the messy hair and loose tie, he looked like a detective, one who had been awake for forty-two hours and was stressed the hell out.

If it were any other friend of mine I probably would've interfered. I might've said, "She's with me," so that Arthur wouldn't bug her. No matter how serious he could be, it was rare. Arthur had a sense of humor that didn't just disappear. I crossed my arms over my chest. Lenorre was a big vampire. She could take care of herself.

Lenorre took a step back and looked down at the hand that hovered between them. "We have already met, Detective. I will forgo the handshake."

Arthur frowned and let his arm fall to his side.

"We spoke on the phone earlier," Lenorre said, "when you called to speak with Kassandra."

The frown shifted into a smile, and then a cheesy grin.

"Ooooooooh." He looked at me. "I get it."

I looked impatiently at him. "Are you done?"

"Yeah, I'll leave Vampira alone. Holbrook is waiting in the interrogation room." He walked past me. "Let's go before he gets his tighty whities in a wad."

I made a disgusted face. "That was more than I needed to know."

He looked back at me and grinned.

I caught up with him. "You do realize that you just called the Countess of Oklahoma, Vampira?"

Lenorre walked quietly behind us.

"Yep," he said with his usual cheesy ass smile.

I blinked. "Why?"

"I didn't think she'd take to me calling her Fangs."

I rolled my eyes. "Sometimes, Arthur, I'm convinced you're just a little boy trapped in a big boy's body."

He grinned widely. "Shh. Didn't you know that's supposed to be a secret?"

"Arthur," I said, "don't shush me."

I stopped when he stopped in the middle of the hallway. Lenorre caught up to us. She was tall enough, especially in the heels, that she had to look down at Arthur.

"Even if I didn't know who you were," he said, "I'd still know what you were."

Lenorre smiled rather coyly. "You are not a sensitive, Detective. I find it terribly difficult to believe that if I did not want you to know, that you would."

He blinked. "A sensitive?"

"Psychic," I explained.

He shrugged. "No, I'm not, but I had a friend in college. He was real different afterward."

Her dark brows went up. "How so?"

"He wasn't as much of a klutz." He shrugged again. "It's in the eyes. There's a look to the eyes, like Kassandra." He motioned to me. "She's got this dominant and powerful look," he said, "this look that she won't let anyone push her around. A good cop can tell just by looking at her. When they look down, that is, so that they're not looking over her head."

"Hey!" I said, giving him a dirty look.

"Sorry, Kass, but you're short."

"I'm five-one," I said.

"You're tiny. You need to eat more doughnuts."

I frowned.

"Doughnuts with sprinkles on them, right?" he joked. I narrowed my eyes at him. It was kind of an inside joke. Let's just say that once I made the mistake of specifically requesting a certain type of doughnut when he'd offered to get breakfast. Of course, Arthur and the rest of the department that he told thought it was a freaking hoot. I should've known I'd never live that shit down.

I sighed. "All right, but only if they have sprinkles on them."

Arthur laughed and I rewarded him with a grin. There was a look on Lenorre's face that said she either didn't get the joke or didn't find it particularly funny.

"I'm cool with it," Arthur said, looking at Lenorre. "I promise not to post a bulletin, but there are going to be cops here who recognize you."

Lenorre offered a slight nod. "I am aware of that, Detective."

"Let's go before Holbrook gets even more pissy," he said. I agreed with him. The last thing I wanted to deal with was a grumpy ex-boss. I was going to do my best to keep that off the agenda tonight. I was surprised to find that my nerves weren't freaking out about Arthur recognizing Lenorre. It shocked me the most to find out that he wasn't vampire racist. A lot of cops thought vampires were monsters. Hell, a lot of people thought anything preternatural was monstrous and evil. I wasn't going to tell Arthur that I'd been a werewolf for three years. I didn't feel that safe with him. Besides, it was best that he didn't know. How did I know he hadn't spotted me for what I am? I just knew. Call it intuition, call it instincts, but I knew Arthur didn't know, even though he'd mentioned that thing about me being dominant. It was interesting that he saw a similar power in my eyes that he saw in Lenorre's. It made me wonder if he'd seen that before or after I had been infected with lycanthropy.

Arthur stopped outside a pale brown door that had paint chipped in areas to reveal the pale wood underneath. He looked at me. "Ready?"

"As ready as I'll be," I said.

He looked back at Lenorre, who had settled herself in a seat against the wall to wait. "What's it like?" There was curiosity in his eyes.

"What's what like?" I asked.

"Banging a vampire."

I told him the truth. "I don't know."

The look he wore said that clearly, he didn't believe me.

"What?" I said, "I haven't done anything with her."

"Kass," he said getting all serious on me again. "If you're not sleeping with her, what are you doing with her?"

I smiled at him, turning the doorknob. "Investigating."

I opened the door and stepped into the room beyond.

CHAPTER TWENTY-ONE

The walls of the interrogation room were a disgusting shade of off-white. No, there wasn't one of those nifty little one-way mirrors. The station hadn't been able to afford one when it was first built. Dan Holbrook was sitting across the table from a petite brunette. I recognized the outline of her features and the light scent of her perfume. There was still a hint of fear to her smell, but it was such a small amount that the flowery perfume overrode it.

Dan turned to look when I walked into the room. He didn't get up, or offer to shake hands, but that didn't surprise me. His dark brown hair was in the same short cut it had been for years. The black slacks he wore were ironed and obviously tailored. He'd taken the suit jacket off and draped it over the back of the chair so that the charcoal dress shirt and shoulder holster were in open view. I remembered from years of working with him that he often did that during any sort of interrogation, be it victim questioning or suspect questioning. He left his gun in plain view. I didn't agree with flaunting a weapon in front of a victim. In my opinion, it's rude, but I've seen it work in front of a suspect. When a suspect is placed on the opposite side of the table, their eyes fill with worry, darting back and forth from face to gun. Dan flaunted his gun for that reason and to display that he was in charge. It irked me that he was doing it in front of a woman who had been attacked.

She huddled over a mug of coffee. Her eyes darted to me and relief slid into their hazel depths. I thought I understood the relief.

Women generally feel more comfortable around other women, especially women who have just been attacked by a man. Her long hair was pulled out of her face, tied back at the nape of her neck. It emphasized her triangular features, bringing the full mouth and wide eyes into view. There was a scratch across her left cheek. It looked like it had just stopped bleeding.

"Lyall," Dan spoke and his tone was thundering deep, "have a seat."

He stood and removed his jacket from the back of the fold-out chair. The chairs were uncomfortable.

"Claire Delaine, this is Preternatural Private Investigator Kassandra Lyall. She'll be interviewing you from this point on."

I didn't exactly take kindly to the fact that he'd given a complete stranger my first name, but I kept my mouth shut. If you know what's good for you, you don't argue with Holbrook.

I sat down as Dan folded out another chair that had been against the wall. He took a seat in the corner of the room, placing the clipboard in his lap so he could take notes. I forced myself to smile at Claire.

"Ms. Delaine, can you tell me what happened to you this evening?"

She looked at Captain Holbrook. "How many times do I have to tell you what happened?"

I spoke before Holbrook could respond. "Ms. Delaine, I understand you're tired, irritated, and that you've probably told the story a million times. That's how interviewing goes. I've been called in to help work this case. I'm the one that needs to know what happened to you tonight. If you don't tell me, I don't think Captain Holbrook is feeling generous enough to fill me in. So it comes down to this—you want my help or not?"

Her fingertip circled the edge of the coffee mug as she gave me a considering look. "Fine," she said. "About a week ago I answered a personal ad in the local newspaper."

"Was it a dating personal ad?" I asked, just to be specific.

"Yes."

I nodded. "Was the ad from a male or female?"

She gave me a look. "The ad was from a male seeking a female."

"You answered this ad?"

She nodded. "We went out to dinner around eight this evening."

"Do you remember his name? Where did you go eat?"

"I don't know his last name, but he said his first name was James, Jay for short," she said. "We went out to dinner at this nice bar and grill. Cattle Horn's Steakhouse." It wasn't obvious but her hand trembled over the edge of the mug. She put her hands in her lap. "Everything was fine," she said. "It was…perfect…romantic…"

"Until?" I asked.

"I found out he was a monster." Her tone was harsh, mingling with an edge of fear, but those hazel eyes burned into my own by the strength of her will. She wasn't willing to play the victim. It was obvious. I wasn't going to mention the park. If I mentioned anything even remotely hinting that I knew where the incident had taken place, suspicions would arise.

Instead, I asked, "What do you mean by that?"

I watched as she struggled to hold herself together. Her shoulders squared and she drew in a long breath of air. "We went to the park after dinner…"

"I need to know what park," I told her.

"Heartland Park. It's not far from Cattle Horn's. We decided to walk. When we got to the park he held my hand and pointed out various trees and plants. He seemed to know a lot about them. I asked him how he knew so much and he told me that he used to work as a park ranger. He didn't specify which park when I asked him, just said one of the parks in Colorado." She looked at me with pleading eyes. "He tried to kill me. I don't understand why…"

"No one ever understands why," I said, not knowing what else to say. If it was the same werewolf that had killed the Nelsons' neighbor, chances were he was just looking for a kill. If the neighbor had been a woman fitting Claire's description I would've said we had a lead. It would have meant that the killer was looking for a certain type of victim.

"You said he was a monster," I went on. "What happened that makes you say that?"

"A werewolf," she said, "I watched as he changed…"

"You saw him shift?" I asked. "Did he say anything before shifting?"

"He told me that he liked me. He said he had a secret he wanted to share with me, and a game he wanted to play. He asked me if I had ever read the story about Little Red Riding Hood. Of course I have, I told him." Her voice was beginning to shake. I was surprised there wasn't a box of Kleenex on the table. She wiped her eyes with the back of her hand, fighting against the tears.

"He changed without warning. He wanted me to watch him change. The fear smelled good, he said. I refused to run when he told me to run, because that's what he wanted. He wanted to chase me, and kill me…" The tears broke and she buried her face in her hands. "I'm sorry," she sobbed, "I told myself I wouldn't cry…I shouldn't…"

"Claire, anybody would cry after what you've been through."

She nodded, keeping her face hidden in her hands. "I don't know what to think." She sounded like a child lost in the dark. I felt her pain grip at my heart and resisted the urge to go to her, to comfort her, to tell her those little lies: everything is all right, it was just a bad dream. The truth was that it hadn't been a bad dream. It was very, very real.

"What did he look like?" I asked. "Do you remember?"

"Tall, muscular, blue eyes," she said. "I think he was in his late twenties, early thirties."

"Do you remember what color his hair was?"

"No. He was wearing a hat."

Carver. It had to be. So, he'd chosen a different name. That made sense.

"Do you know why they asked me to question you?" I asked her.

She looked up at me then, wiping her eyes on the dark blue sleeves of her turtleneck. "No."

"Because," I said, "whoever, whatever did this to you, I'm

going to catch him. I know you're scared," I said. "I've been there." I told her with my eyes that she wasn't the only one that'd been attacked.

She wiped her nose on her sleeve this time. "What happened to you?"

"Let's just say it's dead now. You can't dwell on it too much. I know it's easier said than done, but you get over it, eventually."

"There was more than one," she said.

I pretended to be surprised, widening my eyes slightly, but not overdoing it.

"What do you mean, there was more than one?" I asked, very carefully.

"Werewolf. There was another one that came out of nowhere. It happened so fast... He was coming for me, and the next thing I know this thing slammed into him and I ran." She was looking at the corner of the room like the scene was playing before her eyes. She met my gaze again. "I think it was trying to protect me."

I stood. "Then consider yourself very, very lucky. The other wolf offered no harm to you?" I asked.

She shook her head, eyes glazed. "No, no. If that hadn't happened..." She shuddered. "I don't think I'd be here right now." The tears subsided as she sat back in her seat. "I am lucky," she said.

I nodded. "Not many people survive a werewolf attack."

"You did," she said, then asked, "Didn't you?"

I nodded. "Yes, but that wasn't luck. That was silver ammo."

She looked scared. "What if he comes after me?"

"Does he know where you live?" I asked.

She nodded. "He picked me up from my house earlier this evening."

Shit.

"Captain Holbrook can put you under witness protection," I said. "I'd suggest you go stay with a relative or at a motel under a different name."

"I don't want to be under witness protection," she said stubbornly.

I shrugged. "I don't know what else to tell you."

"We'll make arrangements to see Ms. Delaine is safe," Holbrook said. "Thanks for coming down here, Lyall."

"I have another question."

Claire looked at me and I continued. "How did he pay for dinner?"

"Cash," she said.

I nodded. If he had used a credit card we would've been able to run it and find personal information like his full name, address, etc. Apparently, he'd thought about that too. I stood and Holbrook stood with me. He walked me to the door.

"It took you long enough to get here," he said once we were on the opposite side.

"Dan, I'm not under your supervision anymore. You can't boss me around like you used to."

He actually grunted. "I could stop calling you in to help with cases."

I smiled sweetly. "I'm good help, and you know it. Where would you be without me?"

"Down one royal pain in the ass," he said.

"That might be true, but I know more than anyone in this department about the preternatural."

He was silent long enough that I heard the heater kick on. The heavy whoosh of hot air blew out of the vents and filled the sudden silence. Well, silence aside from Arthur's voice going on about something or another in the other room.

"What do you think?" Holbrook asked at length.

I drew in a deep breath. "I think we've got a serial killer werewolf on our hands."

"You sure about that, Lyall?" He gave me a hard look.

I returned the look. "If I wasn't, I wouldn't have said so. You know me better than that."

He stared at me like he was trying to memorize my face. "What do you know, Lyall?" The question caught me off guard, but I recovered quickly, showing no emotion, no flickering of eyelids.

"Everything I know for sure," I said, "you and your men know."

He gave a sharp nod of his head. I watched as he looked out over the office. His dark eyes stopped on Lenorre, who had her arms crossed over her chest. Arthur was talking to her.

"Is that your new girlfriend?" he asked. "The countess looks a little dark for you, Lyall."

I laughed. "You used to tease me about looking dark," I said. He used to always ask me when I was going to go get a tan, and I always told him that it would never happen. "Besides, why do you presume she's with me? She's talking to Arthur."

Holbrook narrowed his eyes. "No woman in her right mind would willingly talk to Arthur. It doesn't look like your girlfriend is enjoying the conversation."

I ignored the girlfriend bit. "I still talk to him. Are you implying that I'm not in my right mind?"

He scoffed. "You talk to him because you know you're going to get a retainer out of it."

I grinned widely. "Do you tell him that?"

"All the time."

"It's good to know you haven't lost your sense of humor."

"Go save your girlfriend, Lyall."

I nodded and looked over to Lenorre. Arthur's hands were moving around in the air as he described something to her. She ignored him and made her way through aisles of desks to me. I met her halfway and then went for the door.

"Did it go well?" she asked.

"Well enough," I said. "I want to wait outside for a few minutes. Do you know what time it is?" I'd tried to be quick during the interview.

"Kassandra, you do not have to worry about me."

"I wasn't," I said, looking away from her.

"We have a few hours until the sun rises," she said. "I will be fine."

We stopped outside and stood away from the doors, on the

sidewalk next to the building. Lenorre didn't ask any questions. I was waiting for Claire to come out of the building.

Arthur walked out and looked at us. "Loitering?" he joked. He held the door open as Claire walked out.

"What is it, Kass?" he asked.

I looked up at him. "Could you give us a minute?" I asked, looking to Claire.

"You just questioned her," he said.

"Arthur," I said, "let me talk to her for a moment."

He scratched his head. "I don't know if that's a good idea, Kass. If you're asking her something you didn't ask her in there, Holbrook will be pissed."

"It's for her safety," I said. "Trust me. Let me talk to her."

"Fine, but only for a minute. I've got to get her somewhere safe." He made his way toward the parking lot.

"Claire," I said softly, "I need to ask you something, and it's important that you tell me the truth. Okay?"

She nodded, but the look in her eyes was cautious and uncertain.

"What happened to your cheek?"

Her eyes widened like the question had caught her off guard.

"I got scratched," she said. "Why?"

"Shit," I said. "Did the werewolf scratch you?"

I watched as the realization flooded her eyes. "I don't remember," she said, but it came out too fast.

She was only a few inches taller than I. My eyes met hers and I spoke slowly, "If the werewolf scratched you, you're at risk of infection. Do you know what I'm talking about?"

"I already put triple antibiotic ointment on it," she said.

"Claire…This may not be something you want to hear, but I'm talking about an entirely different type of infection."

If I had thought her eyes couldn't get any wider, I was wrong.

"You don't mean…?" she asked.

I nodded.

"Shit," she said.

"Yeah."

"What do I do? Is there any way to prevent it?"

I shook my head. "No, I'm sorry. It either happens, or it doesn't."

She drew in another deep breath. "You're telling me that I could be infected with whatever disease it is that turns people into werewolves?"

"It's called the lycanthropy virus," I said, "and yes."

"How do I know if I've been infected?"

I shrugged. "You don't. You won't know until the next full moon."

She looked at me. It was a long and deep look. I watched as the thoughts slid in and out of her eyes, and knew what she was going to say before she opened her mouth to speak.

"Is that what happened to you?"

Lady knows, I didn't want to lie to her. If she was infected I wanted to help her as much as possible. There wasn't another lycanthrope there to help me through my first shift, or my second shift, or hell, even the third shift. The only person I had was Rupert. I wondered if it would've been easier having another lycanthrope around. The first three shifts had been the worst. The pain had been so excruciating I'd passed out. I could still only remember bits and pieces, like a dream badly broken.

Lenorre's voice was suddenly there, whispering in my ear. "If she has been infected, you can smell the virus in the wound."

I turned to look at her. She was still standing against the wall. An army of chills marched up and down my arms. It was creepy, but I nodded in acknowledgment.

I looked at Claire. "Will you trust me?"

Her eyes were still wide, as if she couldn't quite believe what she was hearing. After a few moments she nodded. I took a step forward and leaned into her. She took a step back.

"Claire," I said, "you have to trust me."

"What are you going to do?"

"Look, I won't touch you. I promise. Just trust me."

I took a step forward to make up for her step back, and she stood still. I inclined my face toward the scratch on her cheek. Up close, I could tell it was deeper than it had appeared at a distance. I drew the air in through my nostrils, sorting through the combination of scents, night air, fear, perfume, and sadness. I realized for the first time that other emotions had a smell too. Fear smelled like something sweet and sour, like sweat and green apple candy. Her sadness smelled like the salt of her tears and something musky. And beneath, her strength smelled like oak trees in spring. I took another careful breath as the smell of antibiotic ointment and petroleum mingled with the light scent of old blood and something else. I focused on the other smell, drawing another breath into my lungs, tasting it at the back of my throat. The smell was faint, but I knew what wolf smelled like.

She was infected.

I stepped back and let out the breath I'd been holding.

"Do you trust me?"

"Why? What is it?"

"You've been infected."

I thought she would argue with me, fight against, pretend it wasn't true, or real. She didn't. I opened my senses and felt her struggle. She conquered the fear quickly, and I felt her strength flow through her. Thank the Goddess.

I watched as she steadied herself like a person bracing against the wind. "I believe you," she said. "Tell me what I need to do."

"She comes with us." Lenorre stood at my side. "This is not something she needs to experience on her own."

Arthur stepped onto the sidewalk as he emerged from the parking lot. I turned to look at him.

"Are you done yet?" he asked. "I've been waiting in the car for over fifteen minutes now."

"We are almost done, Detective," Lenorre said. She turned to look at me.

"Lenorre, this is one mess I don't know how to figure out," I admitted.

Lenorre turned to Claire. "You need to make a decision. Do you want to be alone when the fever takes control of your body, or do you wish to be around people who know how to deal with it?"

"Fever?"

"You're pretty much going to go into a comatose fever," I said. "Been there, done that. It isn't fun and it isn't pretty." I kept my voice low to make sure that Arthur wouldn't hear me.

"This is all stuff that can be discussed on the way home. What is your decision?" Lenorre's gray eyes were all for Claire.

Claire looked away. "Fine. I'll go with you. You'll help me figure out what to tell my family?"

Lenorre nodded and I asked, "And we slide her by the detective…how, exactly?"

Arthur walked up to us. "Whoa, what? What are you talking about?"

Lenorre was a blur of motion as she suddenly stood in front of Arthur. "You will not remember this," she said. "You did not see Kassandra talk to Claire. You took Claire to relatives and now she is safe. Do you understand?"

I took a step back. Arthur's blue eyes were empty of any emotion. There was a glaze to them that a person only gets when they've had too much to drink or smoked too much pot. He was completely gone, taken over by the vampire's powers. Slowly, he gave a nod, once up, once down. Lenorre's magic spilled over my skin and made me shiver. I wrapped my arms around myself as though it would keep me from ever falling under her spell. Right.

"Go back to your car and drive carefully back to your house, remembering only that you took Claire to safety."

My eyes widened. Arthur turned as if he were on strings that Lenorre was pulling. He walked back toward the parking lot, heading for his car.

"We must go," Lenorre said. I was glad that no one else had come through the doors during her little brainwashing episode. I was also glad that she didn't try and touch me. I could tell by looking at Claire that the whole thing had left her a little shaken. Good, I thought, I wasn't the only one.

CHAPTER TWENTY-TWO

It was around four-something in the morning when we arrived back at Lenorre's. I'd parked the Tiburon in the four-car garage on the left side of the house. The door in the garage led into a large and brightly lit kitchen. The color scheme in the kitchen was black, white, and chrome. The tile was white with gray lightning strokes running through it. It reminded me of howlite, a beautiful white gem with streaks of gray. I didn't think howlite was sturdy enough to use as flooring. It was clean, like it had never been used. Growing up, my mother had always been a little OCD about cleaning stuff. I never dreamed that I would see anything cleaner than my mother's house, but I guess I was wrong. Somehow, I couldn't picture Lenorre cleaning. The French maid outfit I could totally picture…the cleaning part, not so much.

I shook the thought away. The last thing I wanted to do was picture Lenorre in something even remotely sexy. After what I had seen of her powers earlier I was a little unnerved. How would I know if she had done that to me?

Lenorre led the way back to her underground hideout. I busied myself with remembering the way, in case I ever needed to get out. We walked through the darkened basement and Lenorre opened the door into the dank hallway. The sound of keys jingled as she unlocked the door at the end of the hallway and opened it as a spill of light flooded out of the room beyond.

"A room will be prepared for you. I will send someone to stay with you. Wait here," Lenorre said to Claire. She nodded and sat down in one of the fluffy armchairs, her shoulders slumped and a look of deep weariness on her face.

I followed Lenorre down the hallway. She opened one of the doors.

"Isabella, a woman is waiting in the main room. I want you and your wolf to go stay with her."

I peeked into the room and saw the blonde from the main room earlier. Trevor looked at us from where he was sitting on a small settee at the foot of the bed. Isabella, the vampire who had been wearing the miniskirt, was now wearing an old-fashioned frilly nightgown and brushing the locks of her long blond hair in front of a vanity mirror. The reflection of her cornflower blue eyes flicked from Lenorre to me. She nodded and I followed Lenorre as she walked down the hall.

"I am going to allow Claire to sleep in the bedroom you were appointed." She stopped at another door. "You need to get your stuff."

I looked at the identical doors lining the hallway.

"This is the room, Kassandra."

"How the hell can you tell?" I asked.

"Practice."

I opened the door and walked in, picking the clothes up off the bed. Lenorre stood in the doorway, patiently watching.

"Where exactly am I supposed to sleep?" I asked.

"That you do not need to worry about," she replied. "Rosalin put your overnight bag in the very last drawer."

She was right. The large backpack I'd kept in a closet at home was in the bottom drawer. I dug my clothes out of the other drawers and tossed them into the bag, draping the coat and dress over my arm. The high heels got crammed into the backpack with the clothes. I tossed the backpack over my right shoulder and shut the door behind me. We turned left down another hallway, and then down another one. At four in the morning my observational skills gave up. There were too many damn doors to memorize. There were a few sets of large double doors here and there. It wasn't until we reached the end of the hallway that Lenorre opened two large shiny black doors.

I froze in the doorway, staring at the dimly lit blackness of her room.

"You are so kidding me," I said.

She gave one of those slow and thoughtful blinks. "Why?"

"You want me to bunk with you?"

She ignored me and walked into the bathroom. The sound of running water filled the sudden silence. Sighing, I dropped the backpack in an armchair at the far side of the room.

Lenorre leaned against the door frame, elbow crooked as she brushed her teeth.

"Well, It's nice to see you have good hygiene," I said.

I think I saw a flicker of a smile around the toothbrush. "I may be dead, but I am not that dead." She walked into the bathroom.

"I thought vampires die at dawn," I said.

"We do."

"And you want me to share a bed with you?"

Lenorre emerged from the bathroom. She was wearing the same robe and nightgown she had been earlier.

"That is an issue?" It was a question.

"If I wanted to sleep with a dead thing I'd go dig a hole in the graveyard and hunker down."

"I assure you, they are not as well preserved as I am," she said and I couldn't tell if she was joking.

I frowned.

"Kassandra, for me to offer my bed to you is a sign of great trust."

I sighed. "Look, what I saw tonight wasn't exactly comforting."

"What you saw tonight is what I am. As much as being a wolf is a part of what you are."

I nodded. "I understand you are being…generous…offering your bed and all, but I just don't think I'm comfortable with it."

"You are not comfortable with me," she said.

I didn't know what to say to that. "I don't know."

"Kassandra, what is it you are not comfortable with?"

"You want me to be honest?" I asked.

"Always," she said.

"I think the whole dying at dawn thing kind of weirds me out."

"How would you feel if I had reacted in a similar manner when you had undergone your change in the park?"

How would I have felt? I drew a deep breath, answering as honestly as I felt comfortable. "The fear might've excited me."

"Your fear or my fear would have excited you?" she asked.

Her stormy eyes met mine.

"Both," I said.

"That is your wolf talking." Her lips curved into a soft smile. "What does the human side of you say?"

"I would've felt rejected."

"And you think that just because I am a vampire, I do not have feelings or emotions?"

I opened my mouth to speak, and then shut it.

"Clever," I said. "That was a smart move."

The look in her gray eyes was questioning.

"Trying to appeal to my sense of compassion to get me into bed?"

"Kassandra, I am not trying to sleep with you."

What? How did that make any sense? It didn't. She was trying to get me into bed with her. I stared into those smoldering gray eyes and tried to figure out what game she was playing. An ache was beginning to start between my eyes and I gently rubbed the bridge of my nose between thumb and index finger.

"I give up. What are you playing at?"

"I am not playing at anything."

"Oh no, obviously, you're playing at something. Out with it," I said. Why was I even staying? I could leave, couldn't I? The only problem was being a little tired, but I could make it home in one piece. I sat down on the edge of the bed, keeping my eyes on the vampire in front of me. We stared at one another for the space of a few heartbeats. She was like some surreal dream that my heart and body cried out for. I didn't feel that with Rosalin. Looking at Rosalin didn't make my groin sink or my knees weak. Looking at Lenorre did.

The problem was that my head didn't believe in that dream, and thought my heart a fool. The damn thing skipped a few beats when Lenorre slowly slid out of the silky robe. My gaze instantly fell to the black-carpeted floor, but nothing could distract my ears from the sound of cloth sliding against skin, her skin. There was fear there, lurking like some great fish against the surface of my soul. She would break me, and I was afraid she'd do it in more ways than one.

I stood, quickly pushing off the bed and heading for the door. Fingers like cold steel wrapped around my upper arms. She turned me to face her. My pulse leapt into my throat.

"I will not harm you," she whispered, eyes glowing with that otherworldly light, misty and surreal. She stepped into me, tightening her grip on my arms, fingers digging painfully into my flesh. Her eyes closed, lashes fluttering.

"Kassandra." Her voice was breathy. The British accent turned my name into something sultry and rich. "Calm down or we are both going to do something we regret."

The fear flowing through my veins was exciting. Oh Gods. My breath came, short and clipped. I closed my eyes, forcing the air slowly, deeply into my lungs. "Let go," I breathed.

Lenorre eased her grip on my arms one inch at a time.

The look she gave me was intense and there was rawness to her eyes when she said, "I just want you to stay with me. That is all, nothing more and nothing less."

"No freaky vampire shit?" I asked.

She inclined her head forward, but not before I caught the corner of her mouth quirk.

"Fine," I said and went to the backpack on the armchair. "Do you have a spare toothbrush?" My hands were trembling ever so slightly.

"Yes," she said, "in the bathroom. Look in the drawer beneath the sink."

After I had accomplished my hygiene duties, I walked out of the bathroom wearing a pair of green plaid flannel boxers. The wolf shirt matched the white patches on the shorts. The wolf on the shirt was black, neck arched as it howled at the full moon. In a nearby tree a raven perched, listening.

The only light in the room came from a lamp that was on the bedside table. The black bars of the lamp's base curved upward, wickedly wrapping around a frosted gray globe from which the light emitted. It bathed the room in deep shadows.

Lenorre was propped up against a mound of satiny black pillows. The curls of her hair pooled out around her body, so that she looked like a fallen angel resting on an ebony cloud. Her pale skin seemed to absorb the light, reflecting it like the moon against a black sky.

The silence was so thick I could hear the blood rushing through my veins. Lenorre closed her eyes. Her long lashes were as shiny as crow's wing, and stood out starkly against her skin.

"Kassandra," she said, "come to bed."

I looked at the empty spot on the other side of the bed. The bed was large enough that I could sleep in it without even touching her. My gaze shifted back to the vampire. She was a lesbian's wet dream. So why was I standing there, frozen in place? I didn't want to climb into bed with her for that exact reason. What lesbian in her right mind would crawl into bed and impassively lie there?

"I am not going to bite," she said, opening her eyes so that I had the full attention of their silvery depths. There was a look in them that I hadn't seen before. She had drawn her guard up. Her face was a blank and expressionless, but beyond the mask she projected was a wariness I could sense.

In the beginning of any relationship or friendship there comes a time where one person silently expects something from the other. If that expectation is not met, it hurts one or the other, and cripples something between them. I suddenly knew that if I turned away from her, it would cripple something between us. If I was not willing to leave my comfort zone at least a little bit, it would stifle whatever was growing. It dawned on me how vulnerable a position she was placing herself in. She had been right that it took a great amount of trust to offer her bed to me. Once the sun rose, Lenorre would be incapable of protecting herself. It was that last thought that made my decision.

On the opposite side there was a small amount of room between the bed and the wall. I crawled up into it, sliding my legs beneath the satin sheets. The sheets were cool against the warmth of my skin. I turned on my side, propping myself up with an elbow on the pillows so that I was able to look at her. She lowered herself, rolling onto her side so that she mimicked my position. A foot of space was between us. If she expected me to close the distance, she was wrong. I slid my arm under the pillow, turning over onto my left side. For several moments I gazed intently at the wall, until finally closing my eyes. It wasn't until my head hit the pillow that I realized I was very tired, but my mind was racing.

There was movement and I lifted enough to turn and look. That little bit of space had dwindled. I rolled back over. Another shudder went through the mattress. I looked again and Lenorre was lying on her back staring at the canopied ceiling. Her eyes flicked to me, and then back to the ceiling.

Movement again. This time, I ignored it, keeping my eyes closed and trying to focus on going to sleep. It was difficult to do with a vampire in the same bed, especially one who kept making the bed move. I was almost asleep when I felt her arm curl around my waist, her hand resting limply against my stomach, as if she was afraid to move any more than she had.

She withdrew her arm when I turned over to look at her. There were only a few inches between our bodies. She was close enough that I could smell the subtle scent of sandalwood mingling with another smell, something like cool night air, crisp and clean. My fingertips brushed her wrist as I took her hand and placed it on my hip. I inched forward, placing the line of my body against hers, and snaked my arm toward her back, resting it at the base of her spine.

"Better?" I whispered, looking up into her pale eyes.

Lenorre rolled over on her back, drawing me into the circle of her arm. The movement placed my head on her shoulder.

"Better," she said.

I touched the front of her body with fingertips, trailing my nails lightly from the edge of her rib cage to the beginning of her hip. The material of the gown was slick against my skin.

"Your heart isn't beating," I said, listening intently to the silence, interrupted only by the sounds of my breath and heartbeat.

"The sun is near," she said as if it explained everything.

"Does it beat?" I asked.

"Yes." Her voice was a breathy whisper. "For you it might, Kassandra."

I tensed.

She peeked through the veil of her lashes at me. "Romance makes you uncomfortable?"

"A little."

"You should become accustomed to it," she said.

"Why?" I asked, trailing my nails lower, down the arched slope of her hip, across the smoothness of her thigh. Why did I feel the undeniable urge to touch her? I wanted to feel her nude body sliding against mine, slick with sweat. I shuddered at the image.

"I can be very romantic." This time, it was she who shuddered as my palm caressed her thigh.

She caught my hand in hers, trapping it. "Do not tease me so close to sunrise."

"I'm not meaning to." I moved my hand, sliding it behind her back, feeling her weight against me.

"I know you do not mean to," she whispered. "Such tender gestures are merely torturous so close to dawn." Her eyes met mine and she swept aside a strand of hair from my face. "Most especially when one cannot follow through."

Her palm swept up my back, drawing me to her. I followed the movement until we were face to face. Her breath was warm against my mouth, smelling of crushed mint.

"There are things I would do to you if there was but more time." I closed my eyes at the promise in her words, at her breath tickling my lips. That pale hand swept across my thigh, threatening to slide under the material of my shorts.

I heard the fear in her voice, barely tangible.

"You're afraid," I whispered, sounding slightly surprised even to myself. I didn't expect that dying at dawn would be enjoyable, but fear wasn't something I expected from a vampire who had done it quite a few times in the last century.

The hair fell around my face as I looked down at her. The smile she offered was wistful. "I am not so much afraid as I am displeased that it is not an enjoyable experience, no matter the time that passes."

The mask she wore faltered a little, allowing me to see the pain buried deep within her stony gaze.

"Does it hurt?" I asked.

Her words were faint. "Somewhat."

I watched as her jaw clenched, and I did the only thing I could think of to distract her from that pain. I cupped the side of her moonlit face in my hand and placed a chaste kiss upon her mouth. Her lips parted and she leaned forward off the bed, securing her mouth against mine. The sharpened points of her fangs glided threateningly over the tip of my tongue. Then her tongue found mine and she locked her mouth to mine, deepening the kiss.

The taste of her mouth was like sweet wine and mint. I felt her mouth open wider and the kiss deepened. Nails dug into the base of my back, causing my spine to bow. Lenorre tore her mouth from mine. Her eyes rolled into the back of her head. I held her body against mine, cradling her head in my hands until I felt a shuddering gasp pour across my skin. A chill of air burst through my body, leaving me breathless and trembling. Just as I could sense emotions, feel people to a particular depth, so too could I feel when Lenorre… *left*. Do vampires have souls? Whatever, I felt it when she died.

Gently, I lowered her to the bed. The look on her face was the peacefulness and stillness that only the dead have. The fear stopped my heart for a moment, constricting around it like a python, making it hard to breathe. I curled against the cold and empty shell of her body. She was not lost. I would not cry. The breath I forced myself to take was like needles in my lungs. I nuzzled my face in the bend of her neck. By nightfall my Lenorre would return to me. It was a temporary death, and she would be reborn.

...My Lenorre?

❖

I woke to the dim lighting of the bedside lamp. Propping myself on my elbows, I looked out at the room. I'd heard something. I listened and another small beeping sound interrupted the silence. I went to my backpack. The zipper sounded like something being shredded in the silence of the room. I had a second to freeze and then shake my head at myself. Lenorre was a vampire. It was three in the afternoon, which meant she was dead to the world. I could probably kill a few people in the room and she wouldn't wake up. I retrieved my cell to find that I had two missed calls and two new voicemails.

The first one was June, asking in a very unhappy tone if I planned on showing up for work at all. If not, she said she was going to call Rit. The second voicemail was from Rit, stating that she was going to go into to the office for a few hours. She told me to give her a call whenever I got her message. I returned the phone call, informing her that I'd been out late helping the police.

"You sound wiped," she said.

"I am," I said. "I was out until nearly four this morning."

"I can't believe they called you in that late." Her tone was sympathetic. "June and I will get things taken care of here. You don't have to worry about coming in."

"Thanks, Rit," I said. "It's greatly appreciated. I'm sorry I didn't notify either of your earlier, but like I said, it was late when I got in this morning."

"That's okay," she said, "go get some rest."

"I'm planning on it," I said. "Again, thank you. I'll talk to you later."

"All right. If you want I'll still come in tomorrow? I need the extra hours, anyhow. Unless you have something you're working on?"

"No, that's fine." I stifled a yawn. "Right now I'm too busy working on this case to take on any new clients."

Rit understood. I shoved the cell into the front pocket of my backpack.

The sheets had grown cool when I crawled back into bed. I stared up the ceiling. What if there wasn't just one or two killers, but more? If I was looking directly at the Blackthorne pack for suspects, I was ruling out other possibilities. As an investigator, I couldn't do that or I'd limit myself and up the chances of overlooking important clues. I had to keep my eyes open and try to look at all sides of the coin. Of course, seeing so many sides and possibilities can be very confusing. Which is where evidence comes into play, but what evidence did I really have? I didn't have any metaphysical or physical evidence that told me that Carver and the wolf I'd confronted in Heartland Park were one and the same. I only had a vague description that seemed to fit the bill.

What if Carver was working with someone else in attempt to take control of the established pack? Rosalin had said that most of the wolves fight and dominate their way to the top. If that was so, why didn't he just challenge her and then challenge the alpha? Was Carver's temper and control so horrible that he became a killer? Had he murdered by accident, or was it a power play that I couldn't understand?

I closed my eyes, as if it would help me to look inside myself and find the answer. What did I feel? What did I sense?

Pack.

Whether it was my thought or some divine whispering, I do not know. But I felt without a doubt that the murderer was someone in the pack.

I curled myself around Lenorre's cold body and prayed for guidance. I fell asleep with images of wolves alternating between sex and fighting, and the sense of foreboding deepening even further.

Chapter Twenty-three

The bed moved violently. A loud gasping breath startled me awake. I woke disoriented, forgetting where I was and whose bed I was in. I looked at Lenorre. She was still on her back, like she hadn't moved. Her eyes flew open and met mine. The look in them made my pulse leap into my throat.

"Lenorre?" I asked softly, afraid to speak any louder.

Her movements were slow as she started leaning toward me. Her gray eyes dropped from my face and to the pulse in my neck.

"Oh, shit." I scrambled off the side of the bed, trying to keep my eyes on her. "This wasn't worth mentioning?" It was more to myself than the vampire.

I was trapped between the bed and the wall. *Smooth move*, I thought. Lenorre was slowly creeping onto her hands and knees, like a cat about to pounce. My lips drew back in a snarl, a warning.

Lenorre hissed at me and the expression turned her beautiful face into something terrifying. I snatched one of the pillows from the bed and held it like a shield. Her body met mine and I shoved that soft shield into her, trying to use my own strength to hold her at bay. When I realized that she was too strong and it wasn't working, I slipped out from behind the pillow and ran into the open area of the room. The last place you want to be in the middle of a fight of any kind is trapped.

She started crawling across the bed, painstakingly slowly, as if she was in no hurry to get to me. The weight of Lenorre's personality wasn't there in her eyes. Instead some predatory beast looked out at me. I knew that look—it was the look of a hunter stalking its prey. Only this time, I was the prey.

Unexpectedly, she came for me. I jumped over the armchair, landing on my feet, but Lenorre was too fast, a blur of motion in my vision. The only thing I could do was try and use her own momentum against her. The sound of my elbows hitting her chest echoed through both of our bodies. I grabbed her shoulders, thrust my arms above my head, and sent her over me.

I turned in time to see her catch herself, but her shoulder caught the painting on the wall. It fell with a loud clash. The glass shattered into a multitude of sharp fragments.

I heard the bedroom door open before Rosalin said, "Kassandra!"

"A little help!" I yelled.

A blur of dark silk and I braced for the impact.

Nothing happened.

Rosalin was there, holding her wrist in front of the vampire's face. Lenorre followed with that predatory look still in her eyes. Rosalin used herself as a distraction, taunting the vampire with the promise of blood. Lenorre's lips parted.

"No!" I yelled, but it was too late.

The sound of skin tearing made me cringe in pain. Lenorre tore the artery in Rosalin's wrist in a spray of bright blood. Rosalin had jerked her wrist back, and that had earned her worse injuries. Her eyes closed as she forced herself not to protect herself, and when she didn't fight, when she made her body go completely still, Lenorre used the grip she had on Rosalin's wrist to pull her in against her body. She brought the smaller woman's wrist up to her mouth and sealed her lips over the wound.

Rosalin whimpered and Lenorre held her trapped against her tall body. She drank, but this was not a gentle embrace. She was hunger-ridden, and any wound that spurted blood would suffice.

The vampire opened her mouth wide and drove her fangs in again, as if trying to make a bigger wound for more blood.

Rosalin's pain-filled eyes pleaded with me. I couldn't just stand there. I walked back to the bed and grabbed the pillow. It was the only object in the room that I could think of using without causing any permanent damage. I didn't want to kill Lenorre—I just wanted her to fucking snap out of it. Vampires, like werewolves, have only a few weaknesses. If it had been any other vampire I would've gone for my gun. But Lenorre wasn't just any vampire.

Cautiously, I stepped up a few feet behind Lenorre. Rosalin's eyelashes fluttered, not in pleasure, but more like she was about to pass out. She saw me and tried to shake her head, tried to put her other arm out, as if to stop me.

The vampire who had been holding her so tightly dropped her. A look of pure bliss crossed Lenorre's profile. Blood dripped in a steady flow down her chin. I reared the pillow back and threw my whole body into it, hitting the vampire with a force that made her stumble. The anger fueled me, pumping through my veins, and this time, I full out charged. The wall shook when we slammed into it. I grabbed a handful of those beautiful dark locks and turned her to face me. I shoved my forearm against her throat. The anger had awakened my beast.

"Kassandra." Lenorre tried to talk over the pressure in her throat.

I growled.

The wolf threatened to spill out of my skin as my body shook with rage. The vampire had hurt another wolf, a wolf we had grown to know, a wolf we had been with, and that was unacceptable.

"Kassandra," she said again, but this time she didn't wait for my response. She spun, and my arm was pulled up behind my back at a painful angle. My cheek met the wall. I tried to push off, to rebound off it, but Lenorre was tall enough that she used the line of her body to pin me.

"Kassandra!" Her words cracked like a whip. "Get a hold of yourself!"

Again, I tried to push off the wall, tried to throw the vampire off me. The wolf didn't like being trapped. Panic made my pulse race, made me fight against her hold. Lenorre's fangs sank into the back of my neck.

The pain arched my spine, caused my hands to spasm against the wall. She growled over the mouthful of skin at the back of my neck. It wasn't the growl of the wolf, but it was a gesture that we understood.

The sensation made my body go slack. The wolf rode me, arching my ass into the woman behind me. A whimper escaped my mouth when her jaws tightened, fangs sinking deeper into my flesh. The blood tickled as it dripped onto the collar of my shirt.

I was suddenly left shuddering and panting. I slid down the wall when she took her mouth from me.

"Why did you stop?" I went to all fours, looking up at Lenorre, who stood a few feet away. "It felt so good." My voice sounded strange. It was too purring, too sexy. I moved and felt every muscle gliding beneath my skin. Stretching, I watched as Lenorre's gaze followed the arch of my body. "So good," I whispered.

"Kassandra," she spoke slowly, "that is your wolf talking, not you."

"When the wolf speaks, is it not with my voice?" My fingers stretched into claws, ripping loudly through the carpet. I leaned forward, out of the stretch.

"She is riding you," Lenorre said.

A throaty laugh that held the edge of a growl came from my mouth. "There's one thing I want riding me, Vampire, and I'm looking at it."

"Rosalin." Her eyes shuddered closed. "Get out."

The other wolf caught my attention, her scent filling my nostrils like fresh pine. A whimper fell from my lips. Why was she leaving? She liked playing with me too.

"Oh no, wolf." Lenorre knelt in front of me. Her arm reached out, grabbing a fistful of my hair. "If it is I you want, that is what you are going to get."

My tongue flicked hungrily across my lips. Oh yes, that's what we wanted.

Rosalin left the room with a single worried glance over her shoulder.

I turned my attention back to Lenorre and growled when she

closed the distance between us. Using the grip on my hair, Lenorre pulled me forcefully to her mouth. I moaned as her hungry lips met mine. Magic spilled out of our skin, washing over us like we were two tiny pebbles on the beach. Blood like delicious ice cream welled between our locked mouths, and I no longer cared whose fangs drew the sweet metallic rush.

Lenorre used her mouth to lure me onto the bed. The shorts I wore tore from my body with a violent jerk. I kissed her neck. I drew that soft flesh into my mouth, drew it in until the tips of my canines drew blood. My tongue curled around the wound as I licked the blood from her skin. I caught two handfuls of her gown. The silk tore in a hiss of fabric.

Lenorre moaned, hands cradling my hips, sweeping upward to caress the skin just below my breasts.

"Please," I whispered, arching into her.

Her tongue drew a wet line across my stomach. "Is this what you want?"

"Yes."

Her hands brushed across my breasts, causing my nipples to harden, summoning a flood of desire from between my legs. Her hand caught the back of my neck, still slick with my blood.

She used that hold to guide me to my knees.

"Look at me." She caught my jaw between her thumb and index finger, forcing me to meet her gaze.

"Is this what you want?" she asked.

I inclined, trying to catch her mouth with mine. She held me back with that harsh grip. I whimpered.

"Kassandra."

"What?" I growled and then whimpered again. "I don't want to talk. I want you to fuck me."

"No." Her tone was harsh.

"You know you want to," I said in a breathy voice, inclining while she held me at bay. "I can smell your desire, Vampire. You've wanted to fuck me since you had my body pressed up against the wall."

Her grip tightened hard enough that it felt like she was

threatening to crush me. She whispered against my lips. "Cage your beast, little wolf, and I will fuck you to your heart's content."

The wolf's growl trickled from my lips.

"You have better control than this," she said, voice firm.

"You shatter my control," I growled, "and my patience!"

Lenorre's hand moved to my throat. Her fingernails dug into my skin. I fell back onto the bed when she pushed me away from her.

I blinked up at the empty air.

"I will not take you like this." Lenorre's voice came from the corner of the room.

A scream tore from me, rage filled, pained, and empty. The bones in my body began sliding, trying to shift. I fought against them. No, the beast would not have me. She would not take me unless I allowed her to come out. I felt her inside me like she was slamming her furred body against my ribs, to tear her way out. A wave of heat flushed my skin as I felt dizzy and light-headed.

"Lenorre." Her name came out strained between my gritted teeth.

"Kassandra?" It was a question.

"What's…" My spine twisted as the wolf clawed through me. I screamed, digging my clawed hands into the mattress. The fabric tore and springs creaked.

"Kassandra, you have to fight her, or she will dominate you."

I tried to shield against her, to quiet my mind, but the wolf howled through me. I did the only thing I could think of…I said a prayer to the Morrigan. I didn't pray for control, I fucking begged for it.

Darkness took my vision. Light like a candle flame sprang to life behind my eyes. I'd felt my prayers answered before, but nothing like this, never like this. The fear sped my pulse.

Then suddenly, the candle was no longer a flickering light but a flame raging through me. Wordless screams fell from my mouth. Magic poured over my skin like melted wax, suffocating, consuming, paralyzing. The wolf looked into that burning flame and cowered. I had a moment to be grateful before the fire intensified, eating me alive.

I opened my eyes to find the shadows swirling around me. The shadow swelled and stretched before swallowing me whole.

I no longer had a body. If I had once had a body, it had been torn apart, atom by atom, cell by cell, and bit by bit. The flame had lifted me up, carrying my essence through a spiral of energy. Everything changed. I was flying through the night air, scanning the blades of grass below like they were beautiful textures on a quilt.

Distantly, I heard voices. I went to them, gliding on currents of air with outstretched arms.

"Rosalin! Do not touch her!" The voice sounded familiar, so I went to it. Something trapped me, pulled me down like a magnet. I tried to break away from it, but it was too strong.

My body pulled at me, sucked me in like some great vortex.

I gasped. I couldn't breathe. There wasn't enough air. The blood pounded in my ears.

"What the…?" Rosalin spoke from the other side of the bed. I opened my eyes and her face loomed in my vision.

Strange, I thought, that I could see Lenorre on the other side of the room at the same time. I blinked hard. They were both looming in my vision, too close to the bed.

"Move back," I said, but what came out of my mouth sounded strange, wrong somehow. I went to touch my mouth with my fingertips. A black wing hovered in my vision.

I tried to sit up, but ended up teetering uncertainly. Lenorre's gray eyes swam in my vision. My heart rate increased.

"Kassandra." Her tone was soothing, tender even. "Calm down. Do you understand me?"

I nodded, closing my eyes tightly. I wouldn't panic. Nope. Not going to panic. One…two…

"What did you do to her that turned her into a bird?" Rosalin asked acerbically.

My eyes flew open. Surely, I was hearing things?

"Bird!?" I screeched. "What the hell are you talking about?" My eyes went even wider. "I am not a fucking bird! I'm a lycanthrope. How can I be a bird?"

"I think she's stuck," Rosalin said. Her hand reached out toward me. It seemed bigger than it should've been. I tried to slap it away and failed. She scooped me up in both of her hands and held me in front of her face.

"Kassandra, stop flapping around like a madwoman." She scolded me as I tried to get away from her.

"Well!" I cawed. "Put me down and I wouldn't be flapping!" The rest came out as short little raspy clicks.

Rosalin grabbed my beak between two of her fingers. "You have got to calm down or you're going to give yourself a heart attack," she said.

I blinked.

"You don't believe us?" she asked.

I tried to shrug, and knew it looked weird. Was I dreaming?

"Was that a shrug?" she asked.

I nodded.

Rosalin walked out into the open area of the bedroom and the next thing I knew, I was airborne. My arms flailed, and for the first time I felt the air catch beneath my wings. I moved them, up and down, rapidly.

I flew.

Holy Morrigan. I was flying.

Spotting the back of the armchair I landed, albeit, a little awkwardly. It took a few hops to catch my balance.

Lenorre came to me, trailing her fingers down my feathered back. It felt weird. I felt weird, like something light and unreal. "Now do you believe us?"

"No," I clicked.

"How does she change back?" Rosalin asked.

Lenorre shrugged. "I've only heard tales about someone receiving a gift from the Goddess," she said. "I have never actually witnessed such. That is something that Kassandra is going to have to figure out."

I closed my eyes. Forever stuck in the form of a bird did not sound like a well-lived life. Maybe it was similar to shifting. I took deep meditative breaths, and instead of a wolf being pushed back in its cage, I imagined a nice little nest on top of a tree. Visualization is everything, sometimes, and surely birds liked nests? I tried to familiarize myself with the energy. Fire. The wolf was more earthy, like rainwater and soil. The bird, or whatever it was, had heat to it. I pushed that energy into the metaphysical nest I imagined.

It wasn't working. Damn it. I wanted my arms and legs back! At least when I was a wolf I felt at home, comfortable in my own skin. This shape was alien to me. I thought about my human body and how much I wanted it back.

A shadowy mist rose around me. Lenorre stepped away from me.

"Fuck," I said and touched my lips. My voice came out in human words and it made me want to cry.

A second later and the back of the chair tipped with me on it. I hit the wall and slid down in a clumsy heap to the floor.

Rosalin laughed.

"Well, looks like she figured it out."

"You think?" I said, standing on wobbly legs, bracing my hands on the back of the chair.

"It is good to see you are back to your normal self," Lenorre said, sounding surprisingly calm.

"And naked," Rosalin added.

I looked down. Sure enough, she was right. I put myself behind the chair, using it as cover. Lenorre went to the closet by the smashed painting. She took something out and then offered me a dark red robe. I took it, gladly.

"Tell me this isn't really happening," I said. "Tell me that one of you just slipped me a roofie."

"A roofie?" Lenorre asked.

Rosalin said, "It's a date rape drug."

"I cannot," Lenorre said thoughtfully, "unless you wish that I lie to you."

"What the hell just happened?" I asked no one in particular.

"I came running when Lenorre called." Rosalin put her hands

on her hips. "You were surrounded by all of this shadowy stuff. Definitely magic."

"What were you thinking when you were about to shift?" Lenorre asked, her expression still thoughtful.

I ran my fingers through my hair, pushing the tangled tresses out of my face. "I don't know. I didn't want to shift. I prayed to the Morrigan for control," I said, then thought about it and finally admitted, "Well, begged, but the wolf is never like that. She's pushy, but not that pushy."

Rosalin said, "You went into a type of metaphysical heat when Lenorre bit you."

I gave her a disbelieving look.

Lenorre said, "Rosalin speaks truth."

"For werewolves," Rosalin continued, "biting the back of the neck is a sign of courtship. When Lenorre bit you, your wolf saw it as a proposal and offered herself." She frowned when she said that last bit.

"Why are you frowning?" I asked.

She actually sighed. "Because the fact that your wolf offered herself to Lenorre means that she thinks she's a fitting mate."

I looked at Lenorre. "But you're not a werewolf."

"No," Rosalin said, frowning, "but she's powerful enough to dominate your wolf."

"What does that mean?" I asked, eyeing her warily.

She shrugged. "A dominant female wolf always goes for a stronger mate. At least, she'll go for a mate that matches her in strength. Lenorre proved that she could match you, if not best you, in that area."

"Great," I said.

"So, you called upon your Goddess's aid." Lenorre swiftly changed the subject, for which I was grateful. "An Irish Triple Goddess who happens to preside over ravens and crows?"

I drew in a deep breath. "Yes." I let the breath out, seeing where she was going. Was that even possible? A headache was beginning to start between my eyes.

If it was the Morrigan's energy that had poured through me, if she had given me this *gift*...Why? Why give me the power to shift into not one, but two animals? And why in the moment when I was trying to cage the wolf did I turn into a bird instead of back into my human form? There was too much to think about. Suddenly all I wanted to do was to sit down, drink a cup of coffee, and pretend I lived a normal life. Any crisis I'd ever met always went better with coffee. And the fact that animals don't drink coffee made me feel a bit more human sitting with a coffee mug in hand.

"I don't want to talk about this anymore," I said. "I'm getting a headache. I still don't feel real and I could really go for some coffee."

Lenorre offered a graceful nod of her head but didn't say anything. She wasn't looking at me, and I found that more disturbing than the way she usually stared at me. Talk about mixed signals.

Rosalin laughed. "I'll go make coffee, then."

I followed Lenorre as she began walking toward the door, busying myself by making sure the robe was tied securely. Lenorre wore a black dressing gown that buttoned up the front. I couldn't remember seeing her change, let alone put clothes on. Sparing a glance at the bed, I spotted the remains of my shorts. The mattress had stuffing sticking out where my claws had torn it. There were black feathers all over the black sheets.

"Sorry about the mess."

Lenorre looked at me with an expression of soft amusement. "Do not trouble yourself with it. It wasn't entirely your fault, after all."

Rosalin fell in quietly behind us as we walked down the hallway.

I sighed, tired to the bone. My voice was more of a whisper this time. "By the way, thank you."

"For what?"

"You didn't take advantage of me," I told her. "Though I probably would've enjoyed it."

The corner of her mouth lifted in a half-smile. "Did I just hear you admit that you would enjoy sleeping with me?"

"We slept together already," I said. "Remember?"

"I remember well what we started," she said in a breathy whisper, "and what we have to finish."

"Finish?" I retorted. "I bunked with you this morning. You got what you wanted."

"Mmm, can you truly say that you have gotten what you wanted?" she asked.

I gave her a look.

"You remember what you said, don't you?" she persisted.

"The wolf said a lot of things."

She whispered against the fall of my hair. "You are the wolf, and she is you. There are desires the wolf will bring to light that you are afraid of."

My stomach did a little flip-flop, and I tried to ignore it.

Had I agreed with the wolf? Had the wolf only spoken my desires out loud?

…Maybe.

Chapter Twenty-four

The dining room was just off the kitchen on the ground floor. The table was large enough to easily seat ten people around it. I sat at one end of the table, huddled over the steaming mug of coffee that Rosalin had poured for me. Even though it had already begun to heal, she had bandaged her wrist with gauze. Lenorre sat next to me, but on the opposite side of the table where the entire kitchen was visible.

Rosalin took a seat, placing the mug of tea she carried on the tabletop in front of her.

"Why does this part of the house feel strange?" I mumbled into my coffee.

"Strange?" Rosalin asked as she took a sip.

I nodded. "I felt it last night. The energy in this area of the house just feels...different than the rest."

Rosalin shrugged. "I don't know what you're talking about."

"How does it feel different?" Lenorre asked.

I tried to find the words that would describe it. If I closed my eyes and focused on the feeling, it seemed tight, warm, like I had just walked into a room where a circle of protection had been cast.

"Magic," I said. "I can't really describe it. It's like the change in the air before it rains."

Rosalin's honey eyes met mine and it was obvious she wasn't quite following my line of thought.

"When the house was built a protection spell was cast around the grounds and within its walls," Lenorre said.

That explained the tight and warm feeling in the air. If what Lenorre was saying was true, then the protection was stronger on this level, because it was on the same level as the grounds around it that had been protected as well.

A cell phone rang. I knew it wasn't mine, because mine was still downstairs in the front pocket of my backpack. Rosalin stood from the table, fishing the phone from the front pocket of her jeans. She answered the phone as she walked out into the living room. I did my best not to eavesdrop on the conversation.

"The wolves are meeting tonight," said Lenorre. I turned and looked at her.

"Has Rosalin talked to the head honcho?"

"If by head honcho you mean alpha werewolf, then yes. She has spoken with Sheila."

"What's the verdict?" I asked.

"Rosalin is taking you with her. I want you to keep your eyes out for anything unusual."

"Lenorre, there's a problem with that," I said.

"Hmm?" She looked at me quizzically. I met that look and found it difficult not to remember the hunger I'd seen in her eyes earlier. With her hunger riding her she would've drunk my blood, whether I consented to it or not. The thought didn't settle well with me. Although it didn't settle well, I understood the darker aspect of both of our natures.

In the end, I'd lost myself to the deeper cravings just as she had.

The memory of her fangs sinking into the skin at the back of my neck clung to me, as if I could still feel the languor infusing my limbs.

I ignored the goose bumps that broke out over my arms and asked, "How am I supposed to know what unusual is, when I don't even know what the usual is?"

Her shoulders rose and fell. "Follow your intuition."

I took a sip of my coffee. "Oh, that'll never lead me astray," I said sarcastically.

Rosalin returned. “That was Paula,” she said, not bothering to take her seat again. “My brother’s girlfriend.”

“I know,” I said, remembering. “Is she available this evening?”

Rosalin took a sip of her tea. “Yeah, we can meet with her at her house before the meeting.”

“We?” I questioned.

“You need to know how to get to her house, don’t you?”

“I’m sure I could figure it out.” I said.

“It saves time,” she said and I didn’t disagree with her.

“Fine.”

Rosalin said, “I don’t mean to trouble you…I know you’re busy working on the case the police hired you on…”

I leaned back in my seat, eyeing her thoughtfully. “Rosalin…” I was suddenly struck by an idea. “Do you think anyone in the pack would’ve taken him to get to you? Say, Carver. He’s gamma wolf,” I added.

Rosalin shrugged. “I don’t know him that well,” she said. “He’s never acted like it, that I know of.”

“It’s a thought to keep in mind,” I told her.

Her eyes shifted uncomfortably to the mug of coffee on the table.

“I’m sure your brother is still alive,” I offered.

“I hope so,” she said. “He isn’t the greatest guy in the world, but he’s my brother. You know?”

I placed my hand on top of hers where it rested on the table.

“I’ll find your brother,” I said, “somehow. First, I’m going home to take a shower. If you want to go with me later, I’ll come back and get you.”

Lenorre moved from her seat and came around the table to stand in front of me. She reached out her hand. I closed my eyes as her fingers swept a strand of hair out of my face. She tucked that tendril of hair behind my ear, brushing the curve of my earlobe in a gesture that nearly buckled my knees. Or would have, if I had been standing.

"You are upset," she said, but it sounded more like an observation than a question.

She cupped the side of my face in her hand and I let her, feeling her cool tapered fingers stroking my cheek. "Confused is more like it."

"I would not have damaged you beyond repair," she said.

I laughed. She gave me a look that wasn't a look of anger. It was a look that told me she didn't understand what I was laughing about.

"Damage beyond repair?" I tilted my head to the side, looking up into her striking gaze. "Is that your way of saying you wouldn't have drained me dry?"

"I cannot drink you dry."

"What is that supposed to mean, exactly?" The words came out a little heated.

"It means that she can't kill us by drinking our blood," Rosalin said. "We're not human. She can drain a human dry, but our bodies pump out blood faster than she can drink it."

"Are you sure about that?" I asked. "It looked an awful lot like you were about to pass out when she was feeding on you. If that was the case," I noted, "I don't think you would've been on the verge of losing consciousness."

Her cheeks turned a light shade of pink. "I stand corrected," she said. "I could've passed out. Blood loss is still blood loss. What I mean is that our bodies would heal that kind of damage."

I gave her a knowing smile and said, "I have hunted and executed a lycanthrope before, Rosalin. I know." I looked at Lenorre. "What am I supposed to do when you feel the sudden urge to rip my throat out?"

She'd stopped touching my cheek and reached out again to catch the ends of my hair between her thumb and index finger. "For one," she said, "I do not suggest running."

The look in her eyes darkened. It wasn't that the color itself darkened, but the look in them was suddenly filled with something dark and sensual.

"And for two?" I asked, barely able to speak through the desire coursing through me.

She bent at the waist, leaning toward me as if she meant to kiss me.

"For two," she whispered against my mouth, "I advise staying calm."

"So not running and staying calm will keep you from ripping my throat out?"

"In the heat of bloodlust, you know as well as I that fear can be quite the aphrodisiac." The scent of cinnamon toothpaste was warm against my lips.

If she hadn't been so close I would've nodded. At the nearness of her body, at the line of her heat so close to mine, my pulse sped.

"And aggression," I said, trying to ignore my rampant heartbeat.

"And aggression," she mumbled and brought our faces together. Her lips brushed mine in a feather-soft caress. She drew back, her eyes serious and intense.

"Be careful, Kassandra."

I resisted the urge to bury my hands in her hair, to pull her mouth back down to mine.

"I will be."

I heard the dishwasher in the kitchen open. Rosalin was no longer in the room. I'd been paying too much attention to the vampire in front of me to notice when she'd left. I let out a shuddering breath and went to get my things.

CHAPTER TWENTY-FIVE

I killed the engine in front of my apartment. Stepping out with my bag and clothes, I pressed the button on the keypad. The car beeped, letting me know it was locked. I unlocked the apartment door and walked into the cool house, turning the light on over the dining room table.

"Where the hell have you been?"

I jumped.

"Good Goddess." I felt my eyes widen. "Rupert, what the hell are you doing here?" The wolf growled quietly, disturbed by someone invading her den. I took a deep breath and soothed her, projecting a sense of pack to her. She settled down, her ears perked but otherwise calm.

"I've been trying to get a hold of you for the past three hours," he said.

I looked at the door, then back to where he was sitting on the couch. "How the fuck did you get in?"

"I don't need a key," he said.

"You picked my lock?"

He nodded. "If you had a chain on the door it would've been more difficult. I'd have had to bust the chain."

"I'll remember that," I said and put my stuff on the table.

"Looks like you stayed the night somewhere," he said.

"I did," I admitted.

"Where?" he asked, "Rosalin's?"

I shook my head and went to the fridge, opening a can of Diet Coke. “Nope. Guess again.”

“The countess?” he asked and even as he asked it he managed to sound like he quite didn’t believe it.

My voice was soft as I sat down in the armchair. “Yeah.”

“I don’t trust her.” His blue eyes had gone cold and hard.

“I’m afraid,” I said.

“Why are you afraid? I haven’t known you to be afraid of anything. Except for spiders,” he said.

“I’m afraid,” I said, “that I do trust her.”

“Kassandra, you can’t trust anyone. Especially not a vampire.”

“Rupert, I think you forget what I am.”

“You’re a different story,” he said. “You didn’t choose to be what you are.”

“Who’s to say Lenorre chose to be a vampire?”

“They’re tricksters, Kassandra.” His voice was calm, as if he was trying to get the words gradually through to me, like if he didn’t remain calm and speak slowly I wouldn’t hear him. I suddenly felt like a crazy woman he was trying to talk down off the ledge. I didn’t like that.

“You don’t know her,” I said, narrowing my eyes. “So don’t start passing judgment and don’t start talking down to me.”

“I’m not passing judgment,” he said. “I’m not talking down to you. I’m just saying that you haven’t known her long enough to really know her either.”

He stood from the couch.

“Wait,” I said and he stopped. “Are you mad at me?”

“That’s not my place,” he said. “I’m just worried. I don’t think you know what you’re getting yourself into.” His shoulders lifted in a shrug beneath the denim jacket. He turned to look at me “You’re like a sister to me and I don’t want to see you to get hurt.”

“Rupert,” I said, “I don’t want to get hurt, either. Trust me on that one.”

“Do what you have to do.” He nodded and opened the door. “Call me if you need anything.”

He shut the door behind him. I got up and locked it, placing the laptop that had been moved to the island on the dining room table. I forgot to ask him why he had been calling me in the first place. If it had been important, he would've told me, but I had a feeling that Rupert was just worried about me. I only hoped that he wouldn't resort to picking my lock again. With a new shifting ability, Goddess only knew what could happen if someone seriously spooked me.

I rubbed my temples. I'd gotten used to going furry once a month. The wolf had become just another aspect of myself, but the raven…

I hoped that the raven didn't come with the same price as the wolf. If it came with the price of going feathery once a month, I wasn't sure how I felt about that.

❖

I spent some time when I got home sipping coffee and doing research on Colorado state parks and killings. Claire Delaine had mentioned that the guy she'd gone out with had worked as a park ranger somewhere in Colorado. Sure enough, there were three killings reported in that area.

In all of them, the victims had been torn apart, and pieces of their bodies were still missing. There was nothing about Carver or any other wolves. In fact, the police still didn't have any suspects.

I turned on the shower. I stood under the spray of hot water, feeling each bead beat against the sore muscles in my back. Shifting into different animals really takes it out of the body.

I thought about Lenorre. I thought about the look of soft affection in her gray eyes as she held me. The way they flinched in pain as the sunlight began to cast its glow on our side of the world. I ran the tip of my tongue across my lips, recollection bringing forth the moment when blood welled between our mouths. There wasn't a nick on my tongue. It had been my canines that had cut her.

The vampire hadn't taken me when she had the chance. She hadn't even taken me when I'd agreed with the wolf and offered myself to her on a silver platter. She had presented herself as a calming presence when I shape-shifted into something strange and unusual. It was still unnerving. Was it permanent? How had I been granted a gift? Was it really a gift? Why would the Morrigan have placed her mark so strongly on me? If I had the energy to freak out about it, I might. I assured myself there wasn't any point in freaking out about it. I'd learned a long time ago that freaking out doesn't fix anything. I had to accept the fact that I was no longer just a werewolf.

I laughed. It seemed that for once in my life I was willing to allow a question to remain unanswered for the time being. Then again, time itself has a funny way of revealing things.

Water dripped onto the floor as I grabbed a towel from the hall closet and headed to the bedroom.

I wore a long-sleeved burgundy thermal and a pair of black jeans. The Mark III in its shoulder holster was hidden from view thanks to the black leather jacket.

I picked Rosalin up, as I said I would.

"Turn here," Rosalin said, pointing to the street on the left. The little blue sign above the red stop sign read *Dillon*. "It's the third house on the left," she said and I guided the Tiburon into the driveway, parking behind a red pickup truck. I turned to look at her while unbuckling my seat belt. "Do they know?" I asked.

"What I am?"

I nodded.

She shook her head. "No." She put her hands in the pockets of her hoodie. "I never told Henry."

"Do you think Carver knows where your brother works and lives?" I asked.

Slowly, she nodded. "The whole pack knows," she said. "We know that type of stuff about one another: where everyone works, what they do for a living, where they live…"

"Terrific," I said.

She looked at me with widened eyes. "If someone from the pack has taken him," she said, "they're breaking pack law."

That much I knew, but I didn't think Carver really gave two

shits about breaking pack law. "I know," I said, stepping out of the car.

The house looked small from the outside. The door opened and the woman looked past me and to Rosalin. Rosalin slipped past me, enfolding the smaller woman in her arms. I heard her whisper, "I'm so sorry, Paula."

Paula stroked Rosalin's back. "I know, sweetie." Paula Meeks stepped back and looked at me. I approached, offering my hand and introducing myself.

Paula took the hand I offered and her fingers were light, her touch tentative and soft. I was guessing she was in her early thirties. "Thank you, Kassandra," she said, "for agreeing to meet with me."

"I'm just glad you found the time." I winced, hoping it didn't sound judgmental. But I found myself hoping that if I went missing, someone would make the time to talk to the people who could help find me. Of course, with the company I was keeping these days, there probably wouldn't be anything left of me to find. I decided to pick up that train of morbid thought later, maybe to lull myself to sleep or something.

She opened the door. "Come in."

I followed Rosalin into the living room, sitting down on the sofa beside her.

"Would you like some tea or coffee?" Paula asked, raising a hand to push the light brown curls of chin-length hair out of her face. Her dark eyes were red around the edges, as if she'd been working too hard and crying too much.

Rosalin accepted the offer of tea. I gracefully declined. I waited until Paula returned, handing Rosalin a mug and sitting down in the recliner on the other side of the coffee table. The house was neat and tidy. Two worn recliners were placed side by side. I imagined Paula and Henry often sat in them, watching television together.

"Paula," I said, speaking softly, "can you tell me what happened?"

I watched as she took in a deep breath, steeling herself. "I came home from work Sunday evening." She looked off to the left, remembering. "He'd already gone into work. He works until midnight at the school."

"Jefferson Elementary?" I asked remembering what Rosalin had told me.

Paula nodded. "Yes," she said, "Henry goes into work at seven in the evening and usually doesn't get home until around midnight." Her voice shook. "I take a sleeping medication," she said. "I'm usually fast asleep when he gets in from work, but when I woke up the next morning he wasn't in bed with me. He wasn't here, so I ran outside to see if his car was in the driveway, and it wasn't. I tried to call him," she said, "and kept getting his voicemail. The last time I spoke with him was earlier Sunday evening, before he left for work."

"He works weekends as a janitor?" I asked.

She nodded.

"I'm sorry to ask you this," I said, "but would there be any reason for you to believe that he left you? Have you been fighting?"

She shook her head, eyes watering with unshed tears. "No," she said, "Henry isn't like that. If he was going to leave, he'd make damn sure I knew it."

"Does he have a history of disappearing for days?" I asked. "Does he drink? Gamble? Is there anyone at work that he's friends with?"

"No, no," she said, shaking her head. "Henry doesn't have very many friends. He's a loner, keeps to himself."

"He's always been like that," Rosalin added.

"Does he have any enemies?" I asked. "Any disputes with anyone at work or anything?"

Paula shook her head.

"My brother is one of those guys that when he does socialize, almost everyone likes him," Rosalin said.

I rubbed my temples. If Henry didn't have any known enemies or friends, I couldn't think of anyone else who would've kidnapped him but Carver. But then, I didn't understand why Carver would kidnap Rosalin's brother. It didn't make sense, unless there was something going on in the pack, some type of power struggle. I looked at Rosalin, wondering, why would Carver take her brother? She'd said he'd made no threats to her. She'd stated that Sheila's brother had, but I had a feeling that was more to do with the whole werewolf power-bluffing shit than any actual real threat. Carver White posed a huge threat. As far as I could tell he was my prime suspect. How many werewolves end up with a dead body on their land? The ones that commit the crime, I say. If Carver wanted her position in the pack—why wouldn't he just challenge her? I had a feeling I would find out soon enough.

I looked at Paula, standing. "Thank you, Paula. I'll call you if I learn anything about Henry's whereabouts."

"That's it?" she asked.

I nodded. "For now," I said, forcing myself to smile.

Gods be damned—what the hell was Carver White up to?

❖

We left Paula's house and headed to the pack meeting. Rosalin informed me that the meeting was at the same place as the one I had spied on before. I drove while she stared out the window, obviously lost in her own thoughts. Once we were on the highway it was pretty much a forward shot until it was time to exit.

"This next exit," Rosalin said.

"That's an exit early," I responded.

"You can park where the others park."

I turned down the dirt road that she was pointing at.

As we drove farther down, the headlights reflected off the other cars and the body of water next to them.

"I didn't know there was a lake out here," I said.

"It's a pond."

Well, it was a big-ass pond.

I parked the car.

She nodded toward my jacket. "You'll have to cover the gun well, Kassandra. I'm sorry, but it's the rules."

I frowned but buttoned up the jacket to hide the shoulder holster. It really didn't matter, because if the entire pack posed a threat to me, well, silver bullets or no, I couldn't pull a trigger fast enough to deal with an angry pack.

Rosalin led the way through the thicket of trees. I wasn't sure if I could've found the clearing from this direction. Though the half shoe prints in the dirt might've helped lead the way if I was that determined. There was always the smell of a group of wolves that wafted on the air, and if I focused I could've tracked it. Roslin put her hands in the pockets of her jeans, ducking tree limbs that jutted out like wicked hands.

I could smell the burning torches before we entered the clearing. A few people mingled here and there. I looked to my right at the stone throne. Sheila wasn't sitting there. I spotted Trevor mingling with two female wolves. Apparently, he spotted us as well. He practically skipped up to us.

"Hey, Rosalin." He looked at me. "Kassandra, right?"

I did my best not to glare, and I think I managed not to.

"Yeah."

"Sheila wants you to introduce her," he said, talking to Rosalin.

"Where is Sheila?" she asked.

"She's not here yet. Said she'd be a little late. She and Lukas had to take care of something."

I looked out over the array of werewolves and spotted Carver White's light hair. His blue eyes met mine, empty of any emotion. I gave him a dirty look.

Trevor said, "They probably got caught up working on the house. They've been doing some remodeling, did you hear?" He looked at Rosalin again. "Sheila's thinking about having our meetings there once the renovations are done." He smiled brightly.

"No. I hadn't heard." Rosalin sounded disinterested. Trevor's girlfriend was still werewolf-sitting. Claire wouldn't be able to meet with the other wolves for a few more days, until the fever finally broke. For now she was on bed rest.

A guy walked up behind Trevor. He smiled at Rosalin and then me.

"Who's your friend?" His voice was a deep baritone. His hair was short and spiky. He was well built. The leather of his jacket thudded against his back when Trevor put half an arm around him.

"Lukas!" he exclaimed. "It's about time you guys showed up. Still remodeling?"

The big man laughed. "Sheila's got this idea that another wall needs to be knocked down to open the dining room up into the living room and den. We're not going to have any walls by the time she's done."

Trevor nodded as if he understood and then looked around. "Where's Sheila?"

"She'll be here soon," Lukas said and then looked at me. "You're Rosalin's friend?" he asked. "The new wolf?"

New? I didn't know how I felt about being called new, but I shrugged. "Yeah."

"Lukas, this is Kassandra. Kassandra, this is Lukas, Sheila's brother."

He offered his palm and I took it, unthinking. He wrapped his hand around mine so tightly that it hurt.

I tore my hand away. "What the fuck, Lukas?"

He smiled, brightly, his blue gaze holding mine. "Just a test," he said, "a lesser wolf wouldn't have taken their hand away."

I slipped my hands in the pocket of my leather jacket. "I'm not very fond of tests," I stated in as cold a voice as I could muster.

Lukas gave a booming laugh, looking to Rosalin. "You didn't warn her, did you, Beta?"

Rosalin's eyes narrowed in contempt and Lukas's smile broadened.

"Warn me of what?" I asked, turning to her.

"They're going to test you. Maybe not today, but as they get to know you," she said, "and some of them, like Lukas here, will be complete assholes about it."

Lukas grinned.

A woman's voice growled out over the clearing.

"Lukas!"

Sheila Morris was sitting in her throne. I hadn't seen her enter the clearing.

I watched as Lukas's shoulders tensed. His eyes narrowed slightly. He turned that look on me. "Well, Kassandra, you've been warned." His voice was a low whisper. He went to stand quietly behind his sister's throne.

Sheila Morris's blue eyes scanned the crowd of werewolves that had suddenly fallen silent. Rosalin grabbed my elbow, and as she went down to her knees she pulled me with her.

I stifled the growl that was beginning to build. The clearing was suddenly hotter, like someone had lit a nearby fire. Rosalin's energy thrummed up my arm where she held my elbow, and I took a deep breath in through my mouth, tasting fur on my tongue.

"Step forward," Sheila said, her eyes meeting mine.

Rosalin let go of my elbow.

I didn't move. I stared very hard at the ground.

I heard her feet on the earth and felt the force of her energy a second before I felt her fingers bury in my hair. Sheila Morris grabbed a handful of my hair and jerked my head back. She lowered her pale face toward mine, close enough that I could feel her breath against my cheek. Somewhere, in the back of my mind, I felt Carver watching.

I felt the wolf inside of me. I felt her anger. A low growl threatened to trickle from my lips. I swallowed.

"Why do you not step forward?" Sheila's blond hair fell around my face as she gazed down at me. I didn't like her that close and resisted the urge to push her away or break her hold.

I spoke very carefully, trying to control my temper, trying to control the heat in my words. "You are not my alpha," I said, "not yet."

Sheila's bright gaze widened as if it was the first time anyone had ever spoken against her. Her eyes narrowed a second later. "If you join our pack," she whispered, "I will be."

"If you're not nice to me," I whispered back, taking a breath in through my mouth, "why would I even want to join your pack?"

She let go of me so abruptly that I almost lost my balance and fell into Rosalin. I caught myself with a hand against the earthen floor.

I glared at Sheila Morris and she glared back.

Oh, I so did not like this bitch.

"Fair enough," she said, smiling. The smile didn't reach nor did it match the look in her eyes. No, there was a look there that said she'd enjoy punishing me for my bad behavior. I stifled a shudder. "Enjoy yourself, Kassandra," she said, and then turned, heading back to her stone throne. She announced out over the clearing, "My brothers and sisters of the Blackthorne Pack, there is a new wolf among us." She smiled darkly as her voice carried clear and unwavering. "Welcome her as you would welcome any other wolf to the Blackthorne pack."

Why did I get the feeling she'd just literally thrown me to the wolves?

I continued to glare. If it wasn't for all of the evidence that pointed toward Carver, I would've so loved the opportunity to hunt Sheila Morris. You know those people you meet once and you know that no matter how many times you meet them, or how nice they try to act, you will never, ever, in your entire life, like them or fall for the good person act?

That's how I felt about Sheila Morris. I was beginning to understand why Lenorre didn't like her. Everything about Sheila rubbed me the wrong way, and knowing that she was a cruel bitch made it ten times worse.

A meteor falling from the sky and striking her would've been icing on my cake.

CHAPTER TWENTY-SIX

I spotted Carver leaning up against one of the trees. He was by himself. So far, it seemed, the whole pack meeting was more of a weekly get-together. I hadn't bothered introducing myself to any of the other wolves, and aside from Rosalin and Trevor, none of them said anything to me. Oh, I caught some of the looks. You know that look people give you upon first meeting, trying to figure you out? Yeah, I got a few of those. The Blackthorne Pack was a tight-knit group, and even though Sheila had told them to welcome me…they didn't, not really. I saw it in some of the glances from male and female alike. A few of the wolves cast their eyes down, but the others seemed to be warning me. I ignored it as best as I could, moving carefully around two female wolves who were talking about work.

I approached Carver.

His blue gaze flicked to me and then back toward the distance. He acted as if he couldn't be bothered, but he said, "I told you the truth. You don't have to stalk me, you know."

"Who said I was stalking you?" I asked.

He scoffed as a look of disgust fell over his features. "Why else would you be here?"

"What do you know about a man named Henry Walker?" I dropped my voice so that, over the happy-chatty werewolves, no one would hear us.

He looked at me. "Rosalin's brother?"

"That's the one," I said, stepping into him. "Where is he, Carver? I'm not fucking with you."

His voice dropped an octave. "How the fuck would I know?"

I closed my eyes, trying not to lose my temper. "Playing the innocent card isn't working in your favor, Carver." I met his blue gold gaze. "I know what you did. I have a witness," I said, then added, "James."

"James?" he looked genuinely perplexed. "Who the fuck is James?"

"The name you gave the woman in the park," I said, "or is that too hard for you to remember?"

Carver bared his teeth in a growl. He stepped into me, so that we were nearly touching. "I…did…not…do…anything."

I stared up at him. "Then, Carver, I suggest you fucking prove it."

A look slid through his eyes, almost too quick to catch, but I caught it. Carver White was afraid. "I can't."

Claire Delaine's words haunted my memory.

He used to work as a park ranger. He didn't specify which park when I asked him, just said one of the parks in Colorado.

"How long have you lived in Oklahoma?" I asked.

"All of my life," he said.

"Shit," I said and with feeling.

I gave him a hard look. "Can you prove that?" But he didn't need to. I could feel it this time. He was telling the truth. *Fuck.*

"Yes," he said and for a moment, my mind faltered. I hesitated as I looked at the man in front of me.

If Carver was the murderer, why didn't he out to me to the pack as a woman that works with the police?

I dug my cell phone out of my pocket and walked past Carver and into the wooded area beyond.

Arthur picked up on the second ring. "Yeah, Kass. What is it?"

"I need you to do me a favor."

"A favor?"

"Yes," I said, "I want you to run Carver's name. You remember

Carver White?" I asked. "The man living in the trailer off Southeast Twenty-sixth?"

"Running it," he said. "What do you need?"

"How long has he lived in Oklahoma?"

"Is he a suspect, Kassandra?"

"I don't know, Arthur, just tell me."

I heard the sounds of computer keys clacking away. I kept walking deeper into the woods, farther away from the pack. Even if I knew it already, I wanted to make sure. If I ended up killing him for some reason, I wanted to know that I'd done all the legal research.

"Carver White has lived here," Arthur said, "since nineteen seventy-nine. That would be the year he was born," Arthur added. "No records of moving in or out of state. I've got a listing of old addresses, do you want them?"

I mentally cursed myself. "No. Any criminal background?" I asked.

"Nope," he said, then asked, "Is Carver White a suspect, Kassandra?"

"Not anymore," I said. "Thanks." I hung up.

If Carver White wasn't my suspect, then who was?

A twig snapped behind me and I spun on my heel in direction of the noise. No one was there.

Gee, me, easily spooked? Nah. I started heading back toward the clearing. I'd put enough distance between myself and the pack that I'd given myself a bit of time to make up an excuse as to my disappearance for the duration of a phone call.

I heard another noise behind me. I turned and someone's beefy fist connected with the side of my face hard enough that the canopy of trees spun and I caught myself on the hard ground with my forearms. I coughed, the pain searing through my bones and flesh. I spat, tasting blood. A heavy booted foot connected with my stomach; the air was knocked out of my lungs and I curled into a fetal position, trying to protect myself.

Something heavy connected with the back of my skull and the world went black.

Chapter Twenty-Seven

I dreamed, and in the dream Lenorre looked at me with worried eyes. Her silver gaze held mine and a look of pity crossed her face.

I looked up into that startling pale face and my heart whimpered. I tried to breathe but couldn't take a deep enough breath. It felt like there was a knife in my side.

Lenorre touched my face with nimble fingers. "Kassandra," she whispered, "Kassandra, look at me."

My heart was pounding. I couldn't breathe. I had to breathe. I tried again and it was like inhaling fire into my lungs; the pain seared throughout my entire torso. There were tears of panic and pain burning at the corners of my eyes.

"Kassandra," she said again, but this time she lifted my face to hers. "You have to wake up."

I opened my mouth to speak but no sound came out. Lenorre reached out, circling her arm around my waist. I felt her energy unfurling like a serpent, wrapping around me, but instead of constricting, a cool breeze of power filled my lungs as she forced the air into me. I drew the breath of her power in a long ragged gasp and said, "I can't."

Her fingers were suddenly cold steel. "You can," she said, eyes growing misty with power, "and you will."

I woke, gasping around the pain in my side. I opened my eyes and blinked into the darkness. The darkness wasn't right. I could see in the dark, but this, this I could not see in. I panicked, trying to move and finding that my hands were bound behind my back.

My pulse quickened, pounding through my aching head like some great bell. I licked dry lips.

Think, Kassandra, think. I took a very slow breath around the pain. Something was not right. No, something was terribly, horribly, fucking wrong.

Where the hell was I?

Someone whimpered, high and pitiful.

I froze. "Who's there?"

"I am." It was a man's voice that croaked from somewhere in the room. I turned my face in the direction of the voice.

"Who are you?" I asked, cautious.

He coughed. "Henry," he said. "My name is Henry."

Oh, Gods! I jerked at the leather binds, trying to break them. The leather creaked, weakening, but it did not break. Whoever had bound my hands had weaved several layers of thick leather from my wrist to my elbows. I didn't think they were attached to the chair, but I couldn't be sure. The knowledge made me aware of the fierce ache between my shoulder blades. I remembered Lenorre's face, her voice telling me to wake.

How long had I been unconscious?

"Miss?" Henry's voice croaked again.

"I'm here, Henry," I said. "I know your sister."

"Rosalin," he said and I heard movement. "You know her?"

"Yes," I said, tilting my head. "She sent me to find you."

Okay, so, that was a little bit of a lie. I mean, yeah, I was sent to find him, but being kidnapped with him was so not the way I wanted to find him. Shit.

"Henry, do you know where we are?"

I heard more movement then. "No, I can't see anything."

Terrific, neither could I. I tried to break the binds again, and this time, it cost me. The knifelike pain turned to something more like a sword.

I had a feeling that when the assailant had kicked me, he'd kicked a few ribs out of place.

A bead of sweat trickled down my forehead.

I heard a door open and close to my right. I heard the sounds of heavy footsteps as someone walked into the room. My nostrils flared slightly. A cricket chirped, which meant it was still night, unless it was one of those crazy crickets. If it was a crazy cricket, it didn't matter if it was day or night—the sucker was going to chirp regardless. The side of my face ached. The sound of footsteps was closer.

Who the fuck was it?

I sniffed again and caught the scent of strong woodsy aftershave. The smell of moist soil and patchouli wafted like undercurrents in the air. I hadn't paid much attention, but I was pretty sure Carver hadn't been wearing any aftershave. I was trying to remember when another memory swam to surface. A man with blue eyes and spiky hair offered his hand to me.

"Lukas," I said, sensing him kneel in front of me, disrupting the currents of air.

"Oh, that's very good work, Kassandra." I heard his smile in the dark.

Sore and trapped, my mind started going ninety-to-nothing.

"It was you all along," I said. "It was never Carver."

Gods, Lukas had moved here from out of state!

He offered a booming laugh. "Carver has a bad temper," he said. "It makes it hard for him to control his wolf."

I agreed with him. Carver's temper was what initially had set me off. It dawned on me in one of those moments where everything just becomes so clear and you have no idea how you didn't see it earlier.

"You targeted Carver," I said. "You tried to make him your fall guy, tried to make it look like he had lost control of his beast and killed that woman."

"Brava," he said. "He is also the pack's gamma."

"What sense does that make?" I asked. "Your sister is the pack's alpha. Speaking of which, does she know about this, Lukas?"

"Why do you want to know, Kassandra?"

I smiled, blindfolded and bound to a chair, seeing very little escape, and despite myself—I couldn't help it. "I like to know who to kill." The beast woke from her sleeping den somewhere deep inside me, spilling out of my mouth in a guttural growl.

Lukas Morris smacked me across the face, hard enough that he almost knocked me out of the chair. He caught the edge of it and set me upright.

"No shifting," he said, "not yet."

I spat the words, "Fuck you."

He slapped me again and my eyes rolled into the back of my head.

If he fucking hit me one more time… I forced myself to count to ten.

I decided to talk. "So, Carver would've been your fall guy?" I asked.

"Would've been?" he scoffed. "He will be. In fact, thanks to you, the police will more than likely conclude he's their prime suspect."

I closed my eyes. He was right. The last person I had mentioned to the police was Carver. Shit. Shit. Shit. If I made it out alive, I owed Carver a huge apology.

"Carver is your fall guy," I whispered, "and Rosalin's brother?" I asked, knowing that he was somewhere in the room. I could smell his fear if I focused on it, but fear was too tempting to the wolf, and I wouldn't risk shifting, not yet.

"Think of it as leverage," Lukas said, thoughtfully.

"Leverage?" I asked.

"Oh, yes," he said. "It's enough leverage to get Rosalin out of my way, don't you think? The life of her brother for her title in pack," he mused with a smile in his tone.

Sick bastard.

"Why didn't you just challenge them?" I asked. "That's what you're after, isn't it? You're trying to work your way up the pack ladder."

Lukas was suddenly so close I could smell the spearmint gum he was chewing. I'd never like spearmint again.

"How would you know anything about the pack structure? Did Rosalin tell you?" he asked, an ugly happiness in his tone.

When I didn't answer, his fingers wrapped around my throat, pushing me back into the chair and threatening to crush my windpipe.

"It had to be her," he said, giving me a shake.

I hissed in through my teeth as the pain in my head and ribs soared again. He let me go so abruptly that my body swung forward. I heard him take a step back.

"Yes," he said, "I will tell you something that you did not know. My dear, dear sister extracted a promise from me before I joined up with her pack," he said. "We were changed at the same time, did you know that?"

I blinked behind the blindfold, trying to keep up. "No, I didn't."

"Oh yes," he said, "our uncle liked to do things to us. One day, well…" He laughed. "One day when we were little, things got a little out of hand, if you know what I mean."

I shuddered to think on it. No wonder they both had issues. It made me feel a small sense of pity, but not much. Ultimately, I'm a firm believer that people choose who they want to be.

"What was the promise?" I asked, focusing on the important part and not his life story. Point for me.

"Did Rosalin tell you what the Rite of Challenge is?"

"I know what it is," I said, avoiding bringing Rosalin into it.

"I had to give my oath that I would not throw the Rite of Challenge at any of her pretty little wolves."

"You don't think you're going back on your oath, just a little?" I asked.

"Oh, no," he said, "I'm sure I'm not. You see, I haven't challenged anyone."

"You're going to use Rosalin's brother to get her to step down in the pack hierarchy. That way, you're not breaking your oath to Sheila."

"Brava again, Kassandra." He chuckled softly. "If there is one thing you should know about the Lykos, it is that we are not oath breakers."

That might've been true, but some of them were certainly whack-jobs.

Henry chose that moment to scream. "If you hurt her, I'll kill you myself! You monster!"

I turned my head, following Lukas's fast and heavy steps across the wooden planks of the floor. I heard Henry give a small cry of pain. Lukas laughed.

"Lukas," I said coldly. "If he's dead, he's not leverage. Remember?"

Henry's body hit the floor with a heavy thump. He whimpered.

"So weak and pathetic," Lukas growled. "You can't do anything, human."

I bit my tongue. I didn't think Lukas would like me to point out the fact that he was part human. Another thought crossed my mind.

"James?" I asked.

He came back over to kneel in front of me. "It's my middle name," he said. "How is Claire doing? That was you, in the park." He made it a statement so I didn't say anything. He reached out, touching my hair. I turned away from him. "That white streak gives you away, Kassandra. Did you know that once every alpha werewolf was born with a streak in their hair that reflected the color of their beast's fur?" he asked.

"No," I said, but I remembered Lenorre's comment about the mark of a true alpha.

"Once," Lukas said, "there were those that were born Lykos. Those destined to rule a pack as their leader were born with something that marked them as Lykos. The white in your hair," he said, "is the same color as your fur. That is your mark."

"I wasn't born like this," I hissed.

He sounded amused. "No?" he said, "Then it would seem the virus itself has taken a turn. Do you know that the virus was passed down by those true Lykos? It all began with King Lycaon," he said, "who tried to serve the god Zeus human flesh. But gods do not fall for tricks, do they?" he asked. "No," he answered his own question. "So, Zeus cursed Lycaon, turning him into one of the Lykos, so that he might feast upon the human flesh he revered so much as to try and feed it to the god."

"You're a sick fuck," I said and Lukas gave a deep rumbling peal of laughter.

"We are what we are, Kassandra." I heard him hit his chest with his fist. "I am Lykos!" His voice boomed through whatever prison held me and my skin crawled.

"What about Sheila?" I asked in a quiet but steady voice. "The police take out Carver," I said, "you get Rosalin to step down," I exhaled, "but what about your sister, Lukas? What about your alpha?"

"I will be alpha," he said.

The wolf growled against the inside of my mind, but what she thought was not human words. No, it was my thoughts that translated what the beast inside me felt, and what she felt was: No. No, Lukas Morris would not be alpha. He would never be alpha.

A lonesome howl rang in my ears. Lukas rushed to his feet in a hiss of movement. "What was that?" he said and his footfalls were quick, too quick. Another howl echoed like a blade through the sudden silence, sending chills up my spine, sending a rush of adrenaline through my veins. I tried to break the binds again, and couldn't. Why couldn't I break them?

Lukas cursed as something heavy and solid hit the door.

I could hear them growling. There was another loud thud, loud enough to shake the building around us.

A lone wolf howled her distress call. I felt the beast stir in the pit of my stomach and opened my mouth. The call spilled from my lips, pouring from my heart in an inhuman wolf song.

The house shuddered again.

Lukas rushed back and hit me. "Do not sing to them, wolf!" he yelled.

My beast didn't like that. Behind the blindfold I sensed my eyes bleeding gold and opened my mouth, growling. This time, when he swung, I threw my body to the left. The chair and I clattered to the floor. A surge of mind-numbing pain sailed through my ribs again. I tried to beak the binds at my ankles, breathing shallowly around the pain. Why the fuck couldn't I break through the leather? The door collapsed in a violent sound, hinges screeched an unnerving whine a moment before the wood hit the floor with a sound like heavy thunder.

In the din of it all, I heard Lukas shifting, heard his clothes tearing and the bones of his body popping wet and juicy.

There were snarls like some obnoxious dog fight. Someone touched me and I flinched. "Kassandra." It was Lenorre's voice.

She lifted the blindfold from my eyes and the room came into view like a black-and-white movie. It was night and there were no lights on. She began untying the leather straps at my ankles, fingers moving deftly at the knots. My legs were free. She grabbed the binds at my wrists, working at them.

"Just tear them!" I yelled.

"I cannot," she said. "The binds at your wrists are laced with silver. If I tear the leather and the silver touches your skin, it will burn."

"That's why I couldn't break them."

She freed my wrists, touching my cheek. "Yes," she said.

"How did you find me?" I asked. "Who is with you?"

"Rosalin and Carver," she said. "They found your cell phone and used the scent on it to track you."

"Clever." I smiled, somewhat.

There was a heavy crashing noise and I turned to see some great black bipedal wolf charging the gray werewolf I recognized as Lukas.

I got to my feet, eyes scanning the room. I felt my torso with my hands and winced at the pain. I was still wearing the holster, which meant my gun was around here somewhere. I moved as quickly and light-footed as I could. We were in a shed of some kind. Rosalin's brother lay in a heap on his side, blindfolded and bound as I had been.

"Lenorre." I looked at her. She followed my gaze. I blinked and she was suddenly beside Henry, untying his binds.

I kicked aside my chair, spotting a table beneath an old and rusty window. There was a drawer at the top of the small table. I went for it. Where else would my gun be?

I heard the growl and turned to defend myself, but the black wolf intercepted, leaping onto Lukas's back, its claws scratching at the gray wolf's face. A cinnamon-colored wolf caught Lukas's arm, sinking teeth in and clawing at his legs. Lukas gave a howl of pain. I opened the drawer and found my gun.

The black wolf rode Lukas's wolfman form to the ground and the cinnamon wolf got out of the way of falling werewolves.

"Get off him," I said, clicking the safety of the Mark III, holding the gun in a two-handed grip and aiming down my sights.

The black wolf looked at me with golden eyes. There was a little bit of blue around the edges of his eyes, and I knew without a doubt that it was Carver.

"Carver," I said, "I know you're angry, but please," I added, "let me do my job."

His sunny eyes bore into mine. His furred mouth made the words guttural and clipped. "Make it slow," he said.

I nodded and drew in a deep breath, steeling myself as I slipped into to that place in my mind where I go when it's just me, my gun, and the poor bastard on the other end.

Carver rolled off Lukas.

"Lukas Morris." The wolf inside me combined her eerie voice with mine. My words growled at the edges. "For your crimes, you pay."

His wolfish lips drew back in a snarl as he got to his knees.

I pulled the trigger before he could stand. Once, and the bullet lodged into his chest. His body jerked, reacting to the impact. Twice, and the bullet tore through the skin around his heart like the angry jaws of a predator. I took a few steps closer. My ears rang. I shot again. The bullet exploded his chest into a bloody cavity. Blood and thicker stuff hit my legs like someone had thrown it at me.

I pulled the trigger until the magazine clicked empty. If I had more bullets, I would've kept shooting. I wanted to shoot him until he was more than just dead.

I swayed on my feet and Lenorre caught my arm. "You are hurt," she said. "I can hear your breath rattle. Your ribs are broken."

I was pretty sure they were broken too. I was also pretty sure that tipping the chair over had only made it worse.

I shook my head, biting my lower lip in pain. "I'm fine," I said and then nodded toward Rosalin's brother. "Help him."

She went and helped him to his feet. He stumbled and I took a step forward. "Is he hurt?"

He looked at me with bleary eyes, eyes that were such a mirror of his sister's it was eerie. "A few scratches," he managed to croak in a raw voice. I wondered how long he'd tried screaming the last few days. He turned to look up at Lenorre. "My sister?" he asked. "Where is she?"

Carver sat near the door, licking at a wound in his side. He stopped to look up at me briefly, and with a sharp nod told me that it was over. The cinnamon-colored wolf limped toward Henry on all four of her paws. Her voice sounded so strange, so distorted. "Here," she said, and I wondered if I sounded like that. I shook the thought away.

Henry Walker looked down at his sister and slid helplessly to his knees. "Rosalin," he whispered, reaching out with shaking fingers to touch the tip of her ear. Rosalin ducked her wolfish head and leaned into him.

He wrapped his arms around her. "Why didn't you ever tell me?"

She looked up at her brother and smiled with a wolfish grin, licking his face. His honey-colored eyes glistened with tears.

I met Lenorre's silvery gaze and said, "I need to call the cops."

She inclined her head. "I understand."

"You'll have to go," I said. "I won't risk exposing those who saved my life."

"What will you tell them?" she asked.

"That I was wearing a red cloak and taking a hike through the woods." I gave a quick smile. "Don't worry about me." I clicked the safety back on and holstered the Mark III, nodding toward the door. "Take them and go."

She reached into the pocket of her coat and held something out to me. I looked down to see my cell phone. "You might need this," she said and her red lips curved into a seductively amused smile that made my heart pound.

I met her stormy eyes. "Thank you, for everything."

She touched my cheek with cool fingers. "Your safety is thanks enough." She went to Henry, helping him to stand.

Lenorre's black coat fanned out behind her. The two wolves trailed side by side, following at her heels.

"Lenorre," I said.

She stopped in the doorway.

"Would you mind if I came over later?"

Her lips curved into a beautiful smile that made the breath catch in my throat. "No, Kassandra," she said, "I would like very much to see you after you attend to your health."

I drew a shallow breath. "I will."

I watched as she left with Henry Walker at her side and the two wolves trailing behind her like loyal and imposing guardians.

CHAPTER TWENTY-EIGHT

Arthur and a few cops that I didn't know leaned over the dead werewolf.

"Why is he all clawed up?" Arthur gave me a look.

I shrugged and winced again, wrapping an arm around my stomach like that would help protect me from the pain in my ribs.

"Kassandra…"

I held my hand up. The best excuse I could think of was… "There were other wolves," I said, blinking. "They saved me."

"Where did they go?" he asked.

"I don't know."

One of the EMTs came in and looked at me. He dropped his little bag by the chair that I was sitting in. The leather straps and the blindfold that had been used on Henry Walker were shoved into the pockets of my leather jacket, which I'd found on the floor in the corner of the room. I really didn't want to know how it got there.

"It looks like he was tortured with a spray of bullets," the only female cop in the room spoke. She looked at me with eyes that were crystal blue. Her long red hair fell in a braid down her back.

"Tortured?" I asked. "If I was going to torture him, I wouldn't have used a gun."

Her eyes went a little wide around the edges.

I crossed my arms. "When you're fighting a werewolf, keeping them from coming at you is a necessity."

"Wrap it, folks." Arthur stood, stepping away from the body.

He carefully took the gloves off his hands. They had to examine the body so they could put all those spiffy little notes in their file.

"I'm glad you did what you did." Arthur stepped up to me as the EMT started cutting my shirt. I'd already taken off the holster. The leather jacket was on the floor with it by my feet.

"It's my job," I said. The EMT's cold gloved hands prodded at my ribs. "Ow!" I yelled.

Arthur chuckled. The EMT shook his head. "You have two broken ribs that are going to heal improperly if I do not reset them," he said, and I was glad that he hadn't noticed the fact that they were probably already beginning to heal.

I said, "Just do it."

Which I learned was a complete mistake, because he did.

I think it was the first time Arthur had ever heard me scream.

Once I could breathe again, I turned to look at Arthur. "The wolf's name," I said, "is Lukas Morris. He used to live in Denver, Colorado."

"What about Carver?" he asked.

"Innocent," I said. "It was Lukas the whole time."

"Is Carver a…?"

I shook my head. "I don't know," I lied. "I don't care. I just know he's innocent. You should contact the police in Denver. There were three killings there that match the ones here. It looks like his handiwork."

He wrote it down. When he was done he gave me a long look. "You need a ride?"

I smiled. "That would be nice."

I stepped outside of the small shack and into the blue-and-red haze of the police lights. The shack was a few miles away from the clearing where the pack met. That much, I'd figured out on my own. How else could Lenorre, Rosalin, and Carver have found me? They'd traced my scent through the woods.

❖

It is not an easy thing to take another's life, no matter how many crimes they have committed. No matter how many people they have killed. Ridding the world of some small evil does not ensure a good night's sleep. Neither justice nor vengeance comes with a guarantee that you will not doubt yourself.

What helps is that I know I did what I could for the victims and their families. That I ensured Lukas Morris would never again hurt anyone else.

There wasn't anything I could do about Sheila Morris. I didn't like her, but since Lukas was trying to dethrone her, she hadn't been involved in his little murder escapades. I still didn't trust her, though. There was something about her that I saw in her brother. Not the insanity bit, as Sheila didn't seem like a complete whack-job like her brother, but there was a darkness there that I don't think either of them dealt with in healthy ways. I thought about giving the name to Arthur. That way, he could take her in for questioning. But then I decided that in the future I would keep watch on her myself. If she was innocent, why expose that she's a lycanthrope? It could potentially ruin her life. I only ruin the lives of those that deserve it, when I'm sure they deserve it.

It was the night of the autumnal equinox, a time to prepare for the cold winter months ahead. I would pay my respects to the waning sunlight and honor the moon lady. Soon, her cold fingers would coax the leaves off the trees. The ground would fall asleep under her cloak of frost.

For tonight, everything was in balance.

Arthur pulled up by the gate. "Nice," he said. "I'm starting to see what you see in Vampira." He grinned.

"Arthur," I unbuckled my seat belt, "shut up."

I got out of the car. My entire body felt like I'd been hit by a semi truck. It was a dull ache, which was good, because it meant that the damage done to my body was healing properly. Werewolf or no, I was exhausted, but some exhaustions are of the mind rather than the body. I forced myself to keep my carriage straight as I went to the keypad.

Lenorre had saved my life. Rosalin and Carver had helped her, but I knew without a doubt that she had been the mastermind of my rescue.

The gate opened and I stumbled over a rock. It was a small rock, but one of those little jagged rocks that slip beneath your heel. Usually, I'd notice something like that. I cursed under my breath.

I made it as far as the driveway when the front door opened. Lenorre was suddenly beside me, slipping an arm around my waist.

A muscle in my back spasmed. Sometimes, healing so quickly can be uncomfortable.

"You just did it again," I said.

"Did what?"

"You remember the poof thing we talked about?"

Lenorre shook her head. "I come to help you, and you are more worried about me poofing to your aid than the actual aid itself. Are you truly complaining?" she asked.

I looked up into her misty gray eyes and smiled softly. "No," I said, "I appreciate the aid, whether you poofed to give it or not."

The ground moved out from under my feet. Lenorre cradled me in her arms, holding my body against hers.

"I didn't say you had to carry me."

She gave a slow blink that showed off the richness of her eyelashes. As if that was her response, she began walking toward the house. I let out a deep breath and relaxed. If she hadn't saved my life, I would've gone apeshit for being picked up without warning, for feeling like I was being coddled like a child.

The Countess of Oklahoma carried me into her home, and I knew she wasn't coddling me. She held me not because she wanted to bend me to her will or keep me as a pet.

I looked at her and knew that she held me because she cared.

I rested my head against her shoulder and inhaled the sweet scent of cinnamon and cloves and the smell of crisp night air.

"It is like your detective friend said," she mumbled and I felt her lips moving against the top of my head.

"What is?" My voice was a tired whisper.

"Mmm," she said, "something about doughnuts." I looked up into her shining face. The corner of her red mouth twitched.

I gave a short laugh. "That from a woman who could probably pick up a truck and throw it."

"You are amazingly light compared to a truck."

"That's good to know."

I sank back into the feel of her.

"How did you know?" I asked.

"That you were missing?"

I nodded, not bothering to look at her.

"Rosalin informed me. I told her to search the area. She found your phone."

"What about Carver?" I asked. "He was my suspect."

"He offered to help," Lenorre said. "Mayhap, to prove a point. Who is to know? The fact of the matter is that he did help."

"True," I said. "I owe him an apology."

"You do," she said at length. "Though I do not blame you."

"I do, a little," I said.

"Why?"

"I knew when I met Lukas something was off about him. I just didn't pay attention to it."

Lenorre helped me to my feet before opening the door that led to the basement levels. "Mistakes are a part of life," she said, slipping an arm around my waist as we descended the stairs. "Be grateful your mistake helped you to find and save Henry Walker."

"I am," I said, and meant it.

Lenorre laid me down on the bed and I sighed as I sank into the deep silk bedding. I watched her get undressed. She slid into bed next to me and curled her body around mine.

My muscles eased and my skin warmed where her cold body touched it. Ironic, I thought as I drifted to sleep. I would still have to deal with the crazy shit going on in my life. But for now, I was right where I wanted to be.

About the Author

Winter Pennington is an author, poet, artist, and closeted musician. She is an avid practitioner of nature-based spirituality and enjoys spending her spare time studying mythology from around the world. The Celtic path is very close to her heart. She has an uncanny fascination with swords and daggers and a fondness for feeding loud and obnoxious corvids. Winter currently resides in Oklahoma with her partner.

Books Available From Bold Strokes Books

Witch Wolf by Winter Pennington. In a world where vampires have charmed their way into modern society, where werewolves walk the streets with their beasts disguised by human skin, Investigator Kassandra Lyall has a secret of her own to protect. She's one of them. (978-1-60282-177-4)

Do Not Disturb by Carsen Taite. Ainsley Faraday, a high-powered executive, and rock music celebrity Greer Davis couldn't be less well suited for one another, and yet they soon discover passion has a way of designing its own future. (978-1-60282-153-8)

From This Moment On by PJ Trebelhorn. Devon Conway and Katherine Hunter both lost love and neither believes they will ever find it again—until the moment they meet and everything changes. (978-1-60282-154-5)

Vapor by Larkin Rose. When erotic romance writer Ashley Vaughn decides to take her research into the bedroom for a night of passion with Victoria Hadley, she discovers that fact is hotter than fiction. (978-1-60282-155-2)

Wind and Bones by Kristin Marra. Jill O'Hara, award-winning journalist, just wants to settle her deceased father's affairs and leave Prairie View, Montana, far, far behind—but an old girlfriend, a sexy sheriff, and a dangerous secret keep her down on the ranch. (978-1-60282-150-7)

Nightshade by Shea Godfrey. The story of a princess, betrothed as a political pawn, who falls for her intended husband's soldier sister, is a modern-day fairy tale to capture the heart. (978-1-60282-151-4)

Vieux Carré Voodoo by Greg Herren. Popular New Orleans detective Scotty Bradley just can't stay out of trouble—especially when an old flame turns up asking for help. (978-1-60282-152-1)

The Pleasure Set by Lisa Girolami. Laney DeGraff, a successful president of a family-owned bank on Rodeo Drive, finds her comfortable life taking a turn toward danger when Theresa Aguilar, a sleek, sexy lawyer, invites her to join an exclusive, secret group of powerful, alluring women. (978-1-60282-144-6)

A Perfect Match by Erin Dutton. The exciting world of pro golf forms the backdrop for a fast-paced, sexy romance. (978-1-60282-145-3)

Father Knows Best by Lynda Sandoval. High school juniors and best friends Lila Moreno, Meryl Morganstern, and Caressa Thibodoux plan to make the most of the summer before senior year. What they discover that amazing summer about girl power, growing up, and trusting friends and family more than prepares them to tackle that all-important senior year! (978-1-60282-147-7)

The Midnight Hunt by L.L. Raand. Medic Drake McKennan takes a chance and loses, and her life will never be the same—because when she wakes up after surviving a life-threatening illness, she is no longer human. (978-1-60282-140-8)

Long Shot by D. Jackson Leigh. Love isn't safe, which is exactly why equine veterinarian Tory Greyson wants no part of it—until Leah Montgomery and a horse that won't give up convince her otherwise. (978-1-60282-141-5)

In Medias Res by Yolanda Wallace. Sydney has forgotten her entire life, and the one woman who holds the key to her memory, and her heart, doesn't want to be found. (978-1-60282-142-2)

Awakening to Sunlight by Lindsey Stone. Neither Judith or Lizzy is looking for companionship, and certainly not love—but when their lives become entangled, they discover both. (978-1-60282-143-9)

Fever by VK Powell. Hired gun Zakaria Chambers is hired to provide a simple escort service to philanthropist Sara Ambrosini, but nothing is as simple as it seems, especially love. (978-1-60282-135-4)